Copyright © 202.
All rig

The characters and events portrayed in this book are fictitious. Any similarity to real persons, living or dead, is coincidental and not intended by the author.

No part of this book may be reproduced, or stored in a retrieval system, or transmitted in any form or by any means, electronic, mechanical, photocopying, recording, or otherwise, without express written permission of the publisher.

ISBN-13: 9798841242987

Cover design by Jane Choi @xanichoi

To Tom and Chris,
whose floor I was sat on when I wrote the first sentence and dreamt
up the King George.

Ralph described Mary Woods as 'pragmatic', 'efficient', and above all else 'sensible'. She had never been late for work, her work was airtight, and she'd never given him a reason to distrust her. She was reliable, which Ralph found incredibly important being high up in the corporate world. He had to manage several accountants and auditors and if any of them put a toe out of line, it ended up being him who had to sacrifice a whole lot – business cost, reputation cost, time loss, and so forth. Yes, they also lost their job because of it, but they knew what they were in for when they made such mistakes as 'being kind' or 'doing the right thing'.

He could count on Mary to be 'sensible'. The right thing did not mean putting the business under pressure by succumbing to the wants and will of the customer. She understood that entirely. That's why she was the best in the business, the most highly recommended, the diamond amongst the jewels.

That was also why he called her into his office on a Tuesday morning to discuss the latest business proposal from a customer. She entered his office tidy in a grey business skirt, blazer, and white shirt with a bright yellow cravat – Yellow was for Tuesdays after all. Her brunette hair was done up in a bun to keep out of her eyes, and her glasses sat fitted on the brim of her nose safe from flying around. In her arms she had a simple ruled notebook and a fountain pen; the same pen she'd had for years since her grandmother had given it to her on her twelfth birthday.

On some occasions, Mary had talked about how her parents had expected her to become a librarian given how organised she was. But given the money was in accounting, Ralph admired her career choice. There was that pragmatism that kept her on the straight and narrow. And would hopefully mean he could entrust her with a slightly different contract than usual.

'Mary, please have a seat,' he stated, gesturing a large hand to the chair in front of him.

Mary took it decidedly and put the notebook in her lap ready to take notes, 'How can I help Ralph?'

'I've a new job a little different from the rest. A little quieter in nature to what you're used to,' and he dabbed at his forehead with a handkerchief.

'Seeing as you sent me to audit Paris for the last three months, I'd appreciate quiet,' stated Mary.

'It's a six-week offer from an establishment in the West Midlands. They want a bookkeeper to audit and assess their business and it's been dropping off in the last few years. The landlord is very keen to bring things back in line, and has offered catered boarding to accommodate during the assessment,' Ralph described, confusing Mary.

'What kind of establishment?'

'Public house, an inn,' to which Ralph saw Mary's eyebrows raise, 'I understand it's quite different to what you're used to but you see there are other fingers in this pie.'

Mary put down her pen for a moment, 'what kind of fingers?'

'I can't disclose the details of the client, but we've been approached with an offer of a larger sum to take this job, and make a predetermined assessment.' Mary seemed taken aback and Ralph lifted his hands, 'Now Mary, I would never ask you to break the rules. The inn will still pay for the assessment whatever the conclusion. The contract we'd agreed to states that further payment will be made if the assessment comes to the correct conclusion.'

'What's the conclusion?'

'That the inn must be sold on.'

Mary uttered a laugh, 'They want us to advise the current owner to sell? What for?'

'Undisclosed, but the money for it is hefty.'

'They want it sold to them?'

'Just sold full-stop. Out of the owner's possession. Now Mary,' and Ralph leant forward, 'I understand that this is a strange ask. I come to you because I know if I ask anyone else the assessment will be unfair and may be liable for investigation. You are reliable, and even if you do make a predetermined conclusion, I know you will come to that conclusion methodically so that nobody would even have a notion that it was predetermined,' his eyes hovered expectantly on Mary with a slight quiver, as if he was concerned to how Mary would respond, 'can I trust you to take this on?'

Mary laughed, 'Ralph it's an inn in the West Midlands. One closes a day out there, I daresay it would be easy to see that this is just another pub following the same direction. Of course, I would never sacrifice my reputation and will assess the building as fairly as I can, but I've no doubt it will be like taking candy from a baby.'

Ralph's smile grew on his face with a sigh of relief, 'I'm glad we see eye to eye on this. I'll send you the details and you can report there next week to begin the assessment,' and he placed a pair of reading glasses on to indicate the meeting was over.

Mary finished up writing some preliminary notes and then got up to leave, 'who's the main contact I shall be speaking with?'

'A Mr Stone. Wat Stone,' said Ralph, 'and Mary?' she was half out the door when she turned back, 'it's a very big contract. You appreciate that the cost of coming to a "different" conclusion may put us in a very awkward position?'

Mary nodded with a look on her face that satisfied Ralph, 'of course, but don't worry. I've got this.'

And that was how Mary Woods became the accountant to the Mad King.

TALES FROM THE KING GEORGE

MARY WOODS AND THE UNICORN

STANLEY DODD

WHEN MARY MET WAT

Mary despised rain. The feeling of being damp was uncomfortable and when sitting in warmth it only amplified. And here she was, getting soaked in the rain, waiting for the taxi she called for an hour ago, letting the frustration inside her seethe like a slowly coiling spring. The train had already been late. She'd missed her connection. First Class had been full on the next train. She'd left her umbrella on the platform. And there wasn't a First-Class carriage on her last train.

She was almost seven hours late and she was rarely late. She was punctual and she liked to keep it that way where possible. She reached for her phone to send another text saying she'd be late. She hoped that the landlord was receiving them.

Finally, her taxi arrived and pulled up in front of the station. The passenger window whirred down and Mary peered inside. The driver pulled a face that let Mary know she was looking worse for wear.

'Blimey, couldn't you have waited inside?' he asked casually.

TALES FROM THE KING GEORGE

'I caught the last train. The station is closed,' she stated firmly, 'could you let me in.'

'You want to put bags in the boot?' he asked, opening his door and launching out into the downpour, 'oh lord it's freezing.'

Mary held her tongue as he pulled the lever and she lugged her bags to the back of the car. The driver rounded his side to join her, holding his jacket over his head.

'Where are you wanting going again?' he asked.

Mary fished into her pocket and handed him the address that she'd written so she wouldn't have to further interact with him, meanwhile putting her own bags into the car.

'The King George? Never heard of it,' he stated.

Mary slammed the boot down to get it to click in the latch and ignored the driver's reaction. She opened her door and settled into the back of the car. She felt her hair matted and stuck to the back of her neck, and when she touched her face makeup came off on her fingers. She pulled some tissues out of her bag and began to wipe it off.

The driver jumped in the front typing the address into his phone and starting navigation. Mary eyed the route, seeing it took them through the town onto the other side, where it winded through houses in a suburban area.

'Looks twenty minutes away,' the driver told her.

She nodded as she wiped her face dry and then fished out for her makeup. The driver gave up making any further idle conversation and just focused on his driving, leaving the radio tuned into a music station that was only playing electronic music. After ten minutes she realised the song hadn't changed and it started to drill into her head.

Outside she watched the town pass by. At night she found things took on a whole new life. In the city, that life was one filled with lights and conversation, smashed glasses, and cheers to a new day. In the country, it was quiet, save for the sounds of far-off animals, skies of stars, and the disappearance of civilisation; a strange sense of tranquillity and solitude. In the towns, it was a strange mix as the lights only stuck around the centre of town, and as you travelled into the suburban parts the lights gave out to the shadow. A strange sense of community surrounded by a lonely darkness.

The few people she saw roaming were the odd breed that decided to walk the streets at night; dog walkers, young people, drunkards, and the occasional person you couldn't be sure if they were a murderer or not. She made sure the door was locked.

When they made it to the location on the map, the driver's phone chimed, and he heartily boasted, 'Oh I know this place! This is the Mad King; I've never heard anyone call it the King George.'

'The owner seems to,' muttered Mary as she stepped out of the car.

The rain had stopped so she had an easier time pulling her bags out. The driver had parked up right beside the entrance so she had to step back to get a good look. A light hung on the outside of the building, casting orange over the cream-white walls. Large black-lined windows were lit up on the ground floor seeing into a barroom. The building was three stories, taking up the entire corner of the road – the road going north led over a stone bridge before a terrace began on either side. The road going west had a small alley before again another terrace began on either side. East and south lead back towards the main road.

Hanging above the porchway that covered the entrance was the pub's sign, which displayed a picture of King George but no name. No wonder it was called the Mad King, was all Mary thought.

The taxi driver coughed to grab her attention, as he had the bags out. She paid him and held back on a tip, causing him to scoff and shake his head as he left her to it. Mary was about to enter the building when the front doors burst open and two men stumbled out in each other's arms. Both were laughing about something, and when they almost ran into Mary they each took a step back and looked her over.

'What have we here!'

'Lookie!'

'Fancy dress darlin''

From behind them, another man stepped out, but he took charge and led the two onto the street, where they began to cheer and laugh, shouting 'We'll be back for you!'

'Alright, get off with you two! I don't want you ending up dead in a ditch!' said the third man, grinning.

'Thanks Wat, we'll be back tomorrow!'

He was dressed in a waistcoat and shirt, with suit trousers and leather shoes. His hair was dirty blonde and cut short with a quiff at the front. His eyes were a sharp blue with a glint in them, reflecting the outside light, or so Mary thought. He was tall as well, taller than Mary. She looked up at him as he turned around and said, 'I'm sorry we're closing up. Unless you're looking to spend the night?'

WHEN MARY MET WAT

Mary cleared her throat and presented a hand, giving a firm smile of pride, 'Mr Stone I presume? I am Mary Woods, at your service.'

Wat's grin dropped away and the man grabbed Mary's hand with such enthusiasm, she was sure he was going to pull it off.

'Ms Woods! I'm so glad to see you, I had thought you wouldn't be arriving!'

'Yes, I am much later than I expected, did you not get my texts?'

'I'm sorry, I don't look at my smartphone often,' Wat said, putting a hand in his pocket and pulling out a five-year-old phone, 'I got it recently and I'm not a fan of the thing.'

Mary sighed, seeing what she had to deal with, 'never mind I've made it now.'

Wat lifted his head and met her eyes with such intensity she was mesmerised, before he cried, 'Indeed! Let me show you inside! I'll take your bags for you.'

The man practically tossed her bags through the door along with himself. He held the door open for her and then immediately entered the room on the right. The first room she entered was the barroom; a counter ran on the right-hand side, with a door to a backroom. To the left was a wall with tall tables and stools along it, with two open doorways. Beyond the doorways, down a step, were more booths and tables for drinking. All the chairs were on top of the tables for cleaning.

She followed Wat into the next room. This was half a reception room, half entry to the cellar it looked. Wat dropped the bags by a desk acting as a counter, behind it was a wall with pigeon holes and an opening to stairs that lead down. He disappeared down the stairs and left her to her own devices.

She eyed the room – it was old wallpaper that was peeling a little. The lights all gave a slight yellow hue. The air was musty and thick as if it had been building up for years with nowhere to go. There was also a window to the street, but the blinds were down obscuring it.

When Wat returned, in his hands was a large book that he planted on the desk. He opened it up and flicked to a specific page before taking a fountain pen, shaking it, and then scratching something out.

'Today's the twenty-first of October, correct?' he stated.

'Now it is, yes,' stated Mary, noting the grandfather clock in the room reading the time was almost one in the morning.

'Okay, can I just have you sign the guestbook to confirm your arrival?' he asked, turning the book around.

She took the pen from him and signed where directed, noting the paper and book were incredibly old and yellow.

'Mr Stone, I have to ask, are all your amenities almost a hundred years old?' she questioned.

Wat laughed nervously, 'I shall show you to your room now. It's our best ensuite, dedicated especially for your stay with us! You have no idea how glad I am to have you here, you're doing me a huge favour,' he said and grabbed Mary's bags once more.

He pranced to the right of the room to a narrow staircase leading up to the next floor. Mary followed cautiously after, as the stairs were steeper than she was used to. By the time she reached the landing, Wat was down the corridor in front of her, unlocking a door.

WHEN MARY MET WAT

'I was surprised to have you respond to my advertisement,' he continued saying, 'I wasn't offering much and to have an esteemed agency as your own take it on was a little surprising! I hope that providing lodging does enough to balance the pay by alleviating the expenses.'

Mary reached the room and found it to be rather large. A window opened up onto the stream that ran beside the end of the building and under the stone bridge. The room had cream-coloured wallpaper and the bedclothes were dressed in something Mary would've found in her grandmother's home. She peered around the door into the ensuite and noted that it had a bathtub with a shower attachment, not a full shower cubicle. The toilet at least was modern.

'It's very rustic,' she said.

Wat smiled and then presented a key to Mary; it was a brass lever key that she gave him a raised eyebrow for.

'Yes, we have been looking to do renovations for a while but, as I'm sure you'll find out,' and he chuckled, 'our funds have been a bit constrained.'

'You like to laugh don't you Mr Stone,' Mary observed.

Wat opened his mouth to say something but it looked as if Mary had taken the wind out of it, and so he instead said, 'I'm sorry Ms Woods. I'll leave you to your room, shall I?'

'Yes, thank you. I will find you in the morning when I'm ready to begin my work,' said Mary.

'Very good, breakfast will be served between six and ten in the morning,' Wat stated, 'let me know if you need anything!'

Mary gave him a knowing smile, to which he left the room. When the door clicked close, Mary slouched and dropped onto the bed. It was a little hard, but the duvet was soft. She looked at the ceiling where she could see a great scar in the ceiling's paint. She grimaced at the state. The carpet was also an ugly pattern that she realised was perfect for hiding crumbs and dirt in.

It was not to the standard she had been so accustomed to in the city. Not to worry, soon she'd be finishing off an assessment and settling for a large pay from her agency. Hopefully, the pub would get sold to some wealthy developer and they would knock the place down. She just had to last the next six weeks.

She laid back on the bed and looked at the lamp. The faint strings of a recently dusted cobweb danced in the light.

Perhaps she could finish the work sooner.

She set to prepare herself for bed. She washed off her makeup, dressed in a nightgown, tied her hair up, and then got into bed and turned out the lights. The rain had stopped, and so all she could hear outside was a soft breeze. Outside it was black, but the sky was glowing amongst the room, faint starlight straining to make themselves visible.

A branch tapped faintly against the window, and Mary realised just how difficult it can be to sleep in a foreign area. The darkness contorted the room and she couldn't recognise the furniture she'd seen moments ago. She found herself studying the stars outside, twinkling in the sky above the line of trees. She considered how things change in the dark, how cities never suffered from shrouds to cover everything and instead it was lit up; every inch of it. You can't escape light in the city.

Out here, you can't escape the dark.

WHEN MARY MET WAT

The branch insistently tapped and Mary turned over away from the window and lifted the duvet up to her head. She tried to think of something else. She tried thinking of sheep. Of numbers. She began to count, one, two, three, four-

The window thudded. This wasn't a branch. It almost sounded as if someone had opened it. Mary froze in her bed, her eyes snapped open. She didn't want to turn around; instead, she made the reasonable assumption that the branch had fallen. She thought this to herself even as she felt the breeze float through the room. She had to face reality when she felt her bed dip as someone or something sat down.

She snapped round to flick on the lamp and sat upright, and uttered a short scream before slapping her hand on her mouth.

The man who had unceremoniously sat on her bed, jumped up, his face changing from a charming smirk to a panicked frown.

'Who are you!?' he said.

Mary dropped her hand, and crossly stated, 'Who am I!? Who are YOU!?'

The man took a step back. Mary couldn't stand it any longer.

'Get out! Go away!' she shouted.

'I'm gone,' stated the man with a sneer, and quicker than she thought was possible the man had left through the window he had come in.

Mary took a few minutes, her hand pressed against her chest, to catch her breath. She rubbed her face. Had that really happened? She took a few deep breaths and found her glasses. She'd have to tell Stone about this, she'd have to phone someone. Anyone. Who was that man? How did he get in?

TALES FROM THE KING GEORGE

She closed the window swiftly and then jumped at the sound of knocking on her door. She found her dressing gown before opening it and found a round man with a bustling moustache and nightcap standing groggily in the corridor.

'Everything all right? I heard a scream,' he said in a deep voice.

'Yes, I am now thank you,' she said, 'I need to go speak to Mr Stone,' and she pushed past the round man down the corridor

Another door had opened and a short woman with her hair in a silver bun was eyeing her up, but Mary didn't care about that. She needed to call the police, she had to inform Mr Stone that someone had broken into her room.

At the reception, she slammed her hand multiple times on the little bell on the desk. Shortly, Wat was coming up from the basement, his eyes looking weary.

'Mr Stone, do you have any other staff?' asked Mary.

'I'm sorry, our usual man is ill. How can I help you, Ms Woods?'

'Someone has just broken into my room,' she stated calmly, though her hand was shaking against her hip.

Wat woke up to that, 'did they hurt you? Did they break anything? Are they still here?'

'No, thankfully they left almost immediately. It was almost as if he were looking for someone,' Mary said.

Wat had a hand to his face, 'what did he look like?'

Mary thought about this – she'd not had her glasses on; 'silver short hair, and a long black trench coat.' That smirk, that unnaturally charming smirk that made him irrevocably handsome – no horrible! A horrible face, the face of a criminal. Mary scolded herself.

WHEN MARY MET WAT

Wat looked resigned, 'I see. Let me fetch the phone and I'll ring the police,' he said.

'Thank you,' said Mary, and she folded her arms.

As Wat spoke on the phone, she found herself not able to calm down very well at all. She felt silly, the man hadn't hurt her. The man hadn't even touched her. Yet she couldn't help but find her hand shook and she was biting her lip.

Wat finished up the call, 'Come follow me. Let me get you a blanket,' he said and he went down to the basement.

Mary cautiously followed. Down the stairs behind the desk, it opened to a dark corridor. To her left Wat made a turn into a room with a curtain over the doorway rather than an actual door. She followed and found herself in a lounge, a cabinet filled with glassware sat on the far end next to a record player. A two-seater sofa sat on the rightmost wall flanked by two armchairs.

Wat was at the cabinet and opened the lower section to pull out a glass bottle filled with a brown spirit that Mary assumed was whiskey.

'Take a seat, can I get you a drink?' he asked.

'Just water,' said Mary, though she knew the harder stuff would help she knew she was better off with water. She took the armchair facing Wat and tried to get her shaking under control. Wat poured some whiskey into a tumbler and swigged it. Gasping after, he walked to Mary and then knelt in front of her.

'Are you doing okay?'

She met his eyes and suddenly she felt a wave of ease wash over her. It was strangely calming as if through his eyes alone he was telling her he had everything under control. Her hand stopped shaking and she stole a quick smile, 'Yes I'll be fine.'

TALES FROM THE KING GEORGE

He smiled and patted her gently, before leaving Mary to herself. She took the time to observe her surroundings – the décor definitely fitted a Victorian parlour theme. She was surprised that the walls weren't suffering from damp, being underground. There was a small outdated television that was placed on a media unit, that was currently playing something in black and white with the sound off.

Wat returned with a glass of water that he passed to her. He made another tumbler of whiskey, then sat down on the sofa nearby. He sipped his whiskey, smacked his lips, and then placed it on the coffee table in front of him.

'I know the man who broke in,' he stated.

Mary choked on her drink but managed to keep it from becoming a cough, 'who is he?'

'His name is Richard O'Nerry and he's a thief,' Wat took another sip, 'he's been hounding this pub for the last six months. Unfortunately, my daughter is impressionable and we don't see eye to eye…' he trailed off at this.

It became apparent to Mary that the family had suffered more than criminal activities at the hands of this O'Nerry.

'It was two months ago when I stumbled into that room when the two of them were…embracing. I made it abundantly clear that I forbade the relationship but…' and he shook his head.

'How old is your daughter?' asked Mary.

'Sixteen,' he said.

Mary almost spat out her drink once more, 'that man almost looked thirty! That's awful; he shouldn't be involved with a girl that age.'

WHEN MARY MET WAT

'It's a family problem and it's my responsibility. I'm so sorry it's ended up with you in this awkward situation and I promise this won't happen again.'

Mary gazed at Wat as she thought; no wonder her contractor wanted this place to shut down if criminals had their run of the place. Should she really be expected to stay on to assess the pub if she was threatened like this?

'Mr Stone you understand this puts me in a very awkward situation. How can I continue to assess this pub in such conditions?'

Wat didn't look at Mary. Instead, he nodded his head solemnly and then drank from his glass again.

* * *

The police officers who arrived were a short blonde woman with a heavy chest and face that seemed to drip with fatigue and a lanky young man with a stance that looked as if he would rather be on the move than standing still. The blonde introduced them as 'Officer Duigenan and Baker' to which Baker then waved in a friendly manner. Wat showed them inside and then down to the parlour where he then offered them a cup of tea.

They took the statement from Mary about the situation and her details. Mary did her best to describe what happened. Duigenan noticed that Mary's hand was exhibiting signs of a stressful situation – Mary couldn't stop fidgeting. Her eyes attempted to convey a kind attitude, even with the weight of insomnia.

'Wat said that he is a fugitive,' she said low, 'is he dangerous?'

'Nah,' spoke up Baker suddenly, 'he's a thief that's all.'

TALES FROM THE KING GEORGE

'What my partner here means is that he's only been committed for several accounts of breaking and entering, and burglary,' said Duigenan, looking in Baker's direction the entire time.

'How did he escape from prison then?' asked Mary.

'It's still under investigation,' said Duigenan, intending to drop the subject.

Mary looked to Baker expecting elaboration but the officer shrugged.

'Will he come back?' asked Mary.

Duigenan put her notebook down for a second and looked directly into Mary's eyes, 'We'll have someone patrol the pub tonight, and Wat will put you in a different room. He has never been charged with assault or bodily harm. From the psychiatrist's point of view, he's just a very good thief. We expect he was here to try and steal something.'

'Steal what?'

'We couldn't say,' said Duigenan, 'not right now. Wat, we'll take a look around the room now if you don't mind?'

Wat directed them upstairs and into the ensuite where they looked around for any evidence. Mary pointed out where she had seen O'Nerry come in and where he had been. After ten minutes, they gave up and set to leave the building.

'Thank you for letting us know, every little clue takes us one step closer to catching the bugger,' stated Duigenan.

'Thank you for coming by,' said Wat, 'I do appreciate it.'

'If you could bring Snow by the station tomorrow so we can ask her a few standard questions?'

'Absolutely.'

WHEN MARY MET WAT

The two officers left Mary and Wat by the front door. After he closed it, he gave Mary a long look that said he wasn't sure where to go now. She chewed the inside of her cheek. If her job wasn't on the line, she would be out of the door. But she knew this was going to be a tough job when Ralph had come to her with it. He came to her with nothing but the difficult ones.

'I understand Ms Woods if you decided that the work is not worth it-'

'I'll stay the night Mr Stone as it's far too late to find any other accommodation now, however, I will be evaluating my position tomorrow. Now could you show me another room?'

Wat did so a little less enthusiastically this time and left her alone. This one was on the other side of the building and had no ensuite. She laid back in a single bed and looked up at a crack in the ceiling. She'd have to give Ralph a call in the morning to discuss the matter. For now, she desperately needed some sleep.

WHEN MARY MET MONA

The following morning Mary woke up with a crick in her neck and her body aching all over. She had been tossing and turning evidenced by the fact one of her pillows was now on the floor. She turned off her alarm, stretched to get her joints back in place, and proceeded to ready herself for the day. She was finally dressed and presentable just after seven. Her red cravat was done up neatly and tight, her hair was up in a bun, and she had her glasses hanging around her neck. When she looked herself over in the mirror, she felt discouraged.

Her eyes trawled over the rustic room, the wallpaper with pencil-drawn roses and pansies, the drapes were cream to match the yellowing carpet. The lights flickered gently with a warm glow as if they were really candles. It felt slightly too old and she surprised herself when she considered that she seemed to fit right in. That hurt.

No, she wasn't that old; she shook her head to affirm to herself. Then she stepped out of her room to head downstairs.

TALES FROM THE KING GEORGE

At the bottom of the stairs was the reception room that she recognised from the night before. Behind the counter stood a young girl who looked in her teens. Her hair was platinum blonde, but her lips were small, plump and red. Her eyes when she looked up were a surprisingly dark blue, accentuated by her red cheeks. She gave a sweet naïve smile to Mary, who had no doubt that this was Snow Stone, Wat's daughter.

'You must be Snow,' said Mary.

The girl nodded slowly, 'Yes ma'am.'

Mary stood upright to look her over. The girl was pretty sure but Mary felt there was something else. Something she didn't like.

'Your father has told me about you. A girl your age shouldn't be messing around with men,' Mary said.

Snow's smile faltered for a moment, 'Sorry?'

'You heard me, you should feel ashamed. Now where's your father,' asked Mary.

Snow smiled even sweeter, 'he's in the conservatory. Go down the bar into the billiard's room and turn left.'

'Thank you,' said Mary.

She left the reception and entered the bar. It was empty, but all the chairs were down off the tables. A bartender was cleaning tables on the far side of the room beyond the wall dividing it.

Mary took the right down a hall with doors on her right side and a wall of large windows on the left. Two glass doors were closed but would've opened into a square courtyard with a small tree growing in the centre and two benches on opposite sides of it.

At the end of the hall was a door that she opened into what must have been the billiards room. There was a table in the centre, a dartboard on the wall, a TV mounted in the corner that was currently turned off, and some stools and tables on the outside. Playing the table was a man that looked remarkably like Wat but taller and younger. His hair was rugged and he had a slight stubble around his face. His eyes were small however; when Mary entered they glanced upward for a moment and had Mary catch her breath.

'Hello,' she managed to stutter, 'I'm looking for Wat? Wat Stone.'

The man tossed his head to his right to the door, 'he's in the conservatory.'

Mary slowly meandered to the door, taking her time. The man was playing against himself it looked.

'Are you a relation of his?' she asked.

The man rubbed chalk on his cue, 'he's my dad.'

Mary nodded, 'I'm Mary. Mary Woods, the accountant.'

The man put the queue down and patted his hand for chalk. He lifted his hand as a gentle smile crept over his face, 'Rob.'

Mary took it and gazed at his face. His chin was strong and his cheeks were cut and narrow. When he let her go, she had to recover.

'I'd better go; good to meet you Rob,' she said, and left the room before she made a fool of herself.

Beyond the door was another corridor, but this was older and more open to the elements. It was made of wood painted white and windows covered both sides as well as above her. Green mould coated the glass at the top but the windows on either side were clean as a whistle. The paint needed a new coat as flecks were peeling off all over.

On her left was the courtyard and on her right were the few trees of the woodland. The ground bent down towards the trees as if it were a blanket, and some length of rope was cast over the ground and pulled down, with its grip on the earth tight.

She could see the next room was built from the same white wood and was an octagonal room built on the side of the main building like an extension. Before she made it to the door, a small woman exited and almost ran into her.

'I'm sorry,' she said, adjusting her glasses, 'ooh, are you the new accountant?' she said, peering up at Mary.

Mary gave her hand, 'Ms Mary Woods,' she said.

'Lauren,' said the woman, 'I've heard you had a bit of a scare already. And yet here you still are!'

'Yes, that matter should have remained private,' said Mary, already regretting her stay.

'Oh, not to worry Mary, it's safe with me. I'm so glad to have you here, Wat so dearly needs the help! I have to get to work but if you want to chat or need a haircut you come down to Snippy's! We're on the high street,' Lauren's voice got quieter as she waddled further away.

Mary touched her hair defensively then directed her attention directly to the doors in front of her and the job at hand. She pushed through and found the room was fairly empty. It was filled with a variety of chairs, sofas, benches, an old church pew and all manner of tables to accompany them. At a fine glass table with three finely carved wood chairs, Wat was sitting with the same roundish fellow from the night before; he had a pair of round glasses, a brush-like moustache, and red cheeks. He also seemed to be laughing uncontrollably. Between the two of them was a fine china tea set that was decorated with pumpkins.

'…and before you knew it, he was gone! Turned out he'd run to the next bloody town! That's how scared he was,' the man burst into raucous laughter as Wat chuckled, wiping his eye.

Then Wat noticed Mary had entered and lifted a hand to wave to her, 'Ms Woods! Come over, come over! Octavius, this is Mary Woods, our new accountant!'

The round man stood up. He was wearing brown leather braces with a pair of chinos that only barely managed to hold the flesh within his shirt and when he laughed his belly and jowls wobbled with him.

'Ms Woods, pleasure to meet you,' said the man.

'You too. Mr Stone, I'd like to begin work if I can,' Mary stated.

Wat put down his teacup, 'start? Wouldn't you like some breakfast?'

'If you wouldn't mind Mr Stone, I'd like to know exactly what I signed up for before I have any breakfast. Might I remind you that my stay here is still in question?' stated Mary.

It wasn't, not with that much money on the line. Or her job.

'Right, I'll show you to the office,' he said, 'Octavius it was good to catch up! Bring the veg round the back of the kitchen when you get it.'

'Of course Wat, Miss Woods, I shall catch you at another time!' said the man who Mary gleaned was Octavius.

Wat led Mary down the conservatory and through a set of double doors into a dining area. It was better themed than the conservatory with tables all set nicely and neatly. Doors in front of them read 'STAFF ONLY' and led into what Mary could see were the kitchens. Windows on the left looked back at the courtyard once again. At the end on the left, Wat pushed through a solid door that led back into the bar room.

'I'm happy to give you anything you need,' he was saying during this, 'any questions you ask! Any food or drink, I live to serve! Hah as long as it's not too big a request.'

They returned to the reception and Wat entered the staircase that led down behind the counter. Snow noticed them and gave a quick smile to Wat which disappeared as she looked at Mary.

In the basement, Wat reached the first door on the right and gripped the handle. He pushed it but it appeared to be jammed. He increased the pressure and the door slowly prised open, the sound of rustling paper and ripping coming from just behind it.

'It's been a while since I've come in here,' said Wat, stepping inside.

Mary followed suit and stood right into the yellow sea of old paper. To her left and right were stacks of paper, folders and books, and all over the floor were probably the remnants of one of the taller stacks as it finally collapsed under the weight. In the centre of the room was a desk and behind it two filing cabinets. There was a single light hanging from the ceiling and at the back a small thin window that peered onto the road outside.

Mary closed her eyes and smelt the thick scent of dust and forgotten paperwork and wondered how she was going to manage all of this.

Wat haphazardly made his way to the door, 'yes my grandfather wasn't great at managing files and it's been difficult to organise them,' said Wat, 'but yes if you-' Mary gave him a sharp stare to indicate for him to be quiet. Feeling the daggers piercing his pupils, Wat chuckled nervously and stepped to the door. 'I'll leave you to it.'

As soon as Wat closed the door Mary uttered a deep sigh. She looked around at the colossal mess of papers – at a glance she could see some were dated thirty years ago. Spiderwebs were strung across a couple of the piles and she saw there were more in the ceiling.

'Alright, well let's get started.'

Mary immediately set to work on recreating the piles. As she did, she pulled out any irrelevant information that had been cast into the sea; a couple of kids' drawings, tickets to personal events, photos. She took these and put them on the desk to distinguish them.

Mary liked organising things, she put it down to her librarian spirit. The act of putting things in their correct place was her natural course. Everything has its place; it was simply about finding the correct categorisation system. Sometimes the Dewey Decimal system was not enough. Sometimes it needed a more creative mind.

Glancing at each piece of paper was enough for Mary to paint the picture in her head of the King George's history. It wasn't just financial, you could tell a lot from a person or an establishment from their finances. The older records were much more stagnant with purchases and the profits much wider. The newer ones were reckless and she was having trouble determining where the income was coming from.

It was obvious why Wat was in so much trouble.

By the time midday rolled around she'd completed the piles and begun the process of categorising, moving records chronologically and constructing new piles to provide her an accurate timeline of finances. They became towers of knowledge and she felt much more in control.

Her shirt sleeves were rolled up, her blazer was tossed over the desk chair, and her cravat sat loosely on her chest. Not being on show meant she felt she could relax and dress a little more comfortably. The solitude was doing wonders for her focus. Taking a break, she leaned against the desk and considered the pile she still had to organise. A spider crawled across the wall causing her to wince in disgust. She wasn't afraid of spiders but she would never actively pick one up.

Three friendly knocks introduced the arrival of Wat yet again. He opened the door with a tea tray in his hands holding a teapot and teacup, and a plate of breakfast including eggs, sausages, bacon, beans, a couple of hash browns and a slice of toast along with its own packet of butter.

His face was adorned by a smile of warmth that Mary couldn't help but feel at ease looking at, and seeing the food made her realise she hadn't eaten all day. But she also sighed as there was no room to put the tray.

'Miss Woods, I've brought you something to eat! Some all-day brunch,' declared Wat proudly.

'I see that Mr Stone, but as you can see I haven't the room for it,' said Mary gesturing to her piles that adorned the floor and the desk.

'Not to worry,' said Wat, placing the tray on the floor behind him and then strolling to the desk, 'let's just put this pile of paper on the floor.'

He grabbed a stack of paper from the base and lifted it. Mary didn't have time to protest but she closed her eyes in anticipation – the sound of the air being ejected from his lungs as he pulled the stack into his chest added to her fears.

'These are heavy stacks, Mr Stone-'

'I've got it,' said Wat and he bent his knees to bring the stack to the ground.

He circled the desk to grip another stack, sliding it along the surface into his breast where his arms encircled it to keep it upright. Unfortunately, the success of the first stack told nothing of the second. A discarded piece of paper snuck its way between Wat's foot and the hardwood floor. As his weight shifted, this cunning document found it the perfect time to remove itself and Wat lost his balance.

Mary gasped in surprise as Wat fell like a stone, slamming to the ground against a stacked pile and sending its contents falling into another stack that fell into another. The paper he had been holding cascaded over his body and he was awash in a sea of files.

Wat groaned and slowly picked himself up, 'I'm so sorry Miss Woods, I-'

'Leave. Please,' Mary stated.

Her gaze was fixed upon the scattered remains of her organisational work. Wat said nothing else. He picked up the tray, set it on the empty space, and slunk out of the room, an imaginary tail between his legs.

Mary shook her head and began to pick up the remnants of her hard work. The man Wat was testing her patience. She had dealt with incompetence and ignorance before – they're quite common in the world of business. But they had been dislikeable people. Rude managers and goal-orientated stakeholders. Never had she had to deal with it in such an insufferably nice person.

After half an hour she had repaired the damage and was back on a roll. A couple hours later she had finished the initial chronological organisation and was sitting on the desk setting up a document on her laptop for data entry. The plate was empty and she was fingering the teacup on her desk. Wat hadn't reappeared since his mishap and so she had finished her tea.

She let herself drift off idly as she let her finger trace the pattern on the cup; a fine red apple. She did like Wat's collection of teacups. She considered whether he could suggest a good set for herself.

As she drifted her eyes caught sight of a spider crawling over the paper on her desk. She sighed, not wanting to deal with it at that time, and so caught it under the teacup. Then she returned to her laptop.

'Excuse me?' called a voice, somewhat muffled.

Mary looked up at the door, 'you can come in,' she called.

'Hah, no, could you let me out please?' The voice was a woman's.

Mary frowned, 'Let you out?' and she cast her eyes around the room, 'Where are you?'

'Under the teacup, thank you,' the voice said, 'you just caught me.'

Mary looked at the teacup. Obviously, this was some form of prank.

'Did Snow put you up to this?' she asked out loud, looking toward the door again.

'Not at all,' Mary got up and opened the door to the office; the corridor was empty.

Her brow furrowed as she considered what could be going on. The window to the road was also just as empty. She shut the door slowly.

'I understand this is rather strange but I'd rather you didn't toss me outside or however you wished to dispose of me,' said the voice.

Mary approached the teacup slowly. She was still in disbelief and so after reasoning that there was no way that there was a woman under the teacup, she lifted it up.

The spider was still there; a false widow. It didn't move.

'Thank you,' said the voice. It was no longer muffled. And it definitely came from the spider.

Mary hadn't realised she was no longer holding the teacup until she heard it smash onto the hardwood floor. Her eyes were glued to the spider, her brain frantically attempting to make sense of the situation.

'I see that I've frightened you,' said the spider, 'but if I may be honest, you're the one who destroyed my home.'

Mary lifted her hands as her brain took hold of the only sensible train of thought, 'Destroyed your home?'

'Yes, I had a nice set of webs laid across those stacks,' said the spider.

Mary folded her arms, 'I'm sorry but I had to. I have a job to do.'

The spider made a sound like a huff, 'and that gives you a right to destroy all my work?'

Mary bent down to her knees to look closely at the spider. It looked just like a spider. She couldn't see any wires or miniature speakers attached.

'How do you talk?' she asked, voicing her thoughts.

'I didn't use to be a spider,' the spider said, 'I was cursed by a wizard.'

'A wizard.'

'A life lesson for you darling, don't cheat a wizard. Back then I was well known for playing the field. Nowadays… well I suppose I play a different type of field.'

Mary took a seat at the desk and rubbed her eyes. 'Does Wat know about you?'

'Not at all, when do you think was the last time he was in here? I've been able to hide here for years. Had a good thing going until now,' said the spider.

Mary leant back in her chair, 'I am sorry, is there some way I can make it up to you?'

'Possibly,' said the spider, 'any idea how to break a curse?'

'Not at all.'

'Then maybe I'll think of something else. In the meantime, if you keep my living here a secret that would be much appreciated. In return I'll let you continue your "work",' and the spider suddenly began lifting itself into the air.

Mary realised it actually had run a thread up to the lightbulb above the desk. 'Thank you,' she said.

The spider crawled along the ceiling toward a crack in the corner of the room. Mary watched it go, unable to think clearly. When she looked back at her laptop she couldn't focus on the numbers or letters. All she could think of was the spider.

'What's your name, my darling?' came the woman's voice from the corner.

Mary hesitated. 'Mary,' she eventually spoke. And after another pause, '…yours?'

'I am Mona. It was a pleasure to meet you, Mary.'

Mary didn't answer. As much as the experience had been pleasant, she did not want to admit that she had spoken with a spider.

Mary and the Hunter

As the day wore on, the piles in the office decreased and Mary felt more and more confident in herself. She lost herself in her work, stacking and organising transactions through the King George's long history. The cash flow became a river that she was swimming in, feeling it with every income and expenditure.

But the idea of Mona would keep crawling back. And with her, the thought of O'Nerry. Both sent shivers down her back and she had to take a moment to distract herself.

Mona once again crept into her head when she heard three knocks and Wat peered around the door without an invitation.

'Hello again Ms Woods! Sorry to bother, but I'll be manning the bar from here on. If you would like something to eat, there's a kitchen just opposite here; you're welcome to have anything you fancy. If Snow's around I'm sure she'll fix you up something if you asked her. Or you can come upstairs and I can get something from the pub menu made for you,' said Wat.

TALES FROM THE KING GEORGE

'Thank you Mr Stone, I'll probably help myself down here,' said Mary - she did not want to have to face the patrons of this pub.

Wat nodded and was about to leave when Mary's eyes darted to the corner of the room and she made a noise as if she wanted to ask him something; 'ah.'

'Yes?' Wat said, pausing.

Mary thought for a moment, but then shook her head, 'Never mind.'

Wat smiled and shut the door. Mary listened to him walking away and it wasn't long before a familiar voice piped up; 'You were going to tell him about me, weren't you?' asked Mona from within her hole in the corner.

Mary's head snapped up and then awkwardly shifted, 'I was thinking of mentioning you, but then I'm sure I would look the crazy one. How would he believe me?'

Mona laughed, almost sexily, 'Half the things that go on in this pub, I'd be surprised if he didn't.'

'So there are more things as well as you?' asked Mary, curiosity piqued.

'I couldn't say,' said Mona, 'it's not my place.'

She became quieter after that. A couple more hours of paper sorting later and Mary started to feel hungry. After checking her watch, she decided it was time to find something to eat. She rearranged the piles to let herself out and closed the office door behind her.

Laughter and chatter echoed down the corridor. Some music was playing faintly but she could barely hear it. The thought of all those people pushed Mary into the kitchen.

Through the open door opposite was the kitchen like Wat had said - it was small but it had a fridge, oven with a stovetop, a sink, and several cabinets. To the right was a round table with three chairs around it, most likely the family dining area, but it had a pile of unclean dishes upon it. Mary deduced this was the overflow pile as the sink was almost overflowing with dirty plates and pots.

Mary shook her head in disappointment and approached the fridge. She pulled it open and was met with the horrid stench of rotting and decomposing food. She glanced around; half of what was in it did not look like food, either having been there so long or was never food to begin with, such as the trainer stashed in the back of the top shelf. The fruit and vegetable tray now looked like a compost bin. And there didn't look to be a single bottle of milk (amongst the several brands that were there) that was within its best-before date.

At this point of her search, her hand clutching a handkerchief to her face to keep out the smell, young Snow Stone bounced into the room. Snow stopped halfway through her skip at the sight of Mary who lifted herself up from the fridge to greet the girl.

'Snow,' she said, attempting a smile, 'I was just looking for something to eat…'

She trailed off, indicating the state of the fridge.

'Yeah, I don't usually eat from there,' said Snow, who then opened a cabinet and pulled a packet of biscuits out; chocolate digestives. She snapped one in her mouth.

'I'm not surprised,' said Mary.

'Do you eat a lot then?' asked Snow.

Mary straightened up and eyed Snow. 'No?'

'Oh,' said Snow, who shrugged and then left.

Mary's feelings for Snow were bubbling up into dislike, but she didn't want to focus on that at the present time. She gave a last look for something edible but it wasn't long before she gave up. She resigned to the fact that she'd have to brace the pub.

Mary lifted her shoulders back, readjusted her cravat, and mentally prepared herself. Then she marched out of the kitchen, up the stairs, and out into the barroom.

The place was not as packed as it had sounded. The main room she was in had the bar to her right, where she could see Wat pouring out a drink to a couple of men. One was in a wheelchair, head peeking up above the counter, bald and a little grumpy looking with a silver tooth, his left leg held up in a yellowing cast. The other man was leant on the bar, much happier looking, a rough tasselled grey beard surrounding his chin and a bald head as well, wearing a tweed cardigan and what looked like moccasins. When Wat passed the drink to the man in the wheelchair, leaning over as he did so, he caught Mary's eye.

'Ms Woods! Fantastic, let me introduce you! This is Seamus and Duncan,' said Wat as overjoyed as ever.

The man in the wheelchair with the cast extended a hand, hinting a smile, 'I'm Seamus.'

Mary shook it and then shook the bearded man's, 'And Duncan!'

'Mary; Mary Woods.'

'These two are some of my oldest customers! They've been coming here since my uncle was running the place,' said Wat.

'Aye, since old Saul was manning the taps,' said Seamus, 'he was a good beer tapper. Not like you Wat.' He chuckled hoarsely. 'Can't pour a Guinness to save your life.'

'You're his new bookkeeper, eh?' asked Duncan.

'His accountant, yes,' corrected Mary.

MARY AND THE HUNTER

'I was never good with numbers,' said Duncan reminiscently, 'they always confounded me. You know they have imaginary numbers nowadays?'

'I hear they made them up,' said Wat, and he laughed. Mary smiled politely. 'Anyway, are you hungry? I can rack up anything on the menu for you and bring it out here. Or the dining room if you prefer.'

'Yes, I'd rather the dining room,' said Mary, as she took the menu from Wat's hands. Wat smiled, but she could tell he was slightly wounded.

'How are you finding the place?' asked Seamus, gearing up to take a swig.

Mary paused and said, 'Full of surprises,' putting on a smile.

'Yeah, that's what everyone says,' said Duncan, 'have you met Tilly yet?'

'Tilly?' asked Mary.

'Or Wojciech?'

'Not yet.'

'She's going to have an aneurism if she meets Wojciech too soon I think,' said Duncan.

Seamus dribbled a stream of Guinness down his front and rolled his eyes at himself.

'Ignore these two,' said Wat, 'you can take the menu with you.'

'Thank you Mr Stone, but I'll just have the lasagne if that's alright,' said Mary, passing the menu back.

'Alright, sounds good, I'll have it sent to you in the dining room,' said Wat, ringing it up on the till.

'Good to meet you both,' said Mary and left the three of them at the bar. She followed the directions on the signs for the dining room and passed through one of the doorways in the barroom.

TALES FROM THE KING GEORGE

A step down, she was in a longer part of the bar, also relatively full of people with booths along the left-hand side, and several tables on the right on a raised platform. The walls were painted dark green and the carpet was the classic pub-style carpet, patterned in creams and browns and blacks; the best pattern to hide stains in. The upholstery was mismatched, but there seemed to be a theme of reds and creams.

The people there were mostly elderly, although there were a couple young groups in the booths. One was a group of what looked to be teenagers, laughing about music and voices. She caught the eye of one of the girls, who gave her a questioning look, so she continued through the room.

At the end were two solid wood push-doors; one led into what must've been the kitchen as it indicated 'STAFF ONLY' and the other to the right had a sign reading 'DINING ROOM'.

She pushed on through to the dining room and found it was much less populated. It was right next to the conservatory, with double doors in the corner connecting the two. The room was much more organised than the conservatory with a definite theme; there were tea cloths on each table and they all had at least three chairs to each. It was arranged in a grid-like pattern.

There were two families, one group of loud people, and a couple already eating in the room. Apart from them, it was fairly quiet and Mary felt at peace. She chose a table closest to the windows of the courtyard. The day had ended and the sun had set already, leaving darkness apart from a deep blue sky. She could distinctly see the lights of the gallery and barroom but the rest of the window was her room's reflection.

MARY AND THE HUNTER

Once she sat down, she suddenly wondered how they'd know it would be her to serve to. But in a moment, before she decided to do something about it, a waitress popped out from the kitchens holding a plate of lasagne and brought it directly to Mary, putting it down with a set of cutlery and condiments. She smiled as she did so, her curls falling out of place slightly.

'Lasagne,' she stated.

'Thank you,' said Mary.

The girl smiled and tucked her hair back behind her ear and left her.

Mary ate and, as she did, she ran through the updates on her phone. She messaged some friends who had asked how she was doing. She messaged her father, as he wanted to make sure she was alright. She also messaged her brother, just as an update. But she didn't mention Richard O'Nerry nor Mona. Probably best to keep that under wraps.

When she'd finished the waitress reappeared to take her plate away but hung around for a moment longer than she needed to.

'Are you our new accountant?' she asked, her voice rasping slightly.

'Yes, Mary Woods,' Mary replied, a little off-guard.

'Wat told me about you. Some of the staff are taking a smoke break, do you want to meet them?' asked the waitress.

Mary frowned a little at the notion but then her ears pricked up at the sound of raucous laughter in the barroom and she glanced to the side. The waitress picked up on it. 'Yeah, we'll be a little quieter than he is.'

'Sure,' said Mary, 'I'll come.'

'I'll just take these into the kitchen and then you can follow me,' said the waitress, and she smiled wide.

Mary couldn't help but feel entranced by the girl's white teeth, contrasting so sharply with her skin, and she happened to watch her leave as well. She snapped from it when she disappeared through the kitchen door.

The waitress reappeared and nodded her head behind Mary to the conservatory doors. Mary got up and followed her slow pace.

'My name's Neo,' said the waitress.

'Good to meet you,' said Mary, 'how long have you worked here?'

'About two years now,' said Neo, 'I only work Tuesdays, Thursdays and Fridays, and sometimes occasionally I do a weekend, but not often.'

'How do you find it?' asked Mary.

'Yeah, well you get your ups and downs don't you,' said Neo and grinned. Mary seemed to lose her grasp on reality once more when she saw Neo's smile.

Neo opened up the doors in the conservatory that lead out to a patio area. Three people were already standing out on the decking, underneath an orange lamp that was attached beside the door. It illuminated them but left the area behind them in darkness. It was fairly quiet, with the faint sound of cars and the three laughing when Mary and Neo joined them.

'Hey everyone this is Mary, the accountant,' said Neo introducing her.

Mary instantly recognised Rob, Wat's son, who was wearing a black waistcoat and white shirt with rolled-up sleeves and a cigarette in his hand. Whilst he was definitely tall, he was shorter than the other man, who was built big with a rough-shaven face but rounded features. His hair was short and dark brown and his eyes were sharp, but his smile was slim and sexy. When Mary appeared, she saw his eyes glance up and down at her.

The other person was a tan woman wearing the white clothes of a chef, with big and bright green eyes. Her cigarette stuck out from her mouth, and with Neo arriving she instantly lifted her pack to her, which Neo helped herself to one of. The chef offered one to Mary too.

'Hey,' said the other man, 'I'm Jarrett. This is Rob and Kam.'

'Yes I've met Rob before,' said Mary, 'pleasure. Are you all waiting staff?'

'Kam here's the chef, but as you can see there's not many eating tonight,' said Jarrett.

'That and my dad's on the bar,' said Rob, 'he loves it, so I get away for a while.'

'He seems well-liked,' said Mary.

'Oh yeah, Wat's great, he's a stand-up guy,' said Jarrett, 'he's not got a drop of bad blood in him. He's never raised his voice, never yelled or got angry. I mean, he'll tell you if he needs you doing something differently, but that usually happens like once.'

'Like that time I cooked that woman's steak in peanut oil and she had that allergic reaction,' said Kam, 'I felt awful, but I felt even worse having Wat tell me about it.'

Jarrett lifted his hand, but sighed, 'damn my light went out. Kam?'

'Wait,' said Neo, and she tossed her head to Mary, just as Kam reached out for Jarrett's cigarette and the two of them froze.

'Right, yeah,' and they stopped – Jarrett fumbled at his person with his hands, looking for a lighter. Mary gave a bewildered look to the two of them.

'What?'

'Don't worry about it,' said Neo, 'so what were your other jobs like?'

Mary considered the question before answering. She gave a brief description of the places she'd worked, the companies she worked for, and what she'd done. She toned down the jargon as well so they could understand her. She noticed Neo was visibly interested when she talked about the locations rather than the work and she also kept asking what she did outside of work. But Mary didn't really have an answer to that.

'I just keep busy.'

'They say you're the best of them,' said Jarrett.

'I've been around a bit,' said Mary, a distinct feeling of pride in her voice.

'So,' said Neo, 'you've only been here a day, but have you noticed anything weird yet?'

Mary's mind turned to Mona. 'What do you mean?'

'Well, some things that go on here aren't what you'd call normal. Some of the people too,' said Neo.

'Do you mean like Richard O'Nerry?' asked Mary.

'Oh not that guy,' said Jarrett, 'he's a bastard. Has Wat told you about him?'

'I met him.'

Everyone's eyes widened; 'you met him?' asked Neo.

'Yeah, he broke into my room last night, looking for Snow.'

Mary could see Rob visibly tense up and she felt instantly guilty. Everyone else had a disgusted look on their faces; Jarrett was shaking his head.

MARY AND THE HUNTER

'He should be behind bars,' said Jarrett, 'I wish the police had a better hand on him.'

'Did he hurt you?' asked Neo.

'No, he saw me and then left as quickly as he entered,' said Mary, 'I've heard he's a real piece of work.'

'That doesn't cover it,' said Kam, 'if I ever saw him I'd…' and she raised her thumb and index finger clasped together.

Before Mary had a chance to ask what Kam meant, Neo glanced behind her and then said, 'Looks like we got more customers.'

'Great,' said Kam, 'I'll see you around Mary,' and she winked.

Kam and Neo ducked back into the conservatory to the dining room. Meanwhile, Jarrett and Rob remained where they were. The two men blew smoke up into the air and gave each other a smile.

'What's your man got an accountant for anyway?' Jarrett asked Rob, giving Mary a comforting smile to let her know he wasn't criticising her presence.

'He's not kept track of everything,' said Rob, 'he's said he needs to work out what he has and what he doesn't.'

'Ah, said Jarrett, 'I bet it was the roof in June that got him scared.'

'That and the fence in the common,' said Rob, 'I hope you stay a while Mary.' Mary's eyebrow lifted. 'I can tell it's not been a great first night but we really could do with the help.'

'I think what our friend here needs,' said Jarrett and put a big hairy hand on her shoulder, 'is to meet some of the people around here. I think some will make you want to stay.'

'I think a few people would make her want to leave,' said Rob in a calm but concerned tone.

'Well sure, but what about Tilly?' suggested Jarrett.

'You think she'll stay for Tilly?'

'Jordan?'

'It's dark now, we don't want to mess around in the common.'

'Who's in the bar then? Anyone you could suggest?'

Rob snapped his fingers, 'Van Pelt. He's back in town.'

'Perfect!' said Jarrett, 'you think he's doing billiards?'

'I think he's probably doing darts at this point,' said Rob and put out his cigarette.

'Don't you two have work?' asked Mary.

'Sure, but Wat won't mind. Like Rob says, he loves working the bar,' and Jarrett opened the door for the conservatory. Mary looked back at Rob who shrugged in indifference. She uttered a half grumble before entering the conservatory and letting Jarrett lead the way. They turned left to follow the lightly lit gallery and entered the room at the end with the billiards table.

In the room was a man dressed in tan slacks and a white collared shirt, with black braces holding his trousers up. On his feet were tall, brown leather boots. He looked like he was in his forties with black stubble on his face, a sharp chin jutting out and dark jet-black eyes. His hair was slick and short with a quiff at the front. When Jarrett barged in the man didn't flinch, holding a dart in his right hand and two in his left. The room smelt of cigars and heat which almost caused Mary to cough but she kept it down.

'Therin my man! You're looking brilliant, I heard you were back in town,' said Jarrett, a grin plastered over his broad face.

MARY AND THE HUNTER

The man gave a quick look to see who it was but he didn't seem in high spirits.

'Jarrett, what do I owe the pleasure?' asked the man named Therin, whose strong Cambridge accent threw Mary off. She could definitely notice a tang of sarcasm in the man's voice.

'I just thought you'd like to meet Wat's newest hire – Mary Woods, ace accountant!' said Jarrett, putting his hand on Mary's shoulder yet again, squeezing slightly. This time Mary wasn't having it and threw his hand off; this caught Therin's eye.

'Yes, these two think that meeting you might keep me from disappearing,' Mary stated flatly, indicating the doubt in her voice. However, she did find this man handsome; dashing even. There was a classic kind of style to him as if he'd been dropped off from the nineteen-forties.

'Charmed,' said Therin, and he put the darts down on the billiards table to walk over to her. He presented his hand to take hers, and she let him do so. He slightly bowed with it in a gentlemanly fashion and Mary suddenly felt the blood rush to her cheeks.

'I am Therin L. Van Pelt. I'm a common patron to this establishment but I'm usually away. Why, I've only just come back from the depths of the savannah in Africa in fact.'

The man's dress sense suddenly became more reasonable, 'I see,' said Mary, 'what have you been doing.'

'Why I am a game hunter,' said the man, and he smiled.

Suddenly, Mary felt the respect she might have had for the man dissipate. She frowned.

'I didn't realise such people still existed,' she admitted.

'They are rare, almost as rare as the game I hunt,' Therin said, still smiling proudly.

Mary was unimpressed, 'Is this really the best of the best?'

Rob shook his head in dismissal, 'Therin, can you show her what you brought.'

Therin licked his lips and gave Rob a look that seemed as if he was asking for approval. When his eyes darted back to Mary it became apparent to her that they were hiding something. She would've been extremely annoyed if it wasn't for the fact they were on the edge of revealing it to her.

'It's not going to be a lion's head, is it?' she asked.

Therin laughed, 'no, that's on my wall,' and he walked to the corner of the room where a large brown rucksack was leaning against the wall. He unzipped the top and pulled out a jar that was wrapped in newspaper, held with a large number of elastic bands.

It was at this that Mary swept a glance at Jarrett and Rob. Rob was indifferent but Jarrett had his arms folded and an expectant look.

From the tenseness between them, Mary could tell the two had butted heads in the past but seemed to be on amicable terms. They weren't going to launch at each other's throats at the very least.

Therin put the jar on the billiards table and he held it with one hand around its centre, the other on the lid. 'This is a marvellous catch,' he stated, 'it took me a good solid month of hunting to get these. It was the only prize I've brought back from this venture but it's enough for Oxford that's for sure. I had to skulk around the densest forests I could find. They had to be just the right temperature and with just the right amount of shade. I spent days lying absolutely still and letting them grow accustomed to my presence before I could trap them.'

'Alright, we get it,' said Jarrett, his hand up, 'just show us mate.'

Therin gave him a tired look, then sighed as he pulled the elastic bands off the jar. He gently opened up the newspaper which had hardened and taken the shape of the jar. He was careful not to rip it as he did so.

Inside the jar were three, or four, very bright dancing lights. Mary almost mistook them for fireflies, until she noticed she could not focus on the bodies of the insects.

'These are the very rare, very hard to capture, Kenyan Faeries,' said Therin, 'note the yellow and orange colouration that makes them distinguishable from the European green and white varieties. The yellow and orange mean they are much better suited to the tall savannah grass, and they dim when in the shade to hide amongst the forest. Incredibly fearless as well, they will shy away from perception but animals they will often approach meaningfully.'

Mary looked at him incredulously, 'fairies? Are you trying to make a fool out of me?'

Therin looked offended, 'My lady, I implore, I would never do such a thing. These are real-life faeries, on my heart.'

Jarrett leaned forward, 'Yeah he showed us English fairies two years ago, and those were much more lively. These guys are a little slower.'

'It's a much colder climate here,' said Therin, 'they'll naturally approach warmth in these conditions.'

'So what, these are magical? Do they have strange powers?' asked Mary, her arms crossed, 'what's the mockery?'

'I am being entirely truthful,' said Therin, 'they are faeries. They don't really house any special abilities.'

'Apart from the whole, healing thing,' said Jarrett.

Therin stopped in his thoughts, 'Accelerated healing yes, but that only applies to non-mutated-'

'Can't they also sense water sources?' asked Rob.

'Yes, very helpful in the hotter climates, but otherwise they are simply very shy, rare and,' he tilted his head, 'nice to look at.'

Mary watched the lights dance around one another inside the jar and found them mesmerising. She'd seen fireflies once before but these creatures emitted a much brighter and more enchanting light. She felt calm. Suddenly her mind was rushing back to being nine years old and trying to catch fireflies in the woods. The rush of air as she ran, the itching down her back of sneaky ladybirds and gnats.

She once believed that she could catch fairies in her backyard.

'This is,' she said, then took a step back, 'not real. It can't be.'

'Of course they're real,' said Therin, 'and pricey. I'm going to be getting a hefty sum from my main buyer in Oxford.'

'What will happen to them?' asked Mary.

Therin was about to say something but then caught himself, 'That is not my business.'

Mary narrowed her eyes at him, 'you don't care even a little bit?'

MARY AND THE HUNTER

'My business is procuring and selling them, what happens to them after that is none of my concern. It's none of yours either.'

Jarrett scoffed, 'Don't try and reason with the bloke. He doesn't really care what happens to his game,' and he walked toward the jar. As he did, Mary could have sworn he winked at her.

Rob edged to the door, grabbed the handle and looked outside, 'I'll be back in a moment.'

'I care,' said Therin, and he picked up his dart, 'I care about the big game. The big ones, those I often keep for myself.'

'Not often alive though,' said Jarrett, 'but you're a betting man aren't you Therin?'

The hunter eyed him, 'Are you getting at what I think you're getting at?'

'You've got a good game going on,' said Jarrett, nodding his head to the dartboard.

Mary could see that Therin had gotten sixty and fifteen from an overshoot to the left. She crossed her arms, expectantly.

Jarrett walked to the dartboard and snatched up the second set of darts, 'Come on, one game you and me. You get that head-start.'

Therin raised an eyebrow, 'What's the wager.'

'If I win, the faeries go to Ms Woods here,' said Jarrett.

Mary chuckled at the thought, 'You're going to seriously challenge this man?'

'Very well,' said Therin, 'and if I win? I can't think of much you could give me that equates to the fairie.'

Jarrett licked his lips, gave Mary a knowing look, and squared up, 'You get to take Ms Woods here out on a date.'

Mary was about to object until Therin burst into laughter, leaning back. She narrowed her eyes at the man and his mirth – she could see right into his mouth, spying a golden cap on one of his molars. The reaction he gave rubbed her entirely the wrong way.

'What's so funny Mr Van Pelt?' she asked.

'Oh I'm sorry, but did he clear this with you beforehand Ms Woods? That seemed like the most pathetic attempt…' but Van Pelt trailed off as he noticed Mary's face, 'that is to say on his part. That is no way a slight on yours Ms Woods.'

He cleared his throat and straightened up, a grin still stuck on his face, then presented his hand to Jarrett; 'Deal.'

Jarrett grasped it firmly with both of his and gave it one hard shake, obviously attempting to throw him, but Van Pelt didn't even flinch.

Therin then concentrated on the dartboard and launched his final dart, hitting the mark for sixty again.

'One sixty-six,' he stated out loud.

Jarrett worked his arms around in a circle. He stretched his arms up into the air and across his chest. He clicked his neck back and forth a few times, then readied his throwing hand. Then he switched hands. Then he switched back. At which point Van Pelt uttered a disgruntled noise to indicate this was just a waste of his time; then and only then Jarret took his shots.

He wasn't as good as Therin and ended up not being able to make up any ground. When Therin stepped up again, Mary watched him precisely launch his darts as if he were trying to thread them through a needle. She noted he wasn't perfect, but compared to Jarrett he was a professional.

MARY AND THE HUNTER

''Seventy,' he stated calmly, 'you may want to rethink your strategy, Jarrett.'

Jarrett stepped up and Mary could instantly see he was not taking it as seriously as Therin had. The man's hand tumbled from his arm, as did the dart, and she was surprised he even hit the board. She wondered how Jarrett could have had the confidence to make the bet when he obviously didn't have the skill.

Therin took his turn, but fumbled - he amassed a ten, a fifteen and then shook his head. In the end, he hit seventeen and he seethed. 'Twenty-eight.'

Jarrett tossed his darts haphazardly into the board, 'seventy-five.'

Therin stood up straight and glanced at Mary who was vaguely interested. She felt somewhat flattered that Jarrett was playing this game on her behalf, and she felt Therin's gaze on her occasionally. But she found the whole thing to be ridiculous, especially as she saw Therin getting more and more frustrated. She was not enjoying being the 'reward' like some pretty princess at a tournament, her knights attempting to win her favour. Shall it be the green or the black knight? Neither, she just wanted to go to bed.

She was tempted to just leave them to it but she considered the faeries that were fluttering in their jar. They seemed so eager to get out. Jarrett had a plan and she wanted to see what it was. Perhaps the large man was playing the long feint.

In the next round, Therin instantly overshot, having eight points to go. Jarrett patted him on the shoulder and Mary saw Therin glare at the big man.

'Nah mate, this is how you do it,' and the big man threw two tens, and now he was aiming for the double thirty to check out. He shot Mary a quick look and smile, and she felt a moment of excitement. This was it; this was the play he'd been waiting for. There was almost a little respect for the man, even if he was a little brash around her. With his run-up, she patiently awaited the triumph. She jumped when his dart hit the board. And was instantly disappointed when it was out of bounds.

Jarrett lifted his hands in acceptance, 'it's tricky in the final points.'

Therin ignored the comment and instantly threw a one. The second dart also hit his target of one. He looked to Mary, 'I'm sorry, it's nothing personal.' Then he threw his last dart and this one hit his target - six. He eased up, a smile spread across his face and Therin put his hands on his hips in a victory stance, 'Looks like you owe me a date.'

Jarrett put a hand to his chin, 'looks like I do,' he moved around to the billiards table.

Mary gave him a hard stare, 'splendid,' she said, the word oozing with sarcasm. She also said a small apology in her head to the faeries to say sorry that Jarrett, the complete idiot, had failed them.

'Best two out of three?' Jarrett attempted to bargain.

'No no, our bet was a bet,' said Therin, high on his victory, 'what would you prefer Mary? A tour in the savannah or a cabin in the woods?'

'Come on,' said Jarrett, 'we could switch games? How about billiards?'

It happened before Mary knew it; Jarrett was reaching over the billiards table for the cue but instead when Van Pelt was distracted with her, he grabbed the jar and bolted. The door swung open as Rob entered the room again but he jumped out of the way of Jarrett who launched down the gallery.

Van Pelt didn't notice at first. As soon as it clicked, he ran after Jarrett yelling.

'HEY! You bastard!' he shouted after the man.

Jarrett had already reached the conservatory and slammed into the doors onto the patio. Van Pelt had only reached the conservatory when Jarrett took the jar into the air with both hands and threw it to the ground. It smashed open, scattering glass and the faeries onto the floor.

Van Pelt reached the doorway and couldn't believe what he was seeing. The faeries fluttered up into the air softly, as if dazed, but within seconds they took off into the darkness towards the line of trees at the bottom of the patio. Jarrett had his hands on his hips in triumph.

Van Pelt, realising what the man had done, ran round Jarrett's front and grabbed him by the shirt. Jarrett attempted the same with one of Van Pelt's braces, their faces almost touching. When Mary had arrived on the scene the men were on edge of a brawl. Rob stayed back in the conservatory shaking his head and rolling his eyes.

'How dare you release those; our bet was fair and square! You have just cost me thousands in hunting, and hundreds of thousands in good game! Who the hell do you think you are!?'

'Who the hell do you think you are, trapping those creatures and thinking you can just sell them to the highest bidder!'

'Business is business, you had no right! You think this won't come back to you? You think I won't do everything in my power to-'

'To what, huh? What are you gonna Therin? Shoot me! I dare you.'

'Enough!' shouted Mary, taking it upon herself to step in, 'both of you stop this!' She wedged her hands between the two men to try and prise them apart; she wasn't scared, if they were going to fight, they would've thrown a punch already. When she pushed them away from one another she stepped between them, yet neither could take their eyes off the other; their irises burning with hatred.

'Jarrett just what do you think you're doing!? You should be ashamed of yourself.'

Jarrett was shocked at the reaction, 'You can't side with this guy!? You really didn't care about the faeries?'

'It wasn't your right. And you Mr Van Pelt. I'm ashamed of a man who deals in such things as exotic creatures, especially in things such as faeries!'

'I spent a great deal of money on capturing those things-'

'Then I shall see that you're compensated,' said Mary, 'I agree that Jarrett should not have done what he did. I'll speak with you later but I'm sure we can arrange something, I'm very sorry.'

Van Pelt managed to get a hold of his temper and threw his hands down and adjusted his braces. 'Very well Ms Woods. I think I need to cool off; I shall find you after I get a drink,' he strode to the conservatory, 'I won't forget this Jarrett. This is your third strike. You are not to come near me again, else I press charges.'

He passed Rob without another word, likely headed to the billiards room. Mary gave Jarrett a stern look. At first, he had a boyish grin until he threw up his hands in confusion.

'Come on Mary, don't you have a moral compass.'
'What if he does press charges?'

'What's he going to tell the police, I released his faeries? He can't press anything. Besides, I couldn't let him sell those things. Not after the last time,' and he gestured out to the darkness, 'Look at them!'

Mary looked out and found that in the darkness, the twinkling of orange and yellow lights were bobbing in and out of the trees. So the faeries were still in the area. They were free, that much was true.

'Jarrett, you're brutish and headstrong. If you were trying to make a good first impression, you've absolutely failed.' She squared her shoulders at him. Jarrett's smile softened to guilt. 'But thank you,' she finally said, albeit begrudgingly. She watched the lights until they all but disappeared in the darkness, 'I agree. They should be free.'

Fire in the Kitchen

The next morning, Mary attempted to follow a routine. She got up, readied herself, and headed straight down to the office for seven o'clock. Once sat down she got right back into logging accounts and statements. After a couple of hours, she went to look for a way to make a cup of tea and something to eat. Instead, she found Wat in the kitchen, desperately trying to reach what looked like the last clean plate in the cupboard. After a moment waiting for him to notice her, she coughed.

'Oh Ms Woods!' said Wat, almost losing his footing with one foot on the back of a chair and the other half on the counter.

'Mr Stone,' greeted Mary stoically, 'I was hoping for a cup of tea-'

'Oh say no more!' said Wat, and dropped off the chair to the floor, leaving the plate, 'I'll let the kitchen know and we'll bring some down. Have you already started work?'

'Yes, thank you, I don't faff when it comes to accountancy,' stated Mary.

'Excellent!' said Wat, 'I heard that you met my dear friend Van Pelt last night as well. I apologise if he came across a little aggressive.'

'Mr Stone, so far nothing had been as I would have expected,' said Mary plainly and honestly, 'and if you call Van Pelt a little aggressive you are surely underestimating.' Wat coughed nervously.

'Well, today is Wednesday, which means it should be a little calmer than usual! The middle of the week; people don't usually touch the establishment but I expect our tenants will be walking around,' said Wat, 'I do recommend that, if you take a break, you walk around the common!'

'Thank you, Mr Stone, but tea would suffice,' said Mary.

She could tell Wat was attempting to get her to socialise. Mary knew that it was best not to get too chummy with her clients; made it harder to tell them the facts. Especially when the fact was that the establishment needed to make some major modifications to its budget to stay afloat, or close down. She hadn't yet found all the evidence she needed but the expenditures were racking up.

When she returned to the office, she sat right back down and began to work. But not long after she glanced to the corner in the ceiling with the crack.

'Mona?' she called, softly.

'Darling?' replied the sexy voice almost causing Mary to regret saying anything.

Mary didn't respond immediately for feeling ridiculous but she braced herself, 'What kind of place is this pub?'

She saw the spider scurry out the hole, 'what do you mean?'

FIRE IN THE KITCHEN

'I saw faeries yesterday,' said Mary.

'Oh. Interesting,' Mona responded, unsurprised, 'yes, this pub has its fair share of mystical and mythological creatures passing under its roof.'

'But how? And why?'

'It's just how it's always been,' said Mona.

'Is there anything I should be concerned about?'

'I don't crawl around on the barroom floor so I don't hear a lot but, when I used to frequent, you'd get all sorts. Wat's too accommodating, he won't turn them away.'

Mary sighed and nodded, 'What about you, did he cotton on with you?'

'Hah! No, but he'd never return my advances either,' Mona snickered, 'I used to think he was playing hard to get but now I think he just wasn't interested.'

'Such a shame,' said Mary.

'Oh yes, I missed out on having a shaky financial foundation,' joked Mona, and scuttled away.

* * *

When it came to twelve o'clock, Mary took a break and left the lower level to enter the barroom. Like Wat had said it was practically empty, save for a few couples in the booths and a single man at the bar who was being served by Jarrett. The man looked pretty downtrodden and Jarrett, without drawing attention, motioned he had already had a few pints too many.

Mary smiled at him and followed the gallery, through the billiards room and to the conservatory. Through the room, she exited to the patio she was out on last night. She found that the stone patio had two levels; both with benches, but the lower sat beside the stream. A small wooden footbridge crossed the stream and followed a dirt trail that passed over the brook and between two sets of large and high trees. Beyond the trees was shrouded. It was at this point that Jarrett appeared behind her, slapping a hand on her shoulder.

'What's over there,' she asked, pointing between the trees.

'That's the "lost common". Did Wat tell you about it?' he asked.

'No?'

'Oh, it's a funny story! Back in the 70s or 80s I think, this big old homes developer - actually it might have been a couple of them - well they bought all the land around this common. It used to be pretty big, pretty open. Good place to walk dogs! Anyway, they sneakily cut off bits of the common to give the new homes their own gardens.

'They didn't think about it too well though. Too busy making fences and the houses around the edge, they accidentally cut off the common from the road! All apart from this small entrance. And since the only way to get to it is through the pub, the pub controls the common.

'There's not been any plans to make a new entrance so the council decides to ignore it for Wat's benefit. But they won't pay for its maintenance so that's why Jordan's around, our groundskeeper.'

'I see,' said Mary, 'so it's like a park.'

'Oh yes,' said Jarrett, and he led the two of them down the patio toward it, 'it has a duck pond, shed, little patches of bushes and trees. Very serene, sitting in the middle of town. Apart from the pen.'

They passed between the two tree sets and Mary could see what Jarrett meant. The common had a pond set in the centre, with the other side of it bordered by a cluster of trees that made a small wooded area. The

FIRE IN THE KITCHEN

shed was set on the edge of that and in front of them was level grass. Trails led off into the wooded parts, and she assumed that there would probably be more open spaces and patches of grass, but she was surprised by how big it felt. There were a couple of benches scattered about including one beside the pond on which sat yet another man who looked rather old. His skin was wrinkled and sagged, his nose was long but large, and he wore a grey flat cap and a thick woollen waistcoat. The man saw Jarrett and Mary, and slowly and shakily stood up.

'Jordan!' called Jarrett.

Mary and Jarret circled to meet the old man, in case he ended up falling over before he reached them. When they did, Mary felt good to see the man had a very large and genuine smile on his face.

'How do you do,' said the man, 'my oh my, who is this beautiful young woman.'

Mary introduced herself as the old man took her hand and planted a kiss. Normally she would complain but she let the man have the moment.

'I'm Jordan Mader, I'm the groundskeeper of the common. Nothing happens here without me knowing about it,' the old man chuckled, tongue lolling out.

'It's a lovely space,' said Mary, 'I used to live near a wood when I was a child.'

'And this is a very good wood too,' said Jordan, 'there's not any deer, but we got squirrels, hedgehogs, some owls up there too. Do you care for bird watching at all?'

'I've not really attempted it,' said Mary, and she noticed the binoculars hanging around Jordan's neck.

'What have you spied today then?' asked Jarrett.

'I've seen a spectacular pair of tits,' he said.

Instantly Mary gave the man a look noticing he hadn't taken his eyes off her, and he burst into laughter.

'No really, up there! A couple of blue tits,' he stated, pointing up into the trees. He handed Mary the binoculars. She took the hint and aimed them up. It didn't take her long to find the two small blue birds, sitting on a branch together.

'That is quite spectacular,' Mary stated.

'Ah, now look at that. It's a red-breasted robin and a common cuckoo,' said Jarrett pointing in the opposite direction.

Mary spun around, the binoculars still against her eyes. She didn't see any birds, but she did see Wat. She jumped in surprise and lowered the binoculars. She could see he was across the common, walking out from the woods towards a bench with a woman in tow. The woman was laughing at whatever he was saying. She was wearing a rather light and breezy dress, which Mary found ill-suited to the late-October cold. She had shiny blonde hair, rosy red lips, and her figure was impeccable. Mary was surprised that a woman this attractive was walking with Wat and actually enjoying his company.

'Who is that?' she asked.

'Ah, that's Ms Niamh Glenn-Smith,' said Jordan, licking his lips and stating it over gloriously, 'she and Wat have had regular meetings like this for half a year now. She loves to walk the common.'

'She's a snake,' said Jarrett, 'watch out for her. She acts nice but we know she's lying through her teeth.'

Mary looked the woman up and down. She sure was a sight to see but Mary had dealt with these types of women before. She wasn't new to the idea of a woman using her charm to get what she wanted however she did tend to steer clear of them. What Mona had said to her earlier rang in her head.

'Wat's smart,' she said, 'he won't fall for her.'

'I don't trust her,' said Jarrett.

'You don't need to trust her,' said Jordan, 'if she was talking to me, I'd do whatever she wanted; no questions asked!'

'Even if it was to kill off all the baby hedgehogs hiding out here?'

'You'd find my spade covered in them!' and Jordan laughed.

Jordan then walked off and left Jarrett and Mary, who watched the pair on the bench as they sat together closely.

'What do you think she wants,' she asked.

'She's an estate agent, what do you think?' said Jarrett, 'probably urging him to sell.'

Mary's eyebrows raised. It was intriguing to find someone else with the same goal.

'Van Pelt, this woman - you don't seem to like a lot of people,' stated Mary.

'People tend to be bastards,' said Jarrett.

To take his mind off them, Mary pulled Jarrett away to take her around some more. They passed a wall of trees that covered a part of the common from view and found a set of wooden fencing, twice her height. A great big wooden door was locked by several chains and locks that looked impenetrable.

'What's this?' she inquired.

'A mystery,' said Jarrett, 'Wat had it built a few weeks ago and no one knows why. Only him and Jordan.'

Mary tried to look through the fencing but she couldn't see anything of interest – grass and trees and the fences on the opposite side. In the centre looked like a drum or a trough but she couldn't see it well enough.

'I'll ask him about that later,' she muttered.

* * *

Later in the day, Mary exited the reception to the bustling barroom and found herself bumping into Wat yet again with Niamh on his arm. Niamh jolted in surprise before a large smile spread across her face.

'Hello,' she said in a long and high tone, indicating that Niamh was feigning delight in meeting the one and only Mary Woods, 'you must be Mary! Niamh,' she stated and presented her hand. Mary took it for a soft shake.

'Mary, this is Niamh! She's a local estate agent from down the high street,' explained Wat.

'Is that all you have to say of me?' asked Niamh, playfully.

'An estate agent?' said Mary, following suit in feigning interest.

'Yes, but I'm heading back to work now. Sorry to dash like this,' said Niamh, 'Wat could you grab my coat please?'

'Of course!' said Wat and he briskly walked into reception. Mary glanced at the bar and saw Jarrett there, pouring a drink. He shook his head, giving Niamh a look. Niamh stepped close to Mary and leaned in.

'How are you finding the place?' she asked. Mary instantly thought of the faeries.

'It's quite,' she paused to find the right word, 'curious.'

'Ah yes, curious,' said Niamh and she quickly glanced around, 'here.' She passed Mary a card between her index fingers. Mary would've asked where it came

FIRE IN THE KITCHEN

from, but Niamh leant in further and softly spoke into her ear, 'Come meet me when you can. I would love to ask you what you really think.'

At which point Wat returned with her coat, 'All ready. I'll walk you to your office!'

'Thanks Wat,' and the two of them left the barroom out the front doors, but not before Niamh looked back and gestured to Mary again.

Mary wasn't sure what to make of it, but she took a look at the card. It read as she expected, "Ms Niamh Glenn-Smith, Estate Agent, Harper and Dawn"

She flipped the card over in her hands and looked at Jarrett.

'Bad news,' he muttered.

Mary nodded in acknowledgement, 'She seemed eager to talk to me. I wonder what she wants.'

'She wants to sell the place. Who better to help than the accountant?' said Jarrett, gesturing at her, 'if she could sell it, she could retire on the commission.'

'So could Wat, he'd solve his financial troubles in an instant,' she said

'I'm gonna pour myself a half, you want anything?' said Jarrett, ignoring the comment.

Before Mary could answer with a half-meaningful 'no thank you,' a short tremor jostled her from her feet and it was followed by a loud and low rumble from the kitchen. To Mary, the only possible explanation could be an oven had exploded or the kitchen had burst into flames. Jarrett braced the counter with his hands and literally leapt over the counter, not bothering to run around.

'Stay here!' he ordered and raced through the rooms into the kitchen.

TALES FROM THE KING GEORGE

Mary couldn't see any fire from where she was. The other patrons in the bar were bewildered and looked around, concerned whether they should be doing anything. Mary walked through and said in a calm but stern voice, 'It's alright, no need to worry.'

She had every reason to worry but she was sure if they needed to panic Jarrett would have said. That was until Rob appeared from behind her;

'Alright, I need everyone out the pub quickly. There is an emergency and we need this area cleared now.'

He said it with such power in his voice that everyone rushed to get their belongings and leave the premises. He then pushed past Mary to enter the kitchen as another low and loud growl rumbled from the kitchen.

Mary began to leave with the rest of the patrons until she stopped in her tracks and looked back. The sensible sturdy voice in her was saying to stand outside and call the fire brigade because there was obviously a fire. The sensible voice was urging her, as a professional, to stay out of their business affairs.

But there was the small voice, the voice that had suddenly popped into her head after she saw the faeries, that this was an opportunity. That voice of curiosity. Something strange was going on.

When all the patrons had left and she was alone, she approached the door to the kitchen and listened. She could hear voices, not quite shouts, but loud talking and the sound of something rumbling. You don't talk during a fire. Mary leaned on the door and eased it open.

No one took any notice. Kam, who she'd met the previous night, was beside a great cast iron range. Her hands were on her hips, her hat and hair net were off, and she was sweating heavily. Rob was next to it as

FIRE IN THE KITCHEN

well, and Jarett was as far away from it as he could get. There were also another two people who Mary had not met yet, who weren't involved in the discussion and were standing on the edge of the room. Mary had obviously entered in the middle of the situation and there was a heated debate going on.

'-I don't know, that's what I'm saying,' said Kam, who sounded incredibly irritated.

'How do you calm him down?' asked Jarrett, being poignant.

'He needs space!'

'We can't exactly let him loose at this time of the day, now can we?' said Jarrett, 'there has to be something else!'

'He's choking, how would I soothe you if you're choking?' said Kam.

'Drink some water?' Jarrett suggested.

'Oh sure, let's just put him out then!'

'Would solve our problem,' said Rob flatly.

Mary guessed that whatever the issue was it was to do with the giant stove that was against the wall. She crept towards Rob, who was crouched down near the grating. She knelt down as best she could to see what they were all talking about.

When she could see through the grating, she suddenly understood what they were referring to. Because curled up inside the stove was what she could only describe as a lizard the size of a dog. And it was on fire. She also saw the reason for the tremors when it suddenly lurched, and a rush of flames burst from it, flaring up through the grate and along the outside of the stove. It continued for a few seconds, accentuated by the grumble with short bursts that Mary understood was the choking. The stove groaned at the rush of flames rippling up its surface, charring the iron.

'This is going to get out of hand until we let him out,' said Kam.

'Like I say, we need to do something else,' argued Jarrett.

'I can't exactly give him the Heimlich manoeuvre from out here,' said Kam.

Rob looked round at Mary, 'followed me?' to which she nodded.

Then the door opened once more but this time it was Wat.

'What's going on!?' he spouted.

'Cocharil's choking,' said Kam, 'someone must've dropped something in the oven, he can't spit it out.'

Wat rushed to the stove and put his hands on the grate, immediately pulling them away at feeling the heat. He looked in at the lizard.

'We'll get him out,' he said, 'pass me the oven gloves.'

No one said anything; Kam handed him the gloves. He shoved them on, grabbed hold of the edges of the grate, and yanked it off. He placed it down gently, leaning it against the stove, and then reached in for the lizard.

Suddenly the lizard coughed and flames roared out again. Wat backed off shielding his face. The flames were closer and more violent now there wasn't a grate. When it quietened down he tried again, placing his hands on either side of the lizard's shoulders, and he gently pulled out the lizard. It drooped in front of him.

'Clear the counter,' he ordered.

Kam immediately swept all the objects on the nearest counter to the floor, not giving it another

FIRE IN THE KITCHEN

thought, and Wat gently placed the lizard down. The lizard was on its feet and its head was pointed downward. It began to lurch and then cocked its head up as it coughed, exploding into flames each time. It coughed a few times in succession. Finally, it managed to cough up and spit out what had been lodged in its throat - it was a very charred but distinct piece of broccoli.

'Bloody greens,' said Wat. The lizard began to cool down and its once orange skin started to change colour to a darker red. Wat stroked the creature with his gloved hands.

'Careful Wat,' said Jarrett.

'I know, I know,' said Wat calmly.

He continuously stroked the lizard, hushing it as he did so. Mary could tell it was to soothe the creature. The lizard darkened in colour some more as he did so, turning burgundy, and then a dark brown, and the flames on it died down until it was just smouldering. 'There there,' he hushed softly.

Then he picked up the lizard and tucked it back up into the stove, where it curled up once more. He placed the grate back on firmly and quietly, and he stood back up to Kam and the other kitchen staff's applause. From within the stove, the lizard brightened up to a soft red, and gentle flames emanated from its body as if it wore a hundred birthday candles.

'That was close,' he said with a grin spreading across his face, 'that could've gone a lot worse. Imagine if he'd run loose!'

At which point, almost as if the universe had heard what he had said and decided to make its climactic appearance, the grate popped open and dropped to the floor. Rob jumped back as it did so. Wat, who had already taken off the gloves, rushed to put them back on. But before he could, the lizard hopped down and out of the stove. It looked up at everyone curiously, still half drowsy. The flames rolled over its back and it eyed the door to the dining room.

Mary could see what it was thinking. Everyone could see what it was thinking. Wat most of all as he struggled with his gloves. He whispered quickly but his voice got steadily louder and more erratic, 'no, no, no-'

Then it bolted. Embers drifted in the air behind it as it banged into the kitchen door, squeezed through, and disappeared out of sight, leaving black marks against the wooden door.

'Follow him!' shouted Jarrett, and sprinted after it.

Wat did the same, hands joined by the oven gloves. Rob grabbed a pair of tongs from the kitchen utensils.

'Wait, Rob!' said Kam, but he'd taken off just the same. She sighed and put a hand to her forehead. Then she finally noticed Mary standing in her kitchen, 'Oh Mary! You're here.' Mary raised an eyebrow. 'Probably not the best introduction, but Cocharil is our salamander. He powers the stove and central heating.'

'Explains why your gas bills are so low,' said Mary, arms crossed, 'you locked him up?'

'For his own safety; Wat lets him out on weekends. At night. In the common,' said Kam, arms behind her head, 'if he's loose, he might get hurt.'

'Or hurt someone else,' said Mary, and strode towards the dining room.

'Where are you going?' called Kam.

'To help find it,' Mary called back.

After opening the door, she saw the trail in the carpet from burnt footprints. They ran right down the room, between and underneath tables, down to the

FIRE IN THE KITCHEN

conservatory. Hurrying after, she smelt the scent of burnt fabrics along its path but luckily it hadn't spent too much time in one place to cause much damage. Unfortunately, the trail went cold on the patio, literally; the stone was unaffected by the heat. She looked around for a hint of fire damage somewhere that would indicate the lizard went this way.

Rob was on the Patio and he had his tongs and was crouching lower to the ground, looking this way and that.

'Keep an eye out, if he comes back, I'll grab him,' he said to Mary.

'Where's your father? And Jarrett?' she asked.

'They went over the bridge into the common,' he said, 'better hope the thing doesn't run into the woods. Or Jordan.'

'What if Jordan finds him?' she asked.

'Jordan's not fond of lizards,' said Rob, looking up with a concerned look on his face.

Mary tongued her cheek, 'Why did it choke on broccoli?'

'It only eats coal,' said Rob.

'What does it drink? Kam made it seem like water kills it.'

Rob frowned, 'I actually don't know if it does. My dad usually takes him out.'

'I'm going to talk to him, you stay here.'

She made her way across the bridge and into the common. Wat stood beside the pond looking every which way. Mary rushed to meet him and stood next to him looking in.

'It needs water?' she said, to affirm what she thought.

'I know - Jarrett is looking down the stream. I would've thought he'd come here though, he usually drinks from this bank,' at which point Wat stopped in his thoughts and looked at Mary with shock,' Ms Woods! You were in the kitchen?'

'It doesn't matter. Wat, do you think it can swim?'

'Swim? No, he'd sink but why would-,' Wat then stopped in his thoughts and took another look at the pond. They watched it for a minute, waiting. Then there it was; a bubble.

'Keep an eye out for Jordan,' said Wat. Then he yanked off his jacket, threw it to the ground and dove into the pond. He performed an amateur breaststroke to the middle of the pond before diving below the surface, legs blinking up at the surface for a moment.

'Wat?' called Mary. She couldn't make out where he was until his head bobbed up.

'I think I can see him,' he said, and dove back under.

Mary tried to watch him but she couldn't tell where he was. She scoped around herself again to check Jordan wasn't around but it was just her and Wat by the pond. Time ticked by as if every second was a minute and Mary found herself counting them. After she reached fifty, she got worried. Wat hadn't come back up. But it was a pond, he wouldn't get dragged under. Unless he had gotten trapped.

'Wat?' she shouted,' Wat!'

She had kicked off her left shoe and began pulling off her blouse when he appeared, gasping hard. He had something in his arms. Mary waded into the water to meet him and pulled the lizard onto the side. It was completely black now, eyes closed.

'Damn thing doesn't know he sinks in water,' said Wat, and he knelt down by the unmoving creature.

FIRE IN THE KITCHEN

Then he began to perform CPR, giving the lizard's chest quick presses and blowing in through its mouth and nose. He found it difficult to make a seal but he made an attempt. Mary had her hands over her mouth as Jarrett raced up to them.

'Is he alright?' he asked, towering over them as Wat continued the process.

38, 39, 40, breathe

39, 40, breathe

Mary wished for it to breathe. She prayed.

Breathe

Breathe

The lizard spluttered and Mary heaved a sigh in relief. It rolled over and began nuzzling itself into Wat, remaining a black hue. Wat embraced the creature and lifted it up with two hands, smiling.

'Don't you scare me like that again,' he said, placing a kiss on its forehead.

Then he stood up with the lizard curled up in his arms.

'We'd better get him inside before he ignites again,' he said.

The three of them returned inside, Rob being called with them, and they took the lizard back into the kitchen. Wat placed him back in the stove, his hue now a dark brown, and this time Wat secured the grate hard. He slapped it a couple of times to be sure.

'He'll be burning again shortly,' he said, 'I don't think we'll be able to serve any food until then,' he said to Kam.

'I can make do,' she said.

Then Wat turned to Mary, 'Ms Woods, I should probably have a chat with you about this.'

TALES FROM THE KING GEORGE

'It's alright Mr Stone, I think I now understand the nature of things that go on in this pub,' said Mary, waving her hand in dismissal.

'Yes, things aren't quite what you'd expect,' he stated, 'can I offer you a drink?'

Mary smiled, 'I'll take an explanation thank you. Where and how did you happen to obtain a fire lizard?'

'Salamander,' he corrected, 'now that is a long story.'

THE HIGH STREET

Mary found she had developed a fondness for the Mad King after only a couple of days. She began to take more breaks out from the office to go upstairs and talk to the staff, including Wat, Jarrett, Rob, Kam, Neo and a few others as well. Wat often introduced her to the various locals and patrons who came to the bar and had been coming for years. When she was working, she occasionally found herself having a conversation with Mona, and the two developed a semi-friendship.

When the weekend came around, Mary had the time off. Wat had offered her full reign of the pub; as he had described it, "she was free to go where she pleased and do what she wished." She felt like she could return to the city centre for two days, but it would be too much of a journey for too little gain. Instead, she decided she'd run some errands. Early on Saturday, after having some breakfast, she found Wat just to let him know she'd be out.

'Ah, if you're exploring the area, then you walk down three streets and turn left. It'll take you straight onto the high street,' he said chirpily.

TALES FROM THE KING GEORGE

'Thank you, Mr Stone, I'll see you later,' said Mary, pulling her handbag onto her shoulder and exiting the front doors.

She hadn't really been outside in a while, working and sleeping in the pub meant she had had little reason to. She wasn't familiar with the area so she decided to trust Wat's directions and walk to the high street. She followed his instructions onto a classic, wide, pedestrian-filled high street. Being the weekend, it was bustling with activity. The shop doors were wide open, there was chatter in the air, and a small market was also set up selling wares out in the open. The local people were swimming this way and that, to do their day-to-day business.

She first visited the health and beauty store to stock up on a few things. Then she entered the local bookstore to find something new to read. It was a small self-owned shop that looked like it was trying its best to not be bought out by a chain.

As she was perusing the crime fiction section, which she was particularly fond of, she almost bowled over a short woman whom she hadn't seen.

'I'm sorry,' she sputtered out before noticing it was Lauren, the older woman she'd met previously by almost running into her, and had mentioned cutting hair.

'It's alright dear,' she said, 'my, how are you? I haven't seen much of you.'

'Yes I've been in the office mostly,' replied Mary, straightening her shirt.

'What are you looking for then?' asked Lauren, who was running her finger along the shelf, looking at titles and authors.

THE HIGH STREET

'Just some light reading,' said Mary, 'I enjoy reading before bed.'

'Tim Diamonds is an interesting fool,' said Lauren, pulling out a medium-length book, 'he's a detective! You like crime? I like crime. It's not a very good crime book, but it's a good comedy.'

'I've not read any of his.'

'It's a series by this Ant fellow, I think you'd like it. Do you like fantasy? I'm not big on fantasy but my grandchildren talk my ear off about it! I'd rather have some reality. But no romance, you hear me?'

She placed the book in Mary's hands. Mary didn't think much of it but she decided it was likely as good as any other book she'd pick out.

'Thank you. What are you looking for?' she asked.

'I was looking for these new-fangled Winds of the Winter books, but I can't seem to find any. Here,' she continued speaking, not giving Mary a chance to speak, 'have you discovered some of the Mad King's magic yet?'

Mary eyed the woman, then glanced around the bookstore. She spoke softly under her breath, 'I met Van Pelt. And the salamander in the kitchen,' she said.

'What about Sebastian? Wojciech?' asked Lauren in quick succession.

'Not yet, but I've heard of Wojci–'

'In due time then,' chuckled Lauren, before looking up at Mary's hair and gasping, 'Oh my dear! Look at this, you've got such frayed ends.'

Mary hadn't really done her hair up before coming out and she instinctively reached up and grabbed a strand. She had to admit, she hadn't had anything done to it in a long time and it was getting frazzled.

'I've been busy,' she said.

'Well come with me, let me get it done for you! My place, I've got wonderful people, they have a way with scissors that you wouldn't believe! Come, come!' Lauren urged.

Mary was hesitant at first, but Lauren's enthusiasm gave way, 'Sure, let me just pay for this then.'

After running it through the till, Lauren led Mary outside and back down the high street, towards the edge where the branded stores were thin and the independent shops sprung out in full colour with their various signs and names. Lauren edged Mary to the hairdresser's named "Snippy's", written in pink nineties bubble-writing, with printed pictures sellotaped onto the windows of different hairstyles for women. It had large full windows which through Mary could see there were two salon chairs and a row of seats on the left wall. There was also a tallish man sweeping the floor in a dark green shirt and jeans that looked a little too tight on him.

Lauren opened the door and the bell rang as she called out. 'John! Where's Blue? We've got a customer waiting!'

'Blue!' shouted the tall man with the broom.

'I'm coming!' came a high voice, followed by a younger and large dark-skinned woman who was tying a green apron around her waist. She looked up to see Mary and leant back a little to take her in, 'So what are we looking for?'

'Er, just a trim please.'

'No no, let's style a little! You look like you always keep it in a bun,' Lauren said quickly.

Mary held her tongue. She felt it best not to let on how correct Lauren was.

THE HIGH STREET

'Alright, do you want it styled?' asked Blue, her arms crossed.

'Yes, fine, style it however you think is best,' said Mary.

'I know exactly what she needs,' said Lauren and spoke softly into Blue's ear, who rolled her eyes.

'Fine, let's get started,' he said.

She prepped Mary and began to wash her hair. Lauren took a seat behind her so that she could continue talking and Mary could still hear her.

'The Mad King has always been full of weird things,' she said, 'even when Saul was running it. Do you know about Saul?'

'I've heard of him,' said Mary, her eyes closed.

'You've got Lauren talking on the Mad King? She'll never shut up now,' said Blue, her voice showing a hint of annoyance.

'I'm just saying, after living there for five years, you begin to see that place for what it really is. It's sanctuary,' said Lauren, 'you need to be careful. Most patrons go there BECAUSE it's sanctuary so you don't really want to ruin that. Of course, there's some people who would love nothing more…'

'Like me, after hearing you talking about it non-stop,' said Blue, and she pulled out the hairdryer.

Mary could tell that Lauren was still trying to speak even with the dryer on, but she relaxed. She had been due a haircut for a while now. When the dryer turned off, Lauren was mid-sentence.

'-and that's when we realised they were all in the attic!' she finished off with a chuckle, which Mary chuckled along with, glancing up at Blue who signed that she had no idea what Lauren had said.

TALES FROM THE KING GEORGE

Blue leant her back and she began to cut Mary's hair. Quick snips and Mary drifted off into her own thoughts as Lauren went on about something else that had happened in the Mad King. Mary watched Blue work in the mirror and considered how when she was much younger, she liked hairdressing. She'd pretend to cut her mother's hair, using her fingers as a pair of scissors, and show a mirror to her to see what she thought. Her mother had enjoyed it, and yet she'd kept her hair the same every time she went to the hairdresser's. Come to think of it, she'd never seen her mother wear a different hairstyle in her entire life.

When she came back to reality, Blue and Lauren were arguing.

'If you met her Blue, you'd feel the same way as I do! She's got a nasty air about her,' said Lauren, looking rather serious from Mary's view in the mirror.

'You're suspicious of everyone, I bet you're just jealous,' laughed Blue.

'Of what?'

'That she spends so much more time with Wat!'

'Oh don't be ridiculous,' said Lauren, but Mary could see the old woman smiling and looking away.

'Are you talking about that woman? Niamh something?' asked Mary, curious about the debate.

'Yeah, Lauren doesn't like her. Not surprised,' said Blue.

'Have you met her, Mary? What do you think?' asked Lauren.

'I'm not sure. She said I should see her and talk to her,' recalled Mary. She touched her purse where she'd put Niamh's card.

'Why?'

THE HIGH STREET

'I've no clue, she just wanted to see "what I really think",' said Mary.

'You see! Like I say, there are people who just want to ruin a good thing. Don't go see her!' said Lauren, wagging her finger in Mary's direction.

'Maybe you should,' said Blue shrugging.

'Don't be silly,' snapped Lauren.

'No really. If this woman is up to something, you could find out,' said Blue.

Lauren's face switched emotion, and she sprung from her chair into a quick waddle to approach Mary from the side. She grabbed Mary's hand, causing Blue to moan as she dropped Mary's hair.

'Mary you must go see this woman! Find out what she wants, and whether she is up to no good,' said Lauren with a definite serious tone, 'we can't have someone weaselling in and ruining our good place.'

Mary put a hand on top of Lauren's, 'I really don't think it's a big deal. She's not going to turn out to be a secret agent now is she.'

Lauren gave Mary a knowing look and Mary's face of amusement switched to confusion.

'Lauren,' John called from the back of the room, 'there's a bloke on the phone! Says he's from the council.'

Lauren swore under her breath, 'alright I'll be right there! I'll see you later, but you go find that "agent" and you find out what she wants!'

Then she waddled off into the back room, leaving Blue and Mary. Soon, Blue had finished up, washed and dried Mary's hair again and pulled out the mirror to show her.

'What do we think?'

Mary touched it and felt how much softer it was. It was spilling over her shoulders now and she felt a lot more confident about her appearance with it cascading over her head.

'It's-'

She hadn't worn her hair down in a long time. Not really suited for the work.

'It's perfect. Thank you!'

'I'm sorry about Lauren, she loves to get into these things,' said Blue, 'I think you should take the opportunity and leave now before she gets back.'

Mary paid her and did as she suggested, fast walking back down the high street. As she did, however, her eye caught a sign beside a walk-in office – 'Harper and Dawn'. Retrieving the card from her purse, she recognised it as Niamh's office. Turning to look behind her, in case Lauren was following, Mary turned the card over in her hand. Finally, she decided on what to do and placed it into her pocket as she approached the door. It was glass, so she could see right in. She pushed on the door to enter and the receptionist smiled up at her.

'Hi, I'm here to see Niamh? Er, Glenn-Smith?'

'What's your name?' asked the receptionist.

'Mary Woods.'

The receptionist grabbed the phone and gave a quick call. Mary took a look at the properties on the board; they all seemed to be priced about two-hundred grand, and all in the local area. Not what Mary was looking for in property. She had been considering something out in the country, a heavily wooded area perhaps?

'She's upstairs, first floor,' said the receptionist, smiling and pointing to a flight of stairs to her left.

THE HIGH STREET

Mary followed her instructions, entering the stairwell and climbing the stairs. The walls were painted white with photos of landscapes hanging up. On the first floor was a corridor of offices, to which she aimed for the one with 'Niamh Glenn-Smith' written on it. Before Mary could knock, Niamh was opening it.

'Mary, delightful! Come in, come in,' she beckoned, taking a seat behind her desk.

Her office was very neatly arranged, with an array of potted plants along the windowsill of her only window, and a set of blinds that were wound down so the bottom was just above the plants. She had a white bookshelf to the side filled with books and binders. On her desk was an old computer set to her right, and to the left were a set of photos and a couple of files. Beside the door was a two-seat sofa coloured red, but Niamh gestured to one of the two chairs sitting directly in front of her desk. After Mary closed the door, she took a seat.

'It's wonderful to see you, absolutely delightful,' stated Niamh, 'I was hoping you'd come by.'

'This isn't a bad time?' asked Mary.

'No no, a viewing cancelled on me so I'm free for a couple of hours! A little annoying, but what can you do?' and she laughed, 'So tell me, what do you think of the Mad King.'

'It's lovely, the people are friendly, if a little odd,' and Mary chuckled.

'Ah yes, odd is definitely the word to use,' said Niamh, her eyes wandering off, 'would you say anything unusual has happened during your stay?'

Mary looked away, thinking of Mona, the faeries, and Cocharil.

'Not really,' she said.

'Nothing at all?'

'Why do you ask?'

Niamh looked behind her, then got up and closed the blinds on her windows. She circled around the desk and locked her door shut. Then turned her head to Mary with a comforting smile.

'I've heard that there's more to that pub than meets the eye,' she said, walking back to the desk.

'What makes you say that?' asked Mary, her heart quickening.

Niamh paused before she continued, 'I think that Wat's hiding something. Secrets.'

Mary leant forward, 'What kind of secrets?'

'I don't know, but it's strange. I thought Wat would tell me, but he dodges my questions and avoids talking about the business. Trying to get information out of him is impossible,' said Niamh, 'what about you? Do you know what I mean?'

'I've not really been there long enough to make any decisions,' said Mary.

Niamh stopped talking and looked Mary dead in the eyes. She could tell that Niamh was weighing up whether to let Mary in on what she knew. Then she relented and opened the drawer in her desk.

'Do you want a drink?' she asked, pulling two glasses out.

Interested to hear what she knew, Mary said, 'Sure.'

Niamh also pulled a bottle of scotch whiskey out, 'whiskey. Sorry, I've no ice.'

Mary's eyes widened at the thought of drinking whiskey at all, but she sucked it up. She was on the verge of learning something, perhaps something valuable.

THE HIGH STREET

Niamh sipped the whiskey and shook her head before continuing, 'As their new bookkeeper, I expect you see a lot of what goes in and what comes out?'

Mary nodded in agreement.

'Does it all make sense?' asked Niamh.

Mary frowned at the question, 'What do you mean?'

'The pub staying afloat, does it all make sense? Does the money coming in match the money going out? How well would you say Wat is doing right now?' asked Niamh.

'I'm afraid that's classified information about his business,' said Mary politely but firmly.

'Right, right,' and Niamh took another sip, 'here's the thing. The Mad King is very, very valuable land.'

Jarrett was right all along.

'I've been urging Wat to sell for the whole time we've been an item, but he doesn't want to relent just yet. He's always been "waiting for the right moment" or they've had a "good month". He's hiding something, but whatever it is it's preventing him from actually making a decision.

'But that's why you're here right? You can help him make a decision.'

And it occurred to Mary that the generous benefactor who wished to see the pub closed, the one willing to pay her agency a large sum of money, was sitting in plain sight.

Mary cleared her throat, 'if he made the appropriate changes, his business could survive. From what I know he has regular income from tenants that live in the inn. But there are parts of it incoming and outgoing that don't make sense.'

'Don't make sense?'

'I'm not sure yet and I cannot discuss it with a party such as yourself,' said Mary professionally.

She'd have to stay in Niamh's good books to make sure she didn't lose the job. At least it was good to see who was in charge, even if she would've preferred someone a little further away. The landlord's girlfriend was a little too close, a little too personal. It felt a bit like betrayal.

'I understand completely,' said Niamh, 'oh if I could only sell that pub I would be making a lot of money. Start a new business with those funds. My own estate agency perhaps! I've got big ambitions Mary and I hope,' she leant forward, 'that we see eye to eye?'

'Perhaps,' said Mary, 'I am a professional Ms Glenn-Smith. I will be analysing the property to the best of my ability. But let me be clear,' and Mary took a sip of the whiskey and almost coughed, 'if the pub has any reason to close and sell then I shall find it.'

Niamh's grin widened, 'I knew I could trust you, Mary,' and she indicated with her glass to toast, 'to a fair and accurate assessment.'

Mary attempted the whiskey again. 'Yes,' she managed, 'A fair assessment.'

* * *

Mary felt her distaste for Niamh sit on her tongue the entire walk back from the high street, along with the whiskey in her throat. Something about Niamh felt off and she didn't like it. Something vicious was there.

Mary cursed herself; she'd gotten too involved in their personal affairs. She should've stayed in the middle ground and stuck with numbers, not people.

She was so far removed from the world around her that Mary managed to tumble into a middle-aged man. He had walked out from the takeaway that was opposite the pub. She almost fell over but caught herself. The man muttered as he dropped the boxes down by the stack he'd already arranged. He was a man of Indian descent with a black moustache and bushy eyebrows and, when he spoke, he had a heavy accent which Mary noticed when the man began to berate her.

'Woman watch where you're walking! Can't share a pavement?' he said.

'I'm so sorry,' she said hurriedly.

'I swear, like a bloody circus,' he lamented, 'aren't you that bookie Stone hired?'

'I'm a professional accountant mister…' she trailed off waiting for him to fill in the blank.

'Patel! It's on the sign,' he jerked a thumb up at the takeaway.

'Mr Patel. What business is it to you who I am?' said Mary folding her arms.

'Nothing I want to be a part of,' grumbled Patel, 'you crazies keep your crazy to yourself! My family didn't come here to be involved in your schemes.'

'What schemes might these be?'

'Stone is always messing things around here. I've already seen the planning permission he submitted a few months ago!' and he stood up a little straighter, 'building in that common. I object but the council said I had no grounds!"

'What were your grounds?'

'Disturbing the peace. And you know what they said?' Mary shook her head, 'What peace? Can you believe that? What peace?!'

'I'm sure he's got his reasons,' said Mary.

'I saw the horsebox as well. If he thinks he's starting a race course here, he's got another thing coming!' and Patel scoffed at the idea.

Mary eyed the man up, 'I don't think he's doing that.'

'You can tell him from me, some of us folk here want a calm life. A simple life! No earthquakes or explosions! No wanted men!'

Mary wasn't sure how to reply to Patel with this. 'I'll let him know,' she said.

Patel gave her a look as if to say he knew she wasn't going to, 'why are you involved with Stone anyway? Aren't you from the city?'

'I am Mr Patel, I simply took the job offered,' replied Mary.

'You realise what you've got yourself into? It's downhill from here, do you want to be one of the crazies?'

And the question that had been on Mary's mind all day was spoken aloud. Mary felt strange hearing someone else ask it. She considered Patel, who looked irritated and grumpy as if the antics in the Mad King had been grinding on him for years. There was Lauren, who absolutely loved being a part of it all though. And Niamh who desperately wanted to be a part of it.

'If I'm honest Mr Patel,' she said, 'I've come here with one job and one job only. That's all.'

'Oh sure!' and Patel turned back into the takeaway, 'Don't be waking me up at three in the morning though! I swear, I'll smack Stone's grin right off his face!'

Mary smiled at this. She gripped the bags she was holding tightly and swiftly trotted into the barroom. Wat was at the bar when she entered.

'Ms Woods! Good to see you!' he said, and Mary felt warm inside.

'Good to see you too Wat.'

THE HALLOWEEN PARTY

Mary was unimpressed at the Halloween decorations haphazardly hung about the barroom. The streamers with pumpkins and ghosts on them screamed "pound shop", yet the skeleton that hung unceremoniously from the beam running down the centre looked almost too real. She watched Rob putting them up from the barstool as Jarrett was cleaning glasses.

Halloween was upon them and Mary was no fan. However, she'd now been at the pub for little over a week and she felt that she was expected to attend the celebrations. Wat had warned her at the beginning of the week:

'We're having a Halloween party, a costume party! You're of course welcome to join, or not. Whichever you prefer.'

'I'm not a fan of costumes,' she'd responded, 'especially nowadays it being so Americanised, nobody dresses up to be scary.'

'So, it's okay if you dress up as long as you're scary?' said Wat.

'No, that's not what I meant,' Mary had said, shaking her head, 'you wouldn't find me wearing anything but my own clothes, in my own style.'

'Are you sure I can't tempt you?' asked Wat, lifting a skull mask to his face, 'boo.'

Mary wasn't moved. She gave him a gentle but indifferent look until he took it off, grinning.

'We'll see,' he stated, a little quieter, causing Mary to think he was up to something.

And now here she was, sitting in the barroom as the preparations were underway. She sipped her glass of water and looked back at the newspaper she was attempting the crossword in. It was cryptic. 'Under the side of a fortified wall, find a crab singing' - nine. Had a B and an I which really threw her off. She was tapping her finger against her cheek when she noticed that the rapid tapping of her finger didn't match the sound she could hear. Her eyes flickered up to Jarrett who was also listening out. It was quick taps, almost like a scuttle or a scamper of a small animal. Mary, like her general disinterest in spiders, wasn't necessarily scared of small animals but they weren't preferable company.

'Was that what I think it was?' she asked.

'Sometimes we get pests,' said Jarrett, dismissively, 'it happens in all establishments. They don't get in the kitchen though.'

'Apart from Cocharil.'

'Yes, apart from our central heating system, no animals,' said Jarrett.

Mary raised an eyebrow, just as around the corner came Boz carrying a tray of miniature pumpkins with candles.

'What about Wojciech?' she asked in her strong Polish accent, 'he's allowed in the kitchen.'

THE HALLOWEEN PARTY

She laughed as she began to put the candles on the tables. Boz was another of the staff Mary had met during her stay - she was one of the bartending and waitressing staff working in place of or with Neo. She seemed incredibly excited about Halloween, saying it was one of her favourite holidays, which explained why she was humming 'Monster Mash' as she placed the candles around.

Mary watched her as she did so. Boz was attractive; she was extremely good-looking, but she never seemed to hang around people much. She was rather reclusive. Yet here she was, actually excited to be around a crowd.

'What's your costume going to be Boz?' asked Jarrett.

'I'm thinking zombie,' she said, 'I love zombies.'

Mary watched as she swept around the room and she felt a strange inclination. Something about Boz's movements unnerved her. She was so lost in the feeling that she didn't warn Boz when Rob, who had been holding a hammer at the time, came off the stool he was using. She bumped into him as he turned and the claw of the hammer turned quickly against her bare arm. She seethed, pulling her arm to her chest, grasping it in pain.

'Woah, sorry Boz. Are you alright?' Rob asked.

'It's just a cut,' she said.

'Is it deep?' asked Rob, putting a hand on her arm, but she wrenched it away.

'It's fine, I'll bandage up,' and she whisked off toward the kitchens.

Rob turned to Jarret and Mary and shrugged. Mary sighed, picked up the newspaper off the counter and slid off the barstool.

'I've work to do, I'll see you later,' she said.

TALES FROM THE KING GEORGE

'See you at the party,' said Jarrett.

Mary then retreated down past reception to the office. As she passed the kitchen, she heard a soft rustle from inside but when she glanced in, she couldn't see anyone. She stopped and entered the kitchen, listening for the sound. It was a packet of something rustling in one of the top cupboards. The sound of rapid scampering returned to her mind and she knew that she wasn't going to like what she found.

In the corner of the kitchen, hidden behind the overloaded table, was a plastic broom. She reached over and grabbed it in two hands, holding it defensively, and prepared herself. Her breaths became short and quick as she shuffled toward the cupboard trying to be as quiet as possible. Her grip tightened every time she heard a distinct movement of rodent-on-foil. But she leaned over, her right-hand outstretched towards the cupboard handle. Her fingers clasped it tightly and she began to brace herself.

'Don't scream,' she whispered to herself, and she narrowed her eyes, her eyebrows frowning.

She gently eased the door open, light rolling over its contents. In front of her, amongst torn open bags of crisps, was a large grey rat, and it had heard her open the door. It was on its hind legs looking at her with beady black eyes, standing entirely still. Mary kept her cool. She gave the rat a hard stare with the broom in both hands. She then lifted it up in preparation; she was going to hit it. She was going to smack it right in the head. She won't have rats in her workplace. She was going to do it. Right then and there. She was going to hit it. She was going to hit it right now. Right now.

'For fuck's sake lady, if you're going to hit me, just do it already,' said the rat.

THE HALLOWEEN PARTY

When she was seven years old, Mary's father had scared her witless by jumping out from behind a door dressed as a bear. She had screamed and started crying. Since then, she found bears the scariest thing in all the world, and her father could always make her jump by putting on a bear mask.

But it was when she was eleven that she felt pure terror. She had been in the attic, alone, in the dark. The door shut unexpectedly and a pile of coats fell on her. She hadn't screamed. She froze in place. All her panic was wrapped and trapped entirely in her head. It had taken a lifetime for her to realise she was safe, to prise herself out, and make a run for it.

When the rat spoke, she found herself back in the attic: her body froze, her eyes widened in shock, and she leant back as if to faint. If Wat hadn't just rounded the corner she would've fallen to the floor. Instead, he caught her by the shoulders, gripped her warmly and said heartily;

'Ah, you found Sebastian Ms Woods!'

The rat scoffed at him and rummaged in the nearest bag. Mary slowly turned her head to see Wat's grinning face. 'Sebastian?'

'Yes, he's a pet of one of our oldest tenants. He keeps managing to escape,' sighed Wat, 'you know you're not meant to roam like this Sebastian. What if a cat found you?'

'I'd bite its fucking ear off,' muttered the rat with its mouth full.

Wat coughed awkwardly, 'he enjoys using his wide vocabulary...' said Wat, 'I need to take you back to your cage now Sebastian.'

'At least bring me something to eat Wat, she's starving me up there!' said the rat

TALES FROM THE KING GEORGE

'Alright, alright,' said Wat, pulling the packet of crisps that Sebastian had shimmied his way into, holding the rat in his makeshift sack, 'wouldn't you rather something more wholesome.'

'Yeah fuck off. If you can spare a pint that would also be smashing,' said Sebastian, showing his bottom and tail as he dug to the bottom of the bag.

Wat shook his head and gave Mary a knowing look, 'he's owned by Tilly upstairs.'

He then gestured for her to follow him, which Mary ended up doing while still holding the broom. She was still on edge and not entirely happy with the idea of a talking rat. She of course had already made a connection to a similarly affected tenant, her eyes darting to the office as they passed it, but she didn't expect to meet more of the same condition.

'Was he cursed to be a rat?' whispered Mary.

'Yeah, I was cursed since the day I was born!' said Sebastian, hearing her, 'what's wrong with being a rat!?'

'Nothing, nothing,' backtracked Mary, 'how do you speak?'

'I learnt,' said Sebastian, rising out from his packet, 'hello. How do you do? It's not rocket science.'

'Not many animals are capable of the same,' said Mary.

'Yeah, that's because they don't even try. Idiots, the lot of them,' said Sebastian in disdain.

Wat trotted up the stairs to the first floor, to Sebastian's annoyance causing him to comment that 'it's not a bloody trampoline Wat.' When they'd reached the first floor, Wat took a left turn and headed to room six at which he knocked politely - three raps. Mary cautiously stood behind.

THE HALLOWEEN PARTY

'She won't hear you Wat, she's asleep,' said Sebastian.

Wat nodded, 'Ah, not to worry,' and he reached into his rightmost pocket and pulled out a set of keys. There were only a few, about six or seven. The one he selected was an old brass lever key which he slid into the door and jiggled around in the lock before he could turn it. Even then it looked like it got a little stuck but with another jiggle, he could turn it fully and he opened the door.

The inside was dark apart from a dim orange lamp in the corner on the bedside table which dowsed the room in a half glow. The bed was made but empty, dressed in the same floral pattern Mary knew. There was a bookshelf on the right filled with worn books from the last three decades, various paperbacks that Mary knew would be the same love story in different settings. The room was half a mess with clothes all over the floor leaving not a spot uncovered. Beside the bookshelf was a chest of drawers with a mirror and a large cage with its door wide open. Mary determined it to be Sebastian's home when Wat walked over to it.

Mary gripped her broom hard when she noticed that there was actually a resident; on the left opposite the bookshelf was a rocking chair with a basket of yarn beside it. In the rocking chair, covered in what looked like several quilted blankets, was a very old woman. Her face was wrinkled, her hair was white, and her hands were withered and slender. In her hands, she was holding knitting needles attached to some knitwear but the woman wasn't responding - Mary's first thought was that she was asleep, or considering the woman was extremely old…

'Tilly?' called Wat, as he set Sebastian in his cage with the packet of crisps.

The old woman didn't answer. Mary ambled shyly towards the woman, the broom still in her hands. She glanced at Wat, who was giving her a confused look. Mary tried to mouth, 'Is she dead?' but Wat responded out loud, 'What? You don't need to whisper.'

'Is she alive?'

'She's asleep. She sleeps deeply,' said Wat.

'You're telling me,' said Sebastian, mouth full.

Mary was about to try prodding her with the broom but Wat stepped past her and pushed the broom handle down.

'Stop waving that thing about Ms Woods, she's still a person,' said Wat.

Mary's cheeks flushed in embarrassment. Wat placed a hand beside the woman's neck on her shoulder blade and gently rocked her. 'Tilly?' he called loudly.

Softly, the woman stirred. Her eyelids rolled open and gave Wat a bewildered look until she realised who it was. Her cheeks lifted and she smiled.

'Oh Wat,' the woman spoke, gravelly yet strong, 'my you were only just here.'

'I'm just checking up on you Tilly. Sebastian got out of his cage again, so I'm returning him,' said Wat.

'Thank you, my dear. He's awfully clever isn't he,' she said.

'Don't patronise me,' spat Sebastian.

'How long was I asleep for?' asked Tilly.

'When were you last awake?' asked Wat.

'When you last checked up on me.'

'Then it's been two weeks on the dot,' said Wat.

Mary gave an incredulous look to Wat but he was focused on Tilly and didn't notice it.

THE HALLOWEEN PARTY

'I have felt rather energetic recently, I must lay off the coffee,' she chuckled. Then she turned her head to see Mary, who had been waiting off to the side. 'And who is this charming young woman?'

'This is Ms Woods, she's our new accountant,' said Wat, 'Ms Woods, this is Matilda Oak, our oldest tenant here. She's been living here nigh-on twenty years.'

'Yes, how time flies,' chuckled Tilly, 'I do apologise for my consort. He gets bored being here with me from time to time.'

'That's fine,' said Mary, 'he just startled me is all,' and she realised she was still holding the broom in an offensive position. She moved it so she was holding it in her left hand only and settled herself down. Seeing an old woman talk to the rat like she did, it felt like they were a married couple.

'Tilly, I best get back to the bar. Let me know if you need anything,' said Wat, patting her gently.

'I will do Wat,' she said, 'if I could have a quick word with you dear before you disappear?' and Tilly reached a hand to Mary's arm. The sudden deathly cold touch set her hair on end but Mary nodded. Wat smiled at Mary and left her alone with Tilly.

Mary moved round to the woman's side and knelt down a little so she wasn't standing over the woman. The woman spoke so softly she had to lean in close to hear. The smell of lavender wafted over her and also a smell of earth which threw her off. She also saw, around the woman's neck, was a decorated moonstone that was fastened with silver links.

'I had a dream,' said Tilly, 'it was oh so long, but I saw you.' The woman sounded grave; the smile was gone. 'There was a white horse behind a chain link fence. You were there in front of it as if you were defending it. Before you were three figures; one was a pair of silhouettes, one silver and one midnight-black; one was a beautiful woman wearing a blindfold and holding a hammer; the third was in a long grey coat but the wind was too strong I couldn't make out his face.

'Then you were visited by a cherub and the horse fell over and died. I couldn't say how. But you pointed at the man in the coat. And you screamed wordlessly.'

Tilly gripped Mary's arm tightly and Mary felt the fear creep up within her again.

'Stop scaring her, you old bat,' said Sebastian from across the room.

Tilly then shook her head and let go, 'it was probably nothing,' she said, 'I often have long dreams that don't make sense.'

'You say that,' said Sebastian, 'they do make sense.' Suddenly, it sounded like Sebastian was being empathetic, 'Don't think the worst though, they're always cryptic; it'll end up meaning nothing.'

Mary understood what Sebastian was saying and it comforted her a little. Until Tilly grasped her arm again, with both hands. The woman had a look of concern over her face and she leant forward. Mary tilted her ear towards the woman.

'Just be careful,' she whispered. Mary retreated a little to see Tilly give her such a look of care and concern, it chilled her to the bone. It was the look of apology, the look a doctor might give his terminally ill patients, 'I don't know what it means, but just be careful.' She patted Mary's hand and let go again, allowing Mary to stand up straight once more. Almost immediately Tilly closed her eyes and she drifted off into sleep once more. Mary took a moment to let what she had said sink in before she exited the room, closing

THE HALLOWEEN PARTY

the door behind her. Wat was waiting for her in the corridor, his hands behind his back and with a sympathetic smile on his face.

'She's such a good tenant. She doesn't need a lot of looking after but it's good to check on her,' said Wat, and proceeded to lock the door.

Mary would have questioned what Wat implied but what Tilly had said to her was still running through her mind. The two of them returned back down to the barroom, where the decorations had finished being put up. Rob was nowhere to be seen but Boz was cleaning the bar counter. She noticed the two of them came and greeted them.

'Wat,' she asked, 'Kam wanted to know where the pumpkins are?'

'Octavius should have put them round the back, have you seen him yet?' asked Wat.

'No, but I'll let Kam know.'

She lifted the counter flap to come around and head to the kitchen, at which point Mary noticed her hand was bandaged up.

'Is your hand okay?' she asked.

'Oh it's fine,' said Boz, grabbing it instinctively as she passed them and keeping her distance until she had disappeared out of the room.

* * *

Mary returned to the office and her day continued as normal. The evening arrived and the sounds of people gathering at the bar eventually began to make it to the office, albeit extremely muffled. But as it was just Mary and Mona, she could distinctly tell that it was turning into a party.

'You should finish up and join them,' said Mona.

'Oh sure,' said Mary.

'Dress up in my honour - go as a spider,' said Mona.

'I'll go upstairs in a bit, but not until I've finished with the incomings,' said Mary.

'You need to loosen up,' said Mona.

'Look, I do loosen up. But only when I'm with friends, and only when it's in a controlled environment. Not a local pub,' said Mary, irritated with Mona's constant pressing.

'You have to have it all neatly organised,' said Mona, sailing across the web she was creating.

'Is there anything wrong with order?' said Mary.

'I'm saying sometimes there's nothing wrong with going out of your comfort zone. You've been working all day. Wat definitely would not mind. Go upstairs and have a drink with him.'

The tone in which Mona said this irked Mary and she stopped midway through filing.

'If you're insinuating I'm interested in Stone, you're very much mistaken.'

'Then have a drink with Jarrett, or Wojciech, whatever gets you out of here,' said Mona, 'I want some flies.'

Mary sighed, 'did I mention I met Sebastian?'

'Oh, that bastard,' said Mona, causing Mary to laugh suddenly, 'yeah, he's an arse. Can't stand him.'

'Is he like you?' asked Mary.

'No, he's literally just a rat. Clever though. Said he ate some radioactive waste as a runt and became super intelligent as if he were Splinter. Now he just steals from Wat's beer supply,' said Mona.

'Yeah he didn't sound like a nice person,' said Mary.

'Anyway, stop spending time with me, and spend time with your friends,' said Mona, throwing another line across her web.

THE HALLOWEEN PARTY

Mary considered it genuinely, especially as Mona has referred to them as friends. Then she folded her laptop up and let herself up from the desk.

'Fine, but if I don't like it, I'm going to bed,' she said.

'At least you'll have tried,' said Mona.

Mary opened up the office door, gave Mona a wave, and ventured up the stairs to join in the celebration.

The barroom was packed with people. There were all sorts gathered at the counter ordering drinks, the tables were crowded, and people were even standing out in the courtyard where pumpkins had been hollowed out and spread out in the little square of green. Mary looked around for someone she could recognise but Wat and Jarrett were the only servers at the bar, and they were fairly busy.

Suddenly, a man in a mask jumped out from the crowd in front of her, growling loudly. Mary put a hand to her chest in surprise but the mask was removed and behind it was the round, laughing face of Octavius.

'I got you there, didn't I?' he said.

Mary smiled, but behind it, she was cursing the man. 'Hi, I'm sorry I've forgotten your name.'

'Octavius, we met the other day when I was having breakfast? The pumpkins are by my courtesy,' he said, and he put his thumbs underneath his braces. His dress sense looked to be themed, as he was wearing a bright orange checked shirt, with green trousers held up by a brown belt and braces. The mask was just a skull with red eyes, but jumping out at anyone would scare them regardless of what you wore, Mary noted.

'Yes, of course. It's a lot of pumpkins,' said Mary.

'It was a good month,' said Octavius, 'do you want to join us for some drinks?'

TALES FROM THE KING GEORGE

Mary didn't know who 'us' was, but she agreed and Octavius led her to a group of people who were laughing and drinking at one of the booths. They shifted over, let her in, and she immediately regretted coming up the stairs. Drinking with strangers was not really her favourite pastime, but Octavius was insistent. In a couple of minutes, she was presented with some pumpkin ale which tasted nothing like pumpkin and was privy to a conversation about the best methods for cultivating aubergines.

Boz appeared round a corner, collecting glasses, and Mary was shocked at her costume. She genuinely thought she was a zombie by the way she was dressed and the limp she was putting on. When Boz noticed Mary, she diverted to pass by;

'Hi Mary, good to see you up here,' she said, 'no costume?'

'I didn't have time,' lied Mary, 'you look incredibly believable.'

'I know right, I love dressing up,' said Boz, 'feel!'

She presented her arm to Mary who was a little confused but she still touched the bare skin. It was as cold as ice, colder than Tilly. Her skin was hard as brick and she had to take her hand away due to how unsettling it was.

'Cool right?' she said and continued on.

Mary watched her go and after a moment excused herself from Octavius and his party. She made her way to the bar where Jarrett was pouring a drink for someone. He noticed and leaned towards her, 'Hey, you're here.'

'Yes,' she said, 'nice costume by the way.'

Jarrett had fake sideburns on his face and fake plastic claws on his hands. He had put a little effort into

THE HALLOWEEN PARTY

it but not enough to hinder his work, and he looked tired already.

'Thanks. What's going on?'

'I just saw Boz. She let me touch her arm, but she was absolutely freezing. Plus, she looks bloody convincing,' said Mary.

'Mhm? You got a crush?' asked Jarrett.

Mary shot a glance away, 'no, I think she might actually be one.'

'Be one?'

'A zombie.'

Jarrett almost spilt the pint he was pouring, threw his head in the other direction and stifled a laugh. 'Are you serious?'

'It's not the strangest thing in this pub.'

'Your evidence is lacking,' said Jarrett.

'How would I prove she's a zombie for real?' asked Mary.

'Stab her in the gut, see if she bleeds?' said Jarrett.

'I'm not going to stab her!' said Mary, horrified at the idea.

'She won't bleed, she won't have a pulse, she can't breathe, or she'll eat brains. Pick one and see if it's true,' said Jarrett, taking cash off the closest bloke at the bar as he handed them the pint, 'or here's a crazy thought - ask her.'

Mary turned around and considered Jarrett's point. She watched Boz bustle around before disappearing into the other half of the bar. Her eyes narrowed and she tongued her cheek considering the matter.

* * *

The night wore on and Mary found herself being pulled to and fro - Wat had her introduced to some other patrons, Jarrett made her laugh at the bar, she occasionally saw Neo and she talked to her about her brother, and Octavius occasionally returned, face red and clearly drunk out of his mind.

Eventually, close to midnight, the party died down and the pub started emptying. Mary chatted to Jarrett as he started cleaning up behind the bar when Boz came back with a tray of empty glasses and started putting them in the dishwasher behind the bar. Mary leant to her as she did so.

'Boz?' she asked.

Boz wandered over to the bar, 'yeah?'

Mary's eyes darted a little before she whispered, 'Are you a real zombie?'

Boz hesitated for a split-second, before laughing and shaking her head, 'Wow am I that convincing! No, it's just a costume, right? It's just for show,' and she playfully slapped Mary on the arm.

Mary wasn't convinced. Jarrett had seen the exchange and edged in to whisper his own suggestion. 'Stab her,' and he gestured.

Mary shook her head as Octavius staggered over to her. He extended a hand to her, a smile plastered over his face.

'It was good to meet you, Mary,' he said, 'I must be off now.'

Wat wasn't far behind him, helping keep him steady. He pulled Octavius' arm over his head to give him support.

'Come on Octavius, your cab will be waiting,' he said.

'You're leaving now? In this state?' said Mary concerned. He was way too drunk to be trusted to leave, surely Wat wouldn't intentionally let him leave.

THE HALLOWEEN PARTY

'Yes, I must return back home. Far far away,' he said, 'very far away.'

He said in such a wistful tone that Mary felt like he was hiding something but before he could elaborate Wat was guiding him to the door.

'Well looks like the party's over,' said Jarrett.

* * *

Eventually, Mary found herself in her bedroom getting ready for bed. The hour was late, not long after midnight. She looked for her laptop for a minute before realising she had left it in the office. She sped out of her room and to the stairs, night clothes on. In her head, she noted it would take five minutes until she heard voices from the barroom and jumped back up a few steps to remain behind the wall separating the stairs from reception. They didn't sound like they were coming her way. It was Wat for definite that was in the conversation.

'-it's made up for you, I'll show you up in a second. Did you see your brother as you were coming in?' floated Wat's voice.

'No, we rarely cross paths these days,' said the other voice, a deep and grumbly voice.

'Ah yes, not like the old days. Bear with me one moment,' said Wat.

There wasn't a shadow of him approaching the staircase so Mary assumed he'd gone downstairs towards the office. Mary, curious as to who the new visitor was at this hour, crept down the stairs. She carefully peered around the corner into reception and saw the newest tenant.

It was a man dressed in a very long grey coat, with a lighter grey scarf wrapped around his neck and half his head, masking his nose and mouth. He wore a pair of square spectacles and his head was dark chestnut brown. He also wore gray gloves that he was taking off as Mary observed him.

She found herself instantly intrigued. Unfortunately, as she watched him, her foot slipped and she had to catch her footing two steps down, out behind the wall. This attracted the man's attention. Mary blushed hard; she was dressed in a nightgown and was definitely not in any state to meet someone new. Her mouth was agape in shock. The man eyed her indifferently.

'Hello,' he stated, slightly muffled by his scarf.

Mary couldn't find her words but luck found that Wat jogged up the stairs to the desk to see the two making acquaintances.

'Ah, Ms Woods! Lovely nightwear by the way,' he stated, grinning, 'I see you've just met Mr No-'

'No is fine,' interjected the man. Wat nodded in acceptance and passed the pile of books he'd been carrying to No.

'No, this is Mary Woods. She's our accountant,' explained Wat.

'Accountant?' said No, 'a very interesting occupation.'

Mary found he said it with a pure genuine interest and not with the sarcasm she was used to. Her blush intensified, 'thank you,' she sputtered out and crossed her arms, 'if you don't mind, I was just getting ready for bed.'

'That's perfectly fine, it was good to meet you,' said No.

Mary nodded and then walked slowly up the stairs, before running back to her room. She closed her door and leaned her back against it. Something about that man had given her chills. She cursed herself for going down in a nightgown, what must he have thought? She shook herself out of it and resigned that she'd left her laptop downstairs along with her dignity. Perhaps she'd pick them both up tomorrow.

MARY AND THE ZOMBIE

The next morning Mary dressed in her appropriate fashion, nice and neatly, and proceeded downstairs. The first person she bumped into was Snow, who was at reception idly looking at her phone. Full well knowing she hadn't been on brilliant terms with Snow since she arrived Mary still decided to clear her throat and ask, 'Snow, I don't suppose you've seen a man in grey today? Goes by Mr No?'

'No, I don't know a Mr No,' she replied.

Mary sighed, unsurprised, 'Thank you anyway.'

'You're welcome,' Snow responded without looking up from her phone.

Mary proceeded through the bar to the conservatory and there she found the man. He was dressed almost exactly the same in his long coat and scarf. Here he was sitting at a table, alone, reading a book. She found it strange he was wearing this full ensemble indoors but she approached him all the same.

'Mr No? We met last night,' she said and extended her hand for a handshake.

'Ah yes, Mary was it?' he said and gave her his hand, 'you're dressed a lot better.'

Mary felt the blood rising to her cheeks, 'yes, I apologise for that display.'

'It's alright,' said Mr No.

Mary felt that was the extent of the conversation, but for some reason, she felt a strange notion to try and continue, 'What are you reading?'

Mr No did the usual manner of someone who'd just started a new book and glanced at the cover; 'er, it's Millennium Winds. A book about several men sailing. It's rather good so far.'

'Oh, I've never been sailing before,' said Mary.

'Nor I,' stated No.

Feeling the moment had ended, Mary then nodded and said, 'Well good to see you again Mr No, I hope I do so again.'

She then found herself another table further into the conservatory and sat down. Neo whipped around after seeing her enter, 'Hey, saw you talking to No over there.'

'Yes, I was just making a good impression is all,' said Mary, 'do you know him?'

'Just a regular guest at this time of year,' said Neo, 'A bit quiet though. He likes books, we never see him without one.'

'Mm,' replied Mary, not realising that she had been watching No while Neo had been talking. When she noticed Neo had stopped, she finally turned to her and found Neo with a smirk on her face, 'what?'

'Oh nothing,' said Neo, 'I'll bring some breakfast out to you in a moment.'

After breakfast, she found herself walking to the office as Wat lifted himself up the stairs into reception.

MARY AND THE ZOMBIE

He was dressed in formal attire: a black suit and a black tie.

'Mr Stone?' addressed Mary as she entered.

'Ah, Ms Woods! I have to apologise, I won't be around much of today, me and the family have a funeral,' said Wat.

Mary's demeanour switched from idle curiosity to sympathy, 'Oh I'm sorry.'

'That's alright, he was a great uncle. I only saw him a few times but he was a charming bloke. Fondness for the sea,' said Wat, lifting his mouth's corner.

At this point Rob also appeared, wrapping a black tie around his collar. He nodded to Mary, who gave him an empathetic smile. Then came Snow, also wearing black. Her shining white hair was tied up in a bun on her head with a black ribbon. She recognised Mary and stopped almost dead in her tracks before pushing past her, avoiding eye contact.

'If you need anything, the rest of the staff will be around. You can reach me by phone as well,' said Wat, lifting his mobile.

'Okay, I should be fine though,' said Mary.

'Alright, we best be off; it starts in a few hours and we've got to travel across London. Stay out of trouble!' said Wat, following up with a wink, 'come on kids.'

The two children exited the front doors with Wat following them. He gave a last wave before leaving and shutting the door behind him. At which point Jarrett appeared at the counter:

'Alright, so what do we do about Boz?' he asked.

Mary turned on her heels and looked at him inquisitively.

'What was that?'

'How do we find out if she's a zombie?' he asked, at which point Neo rounded the corner.

'Who's a zombie?'

'Boz.'

'Is she?'

'No we don't know yet,' said Mary, and paused, 'I had a theory though. What should we try and test for?'

'Pulse seems easiest. Grab her wrist and feel for it,' said Jarrett.

'What excuse could I give to grab her wrist?' asked Mary.

'A dance maybe?' suggested Neo, 'you could ask her to a dance.'

'I don't think that'll be happening anytime soon,' stated Mary.

'Don't be so sure,' said Neo, 'did Wat leave?'

'Yeah he just left,' said Jarrett.

'Alright,' Neo grabbed Mary by the hand and looked at Jarrett, 'when you see Boz, ask her to meet us in the ballroom. Don't say why.'

'I can guess,' replied Jarrett with a smile, as Neo led Mary out of the barroom and down the corridor toward the billiards room.

'There's a ballroom?' asked Mary, incredulous.

'Sort of,' said Neo, and she veered them to the right, to the furthest door.

She jerked the handle a couple of times before she pushed it hard. It opened with a loud creak revealing just how disused this room was. Inside, it was pitch black. Neo let go of Mary to reach a cord that when pulled lit the room up.

An old electric chandelier hung from the middle of the room in 80s fashion, and the room was filled with old chairs and tables. There was a small open area, but the rest was full of furniture to the point where it was impossible to get any further into the room. The windows were covered by large, dusty red curtains, which trailed down onto the floor. There was some organisation to the room, evidenced by the fact that Neo immediately walked to the opposite corner where something was lying beneath a white sheet.

Mary, in the meantime, marvelled at the large room. She felt a little disappointed that it was no longer used as a ballroom and only for storage; she imagined it probably looked fantastic when in use. Judging by most of the decor, it looked like they'd stopped using it in the late 80s, or early 90s.

'It used to be used for formal gatherings I think,' said Neo, 'I wasn't around but Wojciech was.'

'Right,' said Mary, 'who is Wojciech?' she asked, but Neo was pulling the cloth harshly off what looked like an old turntable. It was stacked on top of some records that sat on a wooden cabinet full of them. Neo crouched down and pulled out one that was slightly out already. They'd obviously done this before and it had been recently. Mary folded her arms in anticipation.

Neo put the record on the turntable, started it spinning, and then levered the arm onto it. It took a few seconds before it began.

It was not a song that Mary was familiar with, yet it was something classical. In her head, she cursed herself for not recognising it and reasoned she'd need to find out the name of it. After a moment of listening, she raised an eyebrow at Neo.

'We found this about a year ago, that's when we found out-' but Neo was cut off by the sound of approaching footsteps, 'Here she comes!'

Sure enough, in the doorway appeared Boz, dressed as normal. Her hair was tied back and her makeup impeccable. She put a hand to her hip, a little unimpressed.

'Again?'

'Boz! Mary has always wanted to learn the waltz and I told her you do it amazingly, like so good!' said Neo.

Boz sighed, 'It's true, I learned to waltz when I was very little. I don't dance much anymore,' she said softly, 'but it's nice to practise every now and again.'

Mary, who had been thrown into the situation with no preparation or warning, nodded quickly. Boz approached her, 'Do you know much about dancing?'

'Not really,' said Mary, feeling a little out of her depth.

'It's easy. What made you want to learn?'

Mary gave Neo a panicked look, 'er a wedding! I'm attending a wedding and want to dance at it.'

'They'll be doing a waltz at the wedding?'

'Yes, they, er love dancing.'

Boz shrugged, 'alright it's a very common dance,' causing Mary to sigh in relief, 'we'll start with a simple box step.'

She stood in front of Mary with a serious face and motioned to her with her fingers. 'Follow me.' Boz then proceeded to go through the steps of a box step. As she stepped, she explained the movement, 'One, two, three, you see? Back, left, together. Up, right, together. You see?'

Mary attempted to copy but found herself making the box in two steps. She cursed herself and Boz tried pointing it out. When she found that trying to direct Mary wasn't working verbally, she stepped forward.

MARY AND THE ZOMBIE

'Give me your hands,' she said. Mary let Boz take her hands and reposition them; Mary's right hand was in Boz's left palm, and then her left hand was placed underneath Boz's right arm. 'I'll take lead, as that's usually the man,' said Boz, 'now let me show you.'

Boz then took Mary through the box steps again, one, two, three. One two three. She moved slowly, but soon Mary was following Boz's step each time with little overlap. Occasionally she misplaced her foot and it ended up on Boz's but she felt it was actually working.

'Now follow,' said Boz, and her box took her wider.

Mary felt like she was turning; in fact, Boz was directing their box to rotate. She let Boz do so, simply following her steps, but soon Boz cut in, 'Look at me, not your feet.'

Mary suddenly realised she'd been staying straight down the entire time and looked up at Boz.

For a moment Mary understood why dancing was such a romantic gesture. Here she was face to face with this beautiful woman, centimetres from her face, and she felt compelled to lean in. But then she lost her footing, her left foot tumbled from beneath her, and she gripped onto Boz effectively pulling her down.

At that same moment, Boz and Mary were on the floor. Boz lay sprawling over Mary and Mary was staring up at the ceiling in a daze, half overcome with the strange sensation she had had.

'Oh my gosh, are you okay?' said Neo suddenly in a panic.

'I'm fine, are you Mary?' asked Boz, lifting herself up and kneeling to easily stand up. She outstretched her hand to help Mary up.

Mary looked at Boz, then looked at Neo. Neo's eyes darted to Boz's hand and Mary remembered what they were trying to do. Instead of putting her hand in Boz's, she grabbed Boz around the wrist, placing her thumb directly over her veins and pressed hard. Her other fingers wrapped around Boz's arm. Boz frowned in confusion. She couldn't lift Mary in this manner and she looked at Mary's hand. Neo put her hands around her nose and mouth, covering up the fact she was stifling a laugh.

'I see…' said Boz, and put her other hand on Mary's, 'I am flattered Ms Woods, you're a lovely person. However, I already have a girlfriend and I really don't think we would work that way.'

Mary froze and realised that the position she was in made it seem like she was trying to pull Boz in closer, to join her on the floor. Neo choked. Mary began to stutter.

'N-no I was just - I just,' she attempted to spit out.

'It means a lot you feel that way though,' said Boz, and she leant in and kissed Mary on the cheek, sending them crimson. Mary was speechless as Neo turned away.

She allowed Boz to lift her back on her feet and Boz brushed down her clothes before returning to standing up straight, 'shall we return to the dance?'

Mary didn't know quite what to say as she straightened herself out. Even though the plan succeeded, she was too much in a daze to realise they no longer needed to dance, and so Boz started to lead her into another waltz with Neo sniggering in the back.

'You're doing great Mary,' chuckled Neo in support.

Mary tried to throw her a glare but instead, Boz turned her and her eyes ran past the door. There in the doorway was No and Mary almost fell over again. Instead, she simply stumbled a little and brought Boz to a halt, bringing her and Neo's attention to their unnoticed observant.

'I'm sorry, I just heard the music,' said No.

'Mr No,' said Mary, 'what a pleasant surprise, Boz was just teaching me the waltz.'

Mary suddenly pulled away from Boz in a subconscious mind, feeling embarrassed.

'Mr No?' said Neo in disbelief, laughing a little.

At which point No gave her a hard stare before regarding Mary again, 'You were doing quite well. I'm sorry, I'll leave.'

Neo spoke up, 'say No, are you any good at dancing?'

Before he had a chance to leave, No responded, 'I've done the waltz before at a couple of events. I wouldn't say I'm good at it.'

'Maybe you could show Mary what it's like to be led by a man instead of Boz standing in?'

'I think it's pretty much the same,' said Boz.

'I wouldn't mind it,' said Mary quickly, 'if you would be so kind, Mr No.'

The man looked slightly shocked at the notion but he did not leave. Boz halted their movements and stepped back from Mary.

'She's all yours,' she said, crossing her arms a little annoyed.

Mr No crossed the room a little unsure of himself until he reached Mary. His eyes darted around as if he thought it was a trap until they settled on Mary. Then he picked up her right hand, pulled her towards him with his left, and began easing her into the box step. Mary felt herself fall into the rhythm again without keeping track of her own steps. She was watching No's face intently - his eyes were focused on hers. She thought maybe he was looking off in the distance, but there was something more to it. A certain 'je ne sais quoi'. She searched his eyes. In the end, she felt he was searching hers.

His face was rough with short stubble, his cheekbones were sharp and his chin was square and hard. He looked to be middle-aged, probably around fifty-five, but he looked in good shape. And as he guided her around, she felt his confidence and assertiveness like a blanket of safety. She felt secure in his arms and she began to lean in a little closer. It surprised her when he began to pull her closer as well.

That was until the song ended and he drew to a halt. It was eerily silent and Mary could hear No's deep breaths.

'That was,' he began, 'a very simple box movement,' he then said as if finishing off a lesson.

He let go of her and stepped backwards a little awkwardly. His eyes noticed that Boz and Neo were still in the room; Boz crossed her arms with a raised eyebrow and Neo with a crooked smile as if she knew something.

'I must be going now,' said No, tossing his arms to the doorway, and slowly shuffled out of the room into the corridor, where they could hear his quick pace.

'That was pretty amateur,' said Boz dismissively, 'in proper shows you need a lot more flare. More complex movements. But whatever, you need more practice, let me know,' and she left the room.

Neo grinned at Mary, who felt her cheeks flushing again. She licked her lips, stood up straight with her hands on her hips and softly asked, 'What?'

'What was that?' asked Neo, almost whispering as she walked closer to Mary.

MARY AND THE ZOMBIE

'What was what?'

'That was a moment. You two totally had a moment,' said Neo.

'A moment?' said Mary, in a tone that meant she didn't agree, 'what do mean a "moment"?'

'Are you telling me you didn't feel something?' said Neo.

''No I don't know what you mean,' said Mary, crossing her arms, 'we were just dancing.'

Neo nodded, grinning, 'Alright, sure. That's all it was, two consenting adults dancing.'

Mary's jaw fell open, 'this isn't some school! I'm not playing coy so you can tease me about it,' stated Mary.

'Look all I'm saying is it looked like you two shared something,' said Neo, hands in the air, 'I didn't mean to offend you, but you don't need to get all up in a bunch.'

'I'm not all up in a bunch,' muttered Mary to herself.

'So did you find out?'

Mary gave Neo a confused look. Then she realised what she meant.

'I couldn't tell,' she said.

Neo sighed in frustration, 'Mary!'

'It was too quick, and then she took it the wrong way-'

'We'll have to figure out a new plan then,' said Neo, 'never mind we'll leave it for now.'

The two exited the ballroom and Mary pondered whether or not she and No had actually shared a moment. She found herself lost in thought all the way down to the office and whilst she started working. Even when Mona scuttled from her home and tried to speak to her, Mary was having trouble paying attention.

'Mary?' she said, 'Mary!'

'Hm?'

'Did you hear what I said?'

'Yeah, yeah, men are gullible and dim,' replied Mary.

'Okay, but you don't seem to be paying attention,' said Mona, 'are you alright? What happened?'

Mary flicked through some papers idly. 'I guess I was thinking. Every man I've dated has always been so brash.'

'I can empathise there,' said Mona.

'It's just this man, Mr No? He's very,' and Mary paused to think of the right word, 'interesting'.

'Oh really? Is he interested in you?'

'It's hard to tell, we haven't spoken much.'

'I suppose you just need to speak with him.'

'Is there a non-awkward way of doing that?'

'Look, you can either go about it the British way and hope that you bump into him and have the chance to make small-talk with him. Or, you can do like me, the American way, and thrust yourselves into a situation to make small-talk with him. And as I've said before, I had a very big success rate.'

Mary cocked her head to the side, 'really? Is it that easy?'

'Yes, people don't realise it. It's a perfectly reasonable reason to talk to someone because you think they look good.'

Mary nodded in understanding, and they carried on talking. When the day was coming to a close, Mary wandered back up to the main room and found Neo behind the bar. As they had a chat, Wat returned through the main doors and was received by a cheer from the men at the bar. With him walked Niamh who was dressed up nicely in black. She caught a few gazes from the men in the pub and returned them with smiles around the room. Behind them were Snow and Rob who, after getting inside, instantly went their separate ways; Snow down to the reception, Rob towards the billiards room.

'Hi Wat, how are you doing?' asked Neo.

Wat gave a gentle smile, 'it was a pleasant ceremony, his family seemed pleased. The eulogies were also very deep and moving, apart from his youngest grandson…'

'Yes, a little too underthought,' said Niamh, putting her hands on Wat's shoulders and massaging them.

'Exactly, but I wouldn't judge,' said Wat, 'after that it was a sordid affair of drinks and chatting with old family. I don't see them often enough; they mostly live on the west side and up in the East Midlands.'

Mary could tell that Wat was being introspective about the whole experience. She also felt a strange feeling seeing Niamh comforting him. It seemed Niamh's efforts were genuine, but the undertone of her ulterior motive made it seem creepy and dishonest. Mary felt a little uncomfortable and shuffled awkwardly in her spot.

'He seemed a good man, your uncle,' said Niamh, 'you know he served in the Navy during the Falklands? Ended up with a white eye.'

'Yeah he was a brave man,' said Wat wistfully.

At which point Neo lifted a pint she had and a few of the men at the bar followed suit. Wat smiled gratefully at them.

'Alright, I'm gonna get changed and come back up to man the bar,' he said.

'I'll head home then,' said Niamh, and she leant in for a kiss which Wat took before letting her go.

When Wat left Mary unconsciously huffed to which Neo had to respond, 'Jealous?'

'Jealous? No,' she said.

TALES FROM THE KING GEORGE

She just didn't understand how Wat could fall for the woman. She was pleasing to the eye, sure, and Wat himself was a little naïve, but surely he wouldn't just fall for some woman just because she whispered sweet nothings in his ear? She thought better of him than that. Damn woman, coming in here and swanning around with Wat on her arm making it look so easy.

'Easy?'

Mary caught herself, 'Did I just say that out loud?'

'Are you jealous that she has Wat?' asked Neo, 'or envious she has a guy at all?'

Mary gave a hard stare, 'you keep your opinions to yourself.'

Then she gazed around the room. Her eyes locked on No who was sitting in the corner, furthest away from the bar. She gave Neo the eye once more, then looked back at No. What Mona had said struck a chord within her. Giving Neo one more look she then left the bar and walked steadfastly toward No.

Mary was decisive, sure, she knew what she liked, what she wanted, and what she needed. But she wasn't spontaneous. She didn't do things out of turn, she did as directed. She did what was required. It's not so much she didn't have the initiative, she just never needed to. She realised as she walked toward No she'd never asked a man out on a date before. She wondered if that was normal – how many women asked men out on dates? How many women proposed? Was that a problem in itself? She realised she shouldn't contemplate the diverse and problematic gray area of gender studies and tried to remove it from her head when she reached his table and he looked up.

He had a soft but bored gaze. She smiled and then made a spontaneous decision.

'Hi,' she said, 'can I sit with you?'

She swore that some spark lit up in his eye when she said that.

SECRET IN THE LOST COMMON

Mary found Wat sitting in the dining hall with the local newspaper, idly looking at the lower half that was folded toward him, resting it over the front of his right hand. He sipped a cup of tea from the teacup decorated with a white unicorn, likely from the tea set that was placed in front of him. Today it was busier than normal with a few tables sat at by couples. It was around lunchtime which meant that the smell of bacon, sausages and eggs was being overtaken by fish, vegetables and red meats, and one man's curry who was trying his best not to cry from the heat. He had not been aware that when Kam was heading the kitchen the curry special had a touch of fire to it. Not literally of course, but by everyone's reactions, you would believe her.

'It's my family's secret,' she had told Mary after she had burst into the kitchen and chugged several gallons of milk to even start thinking properly. Jarrett had found the entire affair laughable.

TALES FROM THE KING GEORGE

Wat noticed Mary was approaching and his smile widened in a comforting manner. Mary, however, was marching to him on business. In her left arm sat a hefty folder filled with paper, some of which was earmarked but most was clean white with a few colourful binder markers interspersed. Wat didn't seem to take notice and gestured to the seats next to him:

'Mary! Lovely to see you today, I must have missed you this morning. Have a seat,' he said.

'Mr Stone, I'm here to make a full report,' said Mary directly, 'I have finished the organisation of your records.'

Wat sat up straight, excitement burning in his eyes, 'Do tell! Thank you ever so much.'

'Thank you, Wat, but it's why you brought me here in the first place. Ghosts and dragons aside.'

Mary actually felt a deep amount of pride. It was only just last week when she had finished sorting through all of Wat's papers and had begun the art of data entry. She'd spent a good number of hours typing in every expense, every coin of income and tabulated it before organising her graphs and calculators. The technology meant she'd finished the Friday and she'd spent the weekend organising it into clearly readable graphs and notes. She had enjoyed spending her weekend doing it, she even bought a few new markers for the occasion from the local stationary shop on the high street. The end result was the binder which contained all the work of careful analysis of what had been coming in and what had been going out.

But the fun didn't stop there.

Now she needed to talk to Wat and sort out the information that didn't make sense. Report on her initial findings and then build up an action plan to bring the public house under a sensible financial structure, building up assets and perhaps even profits. However, Mary was very much aware of her forgone conclusion; the pub would need to close.

'Now Mr Stone, first things first, you are terrible at managing a pub financially,' she said, 'I appreciate you are brilliant at tending a bar, and your management style does seem to get the work done, but the money is in dire straits.'

Wat put a hand to his chest reflexively and tightened it into a half fist, 'I understand, my father wasn't any good either really,' he half-laughed.

'There are several questionable choices to costs and expenses, and even income. For example, the tenants are all on vastly different payment plans, with some having remained on the same rental agreement for decades and still paying the exact same amount as they did when it began.'

'Is that a problem?' asked Wat, genuinely concerned, 'I couldn't imagine raising the rent on Tilly, she's very old.'

'Yes, but you don't account for inflation. She's still paying barely a hundred pounds a week for lodging, which is incredibly good considering the area and the space. Meanwhile, you charge Lauren close to two hundred a week.' Mary said this all very matter of fact, without emotion. The important thing in this kind of discussion is to declare the fact there is no bias in what you say. You only state the facts.

Wat nodded at what Mary had said and she continued, listing the variations in pricing for various patrons. When she came to salaries, she spoke very plainly that they were "incredibly generous" and "higher than average".

'But the crux of the matter is, even with these losses, you somehow are pulling money from thin air. Accounts have regularly had money deposited into them without so much as a post-it note about what it's in reference to or who it was from,' said Mary, 'it's almost as if you grow money on trees.' She lowered her voice and she looked Wat dead in the eye, 'You don't grow money on trees, do you?'

Wat gave a slight smile and shook his head. The news of his financial mismanagement was dampening his enthusiasm; it was plain for Mary to see. The man wore his emotions on his sleeve and his folded arms and crooked smile indicated that he wasn't feeling confident in his decision-making. Mary wasn't going to go easy on him however, he had to know the situation and believe it was truly as set in stone as she was making it.

Mary continued rattling off various areas that needed improvement - stock, maintenance, staff, pricing, and utilities, up until she reached capital expenditure.

'The last big purchase you made was for several improvements to the common, including fencing and some other amenities.'

This was interesting to Mary, to the staff and no doubt several other regulars to the Mad King. It cut off a good quarter of the common from the public. You couldn't see behind it and so rumours had abounded that Wat was building something; a new summer house perhaps?

But Mary could see by the numbers that whatever he was building was nothing fancy. Jordan had been dedicated to maintaining that no one was allowed in. The gates were padlocked with several chains and he watched the fence during the day. The common didn't get any unsavoury visitors however so the chance of someone being up to foul business was unlikely. Niamh was ever so interested; she'd been pestering Wat to show her constantly. He wouldn't relent.

'That was necessary,' he stated.

'I'm sure it was but it's a huge dent in your finances. What's the purpose of it?' asked Mary.

'I can't tell you that,' said Wat apologetically.

Mary pursed her lips. She had the leverage now, and she was determined to find out what the fence was holding.

'Mr Stone,' said Mary as calmly but as sternly as possible, 'you asked me here to advise you and clean up your financial situation. I can only do that when I have all the information I need. I need to know what the fence is for. I need to know whether it's an asset or yet another liability to add to your ever-increasing list. Now are you going to help me to help you, or am I going to be making my financial decisions half-informed?'

Wat's guilt reddened on his face and he put his hands together to press to his lips. He avoided eye contact for a good minute as it looked like he contemplated the notion. For a brief second Mary wondered if she had offended the man, but she couldn't imagine him being angry.

The man only seemed to be able to express one emotion, and that was pure excitement and euphoria. He'd never been upset, sad, frustrated, not even a little ticked off. Mary wondered if this was all a façade and deeper lay his true emotions. Did he hide his emotions just as he hid the Mad King?

'Okay,' he said, 'tonight. Come and find me at the bar at eleven. And I will show you.'

Mary was stunned and forgot to respond.

'Yes. I will. Thank you,' she finally stuttered.

'Is there anything else?' asked Wat.

Mary then gave the last few notes she had and they entered into discussing the reasoning for many of the other purchases Wat had made in the last year. After an hour Mary had all the information she needed and her binder was now full of notes across the pages in every spot of whitespace that was available. She needed to compile it into her action plan and so she thanked Wat and said she would see him at the bar later that evening.

Before she left, she made sure to just nudge the knife in a little more; 'Wat, just to be clear, its thin ice. I can't be certain if there's much we can do to keep your establishment up.' Wat nodded to what she said, and then she left him to dwell on it.

Mary smiled to herself in giddy excitement. Okay yes, the pub was going to close, but SHE would be allowed to see the secret in the common! It was yet another mystery she would unfurl about the Mad King and one that only she would be privy to as well, unlike every other mystery which everyone else seemed to already be in on.

Because of her excitement, she didn't notice the door of the office was slightly ajar when she walked in and she was shocked to see Niamh leaning against the desk looking passively at some of her filed documents that had been unceremoniously unfiled. The filing cabinet was open and paper was on the desk. Mary puffed herself up and narrowed her eyes.

'Ms Smith?' Mary asked in such a way that it wasn't a question, 'What the devil do you think you're doing?'

The blonde casually looked up at Mary and gave her a sweet yet unnerving smile.

SECRET IN THE LOST COMMON

'Mary, lovely to see you again,' she said, 'I hope you don't mind me perusing.'

'I do, these are sensitive documents, give me those,' she demanded, outstretching her hand.

But Niamh flicked her wrist towards her to pull them out of Mary's reach.

'I'm just taking a look behind the scenes is all,' she said, 'things don't seem to be faring well for the King George. Look at all this expensive garden work.'

Mary knew that Niamh was stalling. 'What do you want Niamh?'

Niamh's ears pricked at the sound of Mary's inquisition.

'What I have wanted and still want. You know about the fence Mary, and so I thought I'd do a little digging of my own. Not literally, of course, couldn't stand the idea of gardening. Flowers are pretty but soil never did it for my skin, it just irritates it,' Niamh touched her wrists defensively, 'Wat won't tell me a thing. I don't suppose you know?'

'No,' said Mary, not wanting to admit that she would do soon.

'It's a pity. As an employee I thought you'd have more of a stake to know, 'Niamh began rummaging in the filing cabinet again, 'see as his girlfriend I can only know so much. I'm "outside" the business, but the staff are all privilege to that,' she then turned slightly to half see Mary, 'what do you think it is?'

'Niamh, look, I'm a woman of my word,' Mary stated as she circled to the filing cabinet, 'and that means I stick to the rules.' Mary placed her hand on the drawer's front as she stepped to the side to look Niamh in the eye. Niamh was taller than her, but she maintained a stern look. When Mary began to push the drawer closed Niamh relented and let her do so, pulling her arms out. 'Let me do my job properly.'

Niamh eyed her and Mary felt the chill of distrust, 'I see,' she finally uttered. She continued to stand beside the cabinet without moving. Mary tensed knowing that she wasn't going to leave; not without being asked at the very least.

'Ms Smith,' said Mary, a lump in her throat that almost caused her to choke on the words, 'if you must know, I've almost finished my full report and as you say,' she looked Niamh in the eye, 'they're not faring well. But I must ask now that you leave if you've nothing else.'

Niamh nodded solemnly, but Mary could see the twinge of a smile prick up the corner of her mouth. 'Okay then,' she looked Mary up and down before walking to the door of the office and touching the frame to leave. 'By the way, there was a spider on the desk. Can't stand the things so it's underneath that pile of paper. You might find it stuck to the bottom; sorry about that.'

Niamh then disappeared, her curls bouncing out behind the door. Mary's heart filled with dread. It took everything to maintain her composure as she heard Niamh's heels echoing down the corridor. When they'd stopped and she was sure she was gone, she shut the office door and pressed her hands to her face.

'Mona?' she uttered.

She reached for the large stack of files Niamh had pulled out and lifted it slowly to see underneath.

'Mona?' she spoke a little louder, trying not to let tears creep into her voice.

On the bottom of the last file, she saw a large black splot, and upon seeing it she immediately dropped the files. Her hands whipped to her face once more as she tried to stop herself from crying too loudly.

'Oh Mona,' she uttered, her trembling lip causing her voice to waver badly. She pressed her hands over her face to wipe away the tears before they overwhelmed her. 'I'm sorry Mona, I'm sorry.'

'Sorry for what?' asked Mona, dropping down from the ceiling on her silk to land on Mary's right shoulder.

Mary turned to her and the relief almost sent her into a frenzy. She caught herself and was able to spit out a half-cackle sound as she realised her friend was still alive and well.

'Oh god Mona, I thought you'd been crushed!'

'As soon as that woman came in, I stayed in the corner. You can tell there's something about her,' said Mona, 'She reminds me of myself.'

Mary sniffed and held up her hand to let Mona crawl onto it, before placing her on the table. Then she lifted up the stack of paper again.

'Was that a friend of yours?'

'I don't make friends with other spiders. Me and them don't seem to mix,' said Mona.

Mary laughed at this and began to tidy up. She and Mona joked together and caught up. The topic of the common came up briefly as Mary took pride in getting Wat to give up his secrets. Mona hadn't seen outside the office in a long time but could recall the common many years ago.

'What do you think is behind it?' she asked.

Mary shook her head, 'no idea but it has got to be something paranormal. That's all it ever is.'

'I'll take that as a compliment,' said Mona.

* * *

Mary settled back down into work. Once she had gotten into the rhythm, she was fully focused on the task at hand, tracking the money. The hours rolled by up until the sounds of people upstairs became too much and Mary found that it was coming close to nine in the evening. She tidied up her work and then proceeded to join in the merriment.

After a couple weeks, Mary had become more and more comfortable with the pub during peak hours. The regulars often were drunk but it never got too rowdy. The football on the TV got people going on the days it was on but Mary found solace in talking to the staff or to some of the older regulars. Also, when she reached the entrance to the barroom, she found one of her favourite people sitting at a table, speaking with Lauren and another woman whom Mary didn't recognise. She locked in and approached the table, catching No mid-sentence.

'-Such a nuisance though, do you enjoy firework shows?' he said in a disgruntled but amicable tone.

Lauren responded, 'I absolutely love them, they always look amazing! Did you see last year's display? It was tremendous!'

'They always look the same to me. It's just a series of colourful explosions and the coordination always leaves more to be desired,' said No, shaking his head.

'I've never met a man who disliked fireworks displays as much as you,' said the other woman, picking up her glass.

'What's all this?' asked Mary, joining the conversation.

'No is telling us his fondness for fireworks,' said Lauren, then leant over and whispered, 'I think it's because he's never had someone to go with.'

SECRET IN THE LOST COMMON

'Well, I've never been fond of fireworks either,' said Mary thoughtfully, 'they always look the same to me.'

No perked up and lifted his glass, 'there we are! Support! Thank you, Mary.'

She smiled and then took a seat at the table.

The conversation continued on until Lauren and her friend disappeared and Mary was left with just No, and their conversation had taken a turn from things-No-didn't-like to things-No-did-like. Mary found herself talking a lot, telling him about her life, her family, and her home in Central, and he made her laugh a few times with some dry comments about the people. There was one point where she almost spat out her wine.

But there was something about No, Mary noticed, he wouldn't talk much about himself. He would often switch the topic to be about her instead. She didn't mind it but it became more and more noticeable that he was avoiding it on purpose, trying to hide something. She didn't feel like he was hiding something terrible, more it was the same sort of feeling she had about Wat; hiding so many secrets because it was habit.

She didn't mind. They were getting on! They were sidled up on the booth's sofa. No made it feel like he wanted to talk to her: he paused often, looking her in the eyes before continuing his sentence.

'I'm old,' he said, 'I've seen a lot of things, met a lot of people, but I've never known a more depressing sight than a crowd of people on the underground waiting for a delayed train in peak hours.'

Mary laughed at his observation, 'no it's not a joyous occasion.'

'They didn't want to be there in the first place, and here they are, having to WAIT for the train to take them to misery.'

'You focus a lot on depression,' said Mary.

'I guess it's the month,' said No, 'November tends to be a very depressing month. So grey and cold.'

'I like November,' said Mary. No gave her a look that she recognised as condescending disbelief. 'I do! I used to love it when I was younger. The air always felt crisp, it was getting close to Christmas, but because of the weather, you could stay in without being weird. It was calmer than December or October.'

'It's grey,' said No, 'it's grey and dull and boring. The popular consensus, let me tell you, is that November is a quiet month but filled with so much pain and sadness. Memorial Day?'

'What about Thanksgiving?'

'Is that a really happy occasion?'

Mary began to twiddle her thumbs, 'My birthday.'

No's eyes widened, 'when?'

'The twenty-third,' she said.

'So, in two weeks then?' said No, to which Mary nodded, 'What are you going to do for it?'

'I rarely do much for my birthday,' she said.

'I think that should change,' said No, 'hey Wat?' Wat, who was standing at the bar serving, looked over at No's call; 'did you know it will be Mary's birthday soon?'

Wat looked almost as if he had heard horrific news. As if No was a doctor informing him there was nothing more they could do for Mary and that she had only a couple weeks left.

'When?' he called back.

'Twenty-third,' said No as Wat clambered over haphazardly to reach their table, at which point he put his hand on Mary's shoulder. Mary had her head in her palm at this point.

SECRET IN THE LOST COMMON

'Don't you worry Mary, we caught it early. We're going to have the most spectacular time. I'll arrange for a party, here in the King George, I'll get everyone together-'

'That won't be necessary,' said Mary, placing a hand on Wat's, with No chuckling beside her, 'I'm going to go back to London to meet with some friends that night, you don't need to worry.'

Wat looked a little crestfallen but the spark never seemed to leave his eyes, 'ah I see. Well, I do hope it's a good day nonetheless.'

And he rose and returned to the bar. Mary gave No a look that let him know just how much she appreciated his interference.

'Wat loves to be involved in everyone's lives. You have to love him for that,' said No.

The night wore on and Mary got a little more and more tipsy, and she and No talked more and more. Eventually, people popped up and joined the conversation; Duncan from earlier in the month joined for a short period talking about the olden days, Neo poked her head in and talked about her plans to travel to China and Vietnam, and even Snow appeared late into the night. Mary thought the girl should be in bed, but No and she shared a short little conversation.

Snow was interested in what No had been up to in the year, and No politely asked her the same. After the small talk Snow turned to Mary, 'By the way Mrs Woods, my dad wanted to see you in the kitchen for a moment?'

Mary ignored the 'Mrs' and checked her watch - it was quarter to eleven. This must be it, she thought.

'Alright, I'll go see what he wants. I'll see you later No,' she said. No responded by nodding in acceptance.

TALES FROM THE KING GEORGE

Then Mary scooched off the sofa and walked slowly with excitement to the kitchens. She pushed on the door and found it empty - they'd stopped serving food an hour ago and so everything was cooling down. Wojciech, who Mary had heard was cooking, likely had already left. There was an open door on the opposite side of the kitchen that looked to lead to a small alcove fenced off beside the pub where the bins were kept.

Mary stepped out the doorway and looked around in the small area, 'Wat?' she said softly, not expecting him to respond. There was no one out there, just the bins and a wooden fence and gate obscuring the view of the street. Mary sighed, shaking her head at the fact Snow must've lied to her. Before she could react, the kitchen door swung closed.

It was a fire exit, so there was no handle. Mary rushed over to the door and tried to pull on it.

'No, no, no,' she said to herself before she gave up trying to get the door open.

She straightened herself out and then knocked politely on the door, three raps before shouting, 'Hello? Could someone let me in?'

Hopefully, someone would walk into the kitchen at some point. Mary sighed in discontent but was startled when a figure fell onto the bins in a crouched stance. She jumped at the sight, holding a hand to her chest as the figure draped his legs off the edge to drop down to the ground onto their feet. When he stood up straight Mary had already recognised the silver hair and the tall stance.

It was the man from the very first night; Richard O'Nerry.

SECRET IN THE LOST COMMON

He grinned in a way that made her incredibly uncomfortable as if she was his prey trapped in a corner. And she very much did feel trapped.

'Mary Woods,' said O'Nerry.

'What do you want?' snapped Mary.

'You stole my room,' said O'Nerry snidely.

Mary had nothing to respond with but she suddenly felt overexposed, almost as if she was standing naked in front of this man. She shied back and realised it was the way he was looking at her. His voice was ominous and slick, yet his gaze gave off wanton desire. She tried to snap out of it and stood straight, but she realised if he were to act on her…

No, he hadn't moved on her. If he was going to, he would've already. Right? What could he want?

'What do you want from me?' she asked, trying to sound as calm as she could.

'Let's say I've an "interest" in you Woods,' said O'Nerry, 'I want to make a bargain. You seem a reasonable woman, you come from a privileged background. You understand that money makes the world go round. I want to hire you.'

'And just what makes you think I would help a disgusting man like yourself,' spat Mary.

'Disgusting!? You've listened to too many rumours,' O'Nerry smiled to himself and, from what Mary could see, he licked his lips.

'I don't make deals with the devil.'

'Oh nor me, not anymore. I can offer you a lot of money, more than anything that Stone can offer.'

'My loyalty cannot be bought,' said Mary sternly.

O'Nerry sneered, 'but it can be won over if the people are dear enough? You're a logical woman, Mary, look at you, you're an accountant! Your whole job is to weigh the pros and cons and you'd be making an honest mistake to miss out on what I can offer you. I may be unlawful but I've come into a lot of money doing so. Part of it could be yours without any strings attached.'

'I make a six-figure salary, you think I can be won over by money?'

O'Nerry slammed a fist against the bin, 'You really want to stick with these freaks!? You want to protect that flamboyant piece of crap Wat and the rest of his frolicking staff!? You think that just because you've spent some time with them, you're one of them, that you actually belong in this hovel of a house?'

Mary felt the pang of a struck nerve, which caught O'Nerry 's eye.

'Yeah, you think that maybe you've found somewhere that's accepted you? Perhaps you have been in the business world too long, Mary, I bet you never thought that the people you work with might actually be friends at one point, hell I bet you never spent enough time with them to know.'

'I have friends.'

'And how often do you see your friends, Mary Woods? Nationally renowned accountant, constantly jumping from one job to another, always got something to be doing. Early to bed, early to rise, or is that just because there's nothing better to do?'

Mary only just noticed but O'Nerry was moving closer to her with excitement in his eyes. He was glaring at her and under those menacing eyes, she was growing smaller and smaller. He was right, she had felt at times like she hadn't the company she had always sought after. Perhaps she did focus on her work too much, but she hadn't known any better. To get better in this fast-paced world you work harder, you work longer. She had never thought that work didn't have to be a constant improvement.

That is until the Mad King. She wasn't constantly improving her methods, hell she was hardly brushing the surface of what she could do. She thought that working at half capacity would be boring but it just meant she was free to use most of the time talking with the other staff, enjoying the pub and its atmosphere rather than letting it smother her. It was relaxing and yet fulfilling all at once.

'But here's the thing Mary,' whispered O'Nerry eerily, 'they don't actually care about you. If you were to leave tomorrow, they would wave goodbye but you'd never hear from them again. This is just a job. You're working for just another business. And therein lies the problem with the business world; it's a dog-eat-dog world.'

Mary found her back pressed against the wall and O'Nerry's face was so close to hers. She thought he would bite her face off, but instead, his mouth slipped past her face, his words slithering out and slipping into her ears. She felt tears welling up.

'I want that thread. Give me the thread. He thinks he can scare me? I will find that thread and burn it, even if I have to burn his whole rotten pub to the ground with it.'

The kitchen door swung open and O'Nerry jumped backward. Mary eased up and realised what had been happening: her body had been tense and pressed hard against the wall, but now she took deep breaths. Her mind cleared as if smoke dissipated and the feelings of doubt and anxiety had just dropped away. She took a step forward, looked at O'Nerry and said:

'No. Get out. Get out!'

'You bastard,' said a rough but deep voice from the kitchen door.

No was stood, hand on the door, his face displaying raw hatred. He immediately tried to take a swing for O'Nerry but the silver-haired man ducked in time and dodged around as No almost lost his footing. O'Nerry, with incredible body strength, lifted himself up onto the bin, and then up onto the wall, careening up to the roof's gutters. No watched him and shouted up, 'Coward!'

'It's tactical retreating,' laughed O'Nerry, showing his physical prowess by pulling himself onto the roof. He crouched to look down. 'I'll be back! Mark my words.'

And then he was out of sight, running along the roof. No gripped Mary's shoulders and looked her over.

'Are you alright? I saw him against you, did he force himself-'

'No, no, I'm not sure what came over me,' said Mary, sniffing to draw back the tears, 'he was just talking and for some reason, I kept listening. How did you find me?'

'Wat was closing up and you hadn't come back. I thought I would see you before I went to bed, so I went looking for you,' he said.

Mary smiled gently at the thought of that.

'I'm fine, he was just pressuring me into...something,' she said.

'What?'

'Nothing, it's nothing,' said Mary, 'no thank you No. Honestly, I'm a grown woman. If I didn't think it was nothing, I would tell you.'

SECRET IN THE LOST COMMON

'I want to let you know I'm here if you need me,' said No.

Mary nodded and she gave him a hug. The two of them held on for a few seconds longer than one would have considered polite and Mary relished the feeling. When they separated, the thought of Wat entered her mind.

'You said Wat was closing up. Did he go to bed?' she asked.

'No, he went outside to lock up the common,' said No.

'I need to go find him,' she said and began to leave.

'I'll come with you,' said No.

'No,' said Mary, lifting her hands, 'no it's confidential business matters,' and she brushed her thighs in a way to say that she couldn't say much more. Or at least she hoped that was what she conveyed.

No shrugged, 'Go ahead. I'll see you tomorrow.'

Mary gave him a smile and then left in a quick pace through the kitchen, into the dining room and then out onto the patio. She carefully trod down the dirty path to the common where Wat was waiting, arms folded.

'Where were you? You're lucky I'm still here, I'm bloody tired,' said Wat, grinning.

'Sorry Wat, I got caught up,' said Mary.

Wat accepted her answer and then he led her into the common. They walked round through the first quarter to the furthest out, where the fence's gates were set. Wat turned off his torch as they approached. Jordan, the gardener, was standing waiting by the gate. Mary could barely tell it was him by the silhouette and the pale light from the moon.

'Mary? You're letting Mary in are you Wat?' he chuckled.

'Unfortunately, she has to know. For "business reasons",' he said, using his hands to place quotes around the words.

'Lucky girl,' said Jordan, 'careful of the buckets now.'

He gestured to the two buckets set beside the gates: one looked to contain water and one some form of powder. Jordan then approached the five great padlocks on the gates and began to unlock them, one by one. Each one took about a minute as he had to deduce the correct key from the thirty he carried. Wat waited patiently, not speaking. Mary found it odd to see Wat not speaking - it carried great weight with whatever was behind the gate.

When Jordan was finished, he unwound the chain and then pulled on the left gate door to open it a narrow way. Wat picked up a bucket and then squeezed in.

'Grab the other bucket?' he asked out loud.

Mary realised he meant her and grabbed it. It was incredibly large, unwieldy and heavy. She struggled a little and had to use two hands so she glanced at Jordan.

'You go on in. I've got to keep watch,' said Jordan.

She also squeezed on through and Jordan then closed the gate behind her. She had to increase her pace to keep up with Wat who was now in the centre of the quarter, but the bucket was bumping into her legs. This mystery was deepening but it felt as if she were working on a farm. She'd seen the farm hands near her childhood home carrying buckets like these in one hand, yet leaning to one side. They would tip them up into troughs for the pigs or the horses depending on where she was. She had admired those men, especially in the summer when they'd been shirtless. She could've been a country girl if she had really wanted.

SECRET IN THE LOST COMMON

The fenced area was just open grass apart from the centre where a little shrubbery and what looked like two troughs were placed. A bright white horse stood by the troughs looking directly at Wat. In fact, Mary noted it was incredibly white, so white it almost looked like it was glowing. In fact, it had to be because there was no light source to make it look that white.

The horse approached Wat warily and revealed him in the horse's glow as if Wat was merely stepping out of a shadow into the sun. Wat put a hand to the horse's head and then continued to the troughs. At the one trough, he placed his bucket down, then fiddled around with the side of the trough. In a moment, the trough emptied itself of water, pouring out onto the grass. After it was done, he fiddled with it some more, then filled the trough with the bucket. Mary realised that he was replacing the water and then rushed to copy him. She presented him with his bucket and Wat did the same thing but, instead, this was grain. Mary looked up at the horse and finally witnessed the horn on its head.

'No way.'

'Mary Woods, this is Wesley,' said Wat flatly.

The unicorn bowed its head down to her. Mary turned to Wat; 'You named it Wesley?'

'No. I call him Wesley because Wesley is his name,' he replied.

The unicorn stomped on the grass with one hoof. She gazed in amazement.

'Mr Stone,' she finally said, 'how did you come to obtain a unicorn?'

'Van Pelt. Two years ago, he was bragging the last unicorn was in the Canadian forests of Banff. I said that was ludicrous. We joked but, in the end, we made a bet; two grand if he could capture the said unicorn and bring it here. I even threw in that, if he did capture it, I would house it here until he found a suitable buyer.

'And here we are,' Wat flourished with a defeated sigh, 'he actually did it.'

Mary felt herself entranced by the creature. 'It's beautiful.'

'He's incredibly rare too,' said Wat.

Wesley stomped on the ground once.

'There are a lot of myths about unicorns. They say drinking its blood can give you eternal life. Or that they can tell the future.'

Wesley brayed and shook his head.

'Yes exactly. That's probably why they're endangered now although they also say that unicorns are as conscious as humans.'

Wesley stomped once.

'And just as smart.'

Wesley brayed, shook his head, and then stomped his foot several times.

'Okay yes, and just as modest.'

Mary had begun involuntarily stroking Wesley's mane as she listened to Wat. Somehow, she couldn't help but feel calm in the presence of the creature.

'He's beautiful,' she muttered.

'And of course, he has to remain a secret. Just like everything else.'

Mary looked Wesley deep into his big dark eyes.

'I promise that I will protect you, Wesley.'

Wesley snorted in acceptance, as Mary embraced the unicorn with all the warmth she could muster. She felt a wealth of serenity bathe her and she stood like that for a long time. When she let go, Wat had his arms crossed waiting.

SECRET IN THE LOST COMMON

'Yeah he has that effect on people,' said Wat, 'unicorns do.'

They then made their way back out of the fenced quarter. Jordan locked up the gate and they thanked him. Wat reiterated his point from earlier, 'we must keep him secret at all costs. Unicorns are extremely sought after and unfortunately often by the wrong people.'

Mary thought of O'Nerry and Niamh, 'I will keep him secret, I promise you that Wat.'

'You know what Mary,' said Wat, 'I truly believe you.'

MARY AND THE WAND

Mary wasn't the snooping type. She felt one's privacy was their own and she never felt the need to get involved in someone else's business without their express permission. Even if they were keeping secrets. In those cases, she felt it best to be upfront with them and explain that keeping secrets was immature and whatever it was they were hiding, they spit out now before it gets revealed under more unsavoury circumstances. This worked well in business and in friendships. However, it did mean that she wasn't privy to 'gossip' as it came.

Here she was, standing above a large wooden chest with a lock on it, and she felt a surge of curiosity that threatened everything she stood for about privacy. She bit her lip, fighting with herself. She desperately wanted to see inside. She desperately wanted to see what it contained.

'If you don't open it, I will,' said Lauren, who was standing next to her, hands clasped together.

'We shouldn't. Rob, tell us that we shouldn't,' was Mary's response.

Rob, who was standing by the trapdoor, shrugged his shoulders, 'I don't really care.'

Mary frowned, 'Rob, come on, you're meant to be keeping an eye on us up here.'

'Dad said that to make sure you don't hurt yourselves on all the crap he keeps up here,' was Rob's response.

'I thought the whole point of being up here was to mark on all his assets,' said Lauren, sarcastically.

That was true, Mary had again exploited her position to get access to Wat's attic. Like the old ballroom, the attic looked like it contained a great number of archaic and antique treasures. Mary wanted to see if there was anything that might be deemed extremely valuable that Wat could then sell to improve his finances. Not that she really thought it would help the cause, but she did want to see what he was hiding amongst the dust. As he himself described;

'I mainly use the attic to store all the things I don't have a use for. There's also a lot of stuff from when my uncle owned the place so who knows what's really up there.'

Wat had said this before leaving to have lunch with Niamh which Mary disapproved of. Lauren had also disapproved but, instead of seething like Mary, had informed Wat just how stupid a man he was. Wat had laughed it off. Sometimes, Mary couldn't help but find the man incredibly naive. The way he had bounded out the door he looked almost fifteen years old running to see the girl down the road for milkshakes.

'Rob, what do you think of Niamh,' Mary had asked, as Rob was opening the trapdoor for the two of them shortly after Wat had left.

MARY AND THE WAND

'She's alright, I don't talk to her much. She's usually with my dad when she is around, so it's always polite talk.'

'Polite talk?'

'How's the day going? What are your plans for the weekend? How's the music going, have you written anything new?'

'You mean small talk?'

'Yeah but the way she does it, she only does it to be polite.'

Mary nodded, then eyed up Rob, 'what was your mum like?'

Lauren swiftly turned her head halfway up the ladder as Rob heaved a sigh.

'Kind of a bitch,' he said, 'At least that's what I get told. I don't remember much, she left when I was pretty young.'

'I'm sorry,' said Mary.

'It's fine, like I said I don't remember much. She wasn't so much a mom to me, just a face. I just remember her and Dad arguing so much that when she left it was nice for the peace and quiet. Plus, Dad got a lot more easygoing and happier when she was gone. When she was here, he was stressed and frustrated all the time.'

'Was that hard on you and your sister?'

Rob gave her a look and then said, 'Oh she wasn't there. We're not full brother and sister.'

Mary gave a low gasp as the cogs in her mind clicked.

'...Who was Snow's mother then?'

Rob gave a strained look and opened his mouth as if to say something, but then shook it, 'it's a little complicated.'

TALES FROM THE KING GEORGE

'Hey Mary, are you coming or what?' called Lauren from the attic.

Mary dropped the topic and entered the attic. She'd have to ask about that at some point.

After a brief look around, they began to try and sort through some of the items. Mary carried a handkerchief with her as every time they shuffled an item, a cloud of dust rose and set off her allergies. She sneezed for a good half a minute when Lauren moved the stacks of clothes off the chest.

It was an old wooden one that looked as if it was a good fifty years old. Straps kept it closed but there was no lock as far as they could see. Etched into the top was the name 'Saul Stone' in gold, meaning it had been Rob's great uncle's. Rob had explained Saul had passed about five years ago, but Mary still felt a little off-put at the idea of rifling through his uncle's possessions. It was likely mementoes from when he was alive, and she felt such an act should be performed by at least a family member.

But still…

'Well I'm opening it,' said Lauren without another thought and unclasped the two straps.

The lid seemed to pop, as if it had been under a lot of pressure closed so tightly, but when Lauren lifted the lid the chest appeared to be half empty. Peering inside they could see mostly letters and papers, along with a couple of other objects; a set of vials, a compass, what looked like a magic wand, a set of scales, a candle holder, a small sword letter-opener and a couple of jewellery boxes. Lauren immediately lifted one of the vials out of its holder and looked it over.

'This is odd stuff,' said Lauren, 'do you think it's magic?'

MARY AND THE WAND

'Wouldn't surprise me,' said Mary, and reached for the wand, 'look at it.'

She lifted the wand and waved it slightly. She felt a breeze waft around her as if great power had been unleashed. Lauren felt it too and looked up at Mary.

'Did you feel that?' Mary asked, to which Lauren nodded.

'You think you can perform magic with that thing?' she asked.

Mary looked at the wand, then looked at Lauren. Then she cracked a smile and the two women dashed for the trapdoor. Rob gave a confused frown as they approached.

'What did you find?' he asked.

Mary brandished the wand, 'we're going to see if we can perform some magic.'

'Where did you get that?' asked Lauren.

In Rob's hands was an old accordion, 'I found it on the side. Thought it might add a little something to my music.'

He then proceeded to produce a very stifled wheeze as he pushed it together.

'Might be a bit old,' he said.

Mary and Lauren exchanged a look before they clambered down from the attic in a hurry. Mary led the charge, wand in hand, racing down the stairs.

'What do we try?' called Lauren.

'I have an idea,' said Mary, and turned down towards the office.

She veered left into the Stone family kitchen. As she expected, dishes and plates were stacked in a mess in the sink and on the side. The mess hadn't been touched in days and Mary wasn't going to go a foot near it. But now she had magic on her side.

TALES FROM THE KING GEORGE

Probably.

'How should I do this?' she asked Lauren.

'Flick it? Like in the movies,' Lauren replied.

'Do you think I need to say something as well?'

'Like what?'

'Clean-it-uppicus.'

'…Just flick it and we'll see what happens.'

She held the wand in two hands with Lauren behind her, just in case things got crazy. Mary then gave a slight flick of the wrist to swish the wand in the air. As before, a strange breeze surged around them. A dish rattled in the sink, and then so did all the others. Suddenly, they lifted themselves into the air and stacked themselves to the left of the sink. The plates followed suit. Then, in some Disney-esque manner, one by one they drifted over to the sink where invisible hands rubbed them with soap and rinsed them under the tap, before placing themselves neatly on the draining board.

Mary gave Lauren an excited look watching the washing up complete itself.

'It is magic,' said Mary.

'What else can we do?' said Lauren.

'Anything, we have a magic wand!' said Mary and she raced out of the kitchen.

* * *

About an hour later, Mary and Lauren were sitting on the patio under the shade of one of the parasols. They'd spent a good hour setting tables in the dining room without touching a thing, had set off a snooker game by itself, and had somehow managed to flick the wand and bring two martinis out to the patio, where they were now sipping them avoiding the sun. The sun was unprecedented as it was bright and hot even if it was the middle of November.

MARY AND THE WAND

Lauren sighed loudly, 'What do we do next?'

'The possibilities are endless,' said Mary, 'what did that kid do in those films?'

'Just sent people flying really,' said Lauren, 'unlocked doors, fought dragons.'

Mary then sat upright in a flash. She gave a knowing smile to Lauren who just watched her in curiosity. Mary then stood up straight and pointed at herself with the wand.

'Levitate,' she said sternly and flicked the wand.

There was a moment where nothing happened. But then she felt her feet get wrenched from the ground and she hovered softly in the air. Mary felt a burst of excitement and pure joy at the prospect that now lay in front of her. She was a kid again, with all the freedom of the world at her fingertips. Lauren was on her feet now, 'no fuckin' way.'

Mary then lifted her wand and pointed it up, and she tore up into the sky. She raced at what felt like a million miles an hour. Mary felt like she was young again, twelve years old racing down a hill on a bike. When she felt she'd elevated high enough, she lowered the wand and looked around. She was a good thirty metres in the air and Lauren was on the ground looking up in awe.

Mary took advantage of her newfound power and pushed the wand forward. The wand continued and pulled her along with it, letting her fly through the air almost gracefully. About as gracefully as you can fly when a wand is pulling you around. Yet when she hovered in the air, she felt as if she was held in place in the world, as if the world could continue to turn and she would remain constant. She pointed the wand onward and looked around. Beneath her stretched the town, the high street, the low street, the common, she could see it all. Behind her hills rose up amongst the patchwork. She could see where the roads bled through the land and where they spread out and became the city, and where they bunched up to become the motorways that shot through the countryside, very finely like needle and thread, but oh-so precise.

The people were not ants, they were dots; they were almost like the drops of water on a car window. They moved slowly and they stopped randomly, but together they made a beautiful constantly moving scene. She paused for a moment to take it all in. It was like being in one of the many skyscrapers but with so much more freedom to move around and see what she wanted to see.

When she was finished, she pushed the wand back in the direction of King George. She gently tapped the wand down and it softly lowered her. She stood in front of Lauren, who had been enjoying the rest of her martini.

'Did you enjoy that?' she asked, smiling.

Mary simply nodded enthusiastically, the wand in both her hands.

'It was amazing,' she said, 'I could see everything up there.'

'Don't you usually work in skyscrapers?'

'Yes, but this was something else. You're free up there! Free to go wherever!'

She sat down and let herself come down from the adrenaline high. Then she realised she was gripping the wand incredibly tightly and frowned. She looked up to find Lauren giving her an expectant look. Mary opened her grip and offered it to Lauren, 'See it for yourself.'

Lauren greedily snatched the wand and then did as Mary had done and lifted it above her.

MARY AND THE WAND

Nothing happened.

She gave Mary a disappointed look, then tried a couple more times punching the air. She didn't rise even a centimetre. She held the wand with both hands, 'what's wrong with it.'

'Let me see?' asked Mary, opening her hand to Lauren.

Lauren jerked the wand out of Mary's reach, 'no, no, I must be doing it wrong.'

'Maybe it won't work for you,' suggested Mary.

'Why not? It worked for you,' said Lauren bitterly, and tried to punch the air a couple more times.

'Lauren, give me the wand. I just want to test-'

'Test what? This should work!'

'Maybe it only works for me?'

'Why? You're not magic.'

'And you are?'

'No,' and Lauren sneered, 'but this is unfair! Why does it only want to work for you!' Lauren waved the wand aggressively in the air.

Suddenly, Neo burst out onto the patio.

'Hey, we've got a situation in here!'

* * *

The dining room was a mess. Tables were overturned, some chairs were broken in half, cutlery was scattered, and even some of the wallpaper was torn. However, Neo left all that and led the women into the barroom. Boz was holding a drinks tray up behind the bar as bottle after bottle was throwing itself at her, not quite hard enough to smash but definitely enough to give her trouble.

'Somebody help!' she cried out.

'What did you two do?' said Neo.

TALES FROM THE KING GEORGE

Lauren lifted the wand and swished it through the air but, instead of ending the tirade, three bottles lifted themselves up and threw themselves down at Mary, Neo and Lauren, smashing at their feet. The three of them jumped. Mary tried to grab the wand.

'You must be doing it wrong!'

'I'm doing just like you did!' said Lauren, and she flicked the wand again.

This time, some barstools lifted up and threw themselves at the three of them. Mary and Lauren dove to their left, Neo to their right into a booth. Now that Lauren was on the ground Mary tried to wrestle the wand out of her hands.

'Give it to me!' she said.

She knew that she might not be able to stop the mess but Lauren wasn't helping it. The older woman would not let go. She struggled to her feet and ran out of the barroom. The bottles had stopped throwing themselves around but the women could hear the sound of objects moving from the end of the gallery. Lauren stopped halfway down as Mary got up to the entryway and the door to the billiards room opened up. All ten balls and a cue fired themselves down the corridor. Somehow they all missed Lauren but Mary had to drop harshly to the ground to avoid getting hit. Lauren turned left and she opened up the doors to the central courtyard. At which point Mary heard the sound of the front door of the barroom opening up and Wat's shocked voice say, 'What on earth?'

Lauren was out in the courtyard looking Mary dead in the eyes, terror coating her face. Then suddenly, without any prompting, she was yanked up into the air. Mary covered her mouth with her hands, then pressed them to the ground to get up and run.

MARY AND THE WAND

'Lauren!' she shouted and she ran out to the courtyard.

She didn't really know what she should do; Lauren was now hundreds of metres in the air. There was no way that Mary could follow her without the wand. She could hear Lauren screaming at the top of her lungs. Shortly Wat, Neo and Boz were outside. Mary turned to meet his stare. It wasn't happy.

'What's going on?' he demanded.

'I'm sorry Wat, I'm so sorry. We found a wand in your dad's chest and we used it. But it's gotten out of control!' said Mary.

'What wand?' said Wat.

At which point something rapped on the stone tiles in front of them. Mary gasped in horror.

'That wand!' she said and looked up. Lauren was screaming and rapidly falling towards them and her doom. 'She's going to die!'

'Wat, do something!' said Neo.

Wat just watched Lauren, a stern look on his face. Mary gave him a confused stare, before blurting out, 'Do something!' He still didn't move.

She turned around so as not to face the horror of Lauren splattering onto the ground. Lauren's screaming rose in volume as she got closer until she was a deafening roar and her body was a blur, coming into view and completely visible, just moments away from her final resting point. But she stopped suddenly, half a metre from the ground. She was hovering, as Mary was before. After a moment she dropped and hit the ground, gasping and panting as she came to realise she was not dead and all the praying she'd done to the Lord in her head had actually come to fruition. She lifted her two hands to the air, laughing and crying at the same time, 'Thank you!'

Mary turned around to see Neo and Boz kneeling down to Lauren, checking she was alright. Wat looked at the wand and picked it up then brandished it at Mary with a slightly confused but annoyed look.

'This wand?' he said.

'Yes, I'm so sorry,' said Mary, 'we were just messing around with it.'

'You mean, you caused the mess?'

'We were using it to clean the dishes and tidy the rooms up and to fly.'

'...How?'

Mary gestured, 'We just flicked it around and it started doing what we wanted.'

'You just flicked it?'

'I don't know how it works, we thought it was magic,' said Mary.

Wat looked her up and down, 'This is a water-dowsing stick. It's not magic.'

Mary's world cracked, 'then, how did we do all the cleaning?'

Wat sighed, 'When you were clearing the attic, what else did you find? Did you touch anything else?'

Mary looked at Lauren, who looked back at her and shook her head. 'We only took this.'

Wat shook his head and left the confused women in the courtyard. He entered back into the barroom and began to look around. Mary quickly followed him.

'I'm confused, if that wasn't magic, then what was that?'

'It was a poltergeist,' said Wat, 'you've been tricked into thinking you've been doing magic.'

MARY AND THE WAND

'But why?' asked Mary. Lauren at this point was too shaken up to speak.

'I need to grab something. You find where that poltergeist is now and get it back out in the open if you can. I'll come find you,' he said, and ran off toward the attic.

Mary was about to protest but he was gone. She looked around and found Neo and Boz propping up Lauren.

'I'm sorry Mary,' said Lauren, 'I was just so upset that it wasn't working. I didn't mean to cause all this-'

'You didn't cause all this, it was a ghost,' said Mary.

'A ghost?' Lauren repeated, and laughed a little, 'Of course it was,' she was still recovering from her near-death experience and so Neo set her down in a chair.

'We need to find it though. Wat has a plan,' Mary then looked around. There was no destruction going on, it was all quiet again. It had to be somewhere, messing with something, 'where would it have gone.'

'It messed up the dining room, the billiards room, the barroom. Threw me in the air. Sounds like it's done a number everywhere!'

'Yeah, just after you two had tidied it up as well,' said Neo.

Mary's mind clicked, 'that's right, we tidied up the dining room. We also set up a game in the billiard room. And we also started doing the dishes-'

'-downstairs!' finished off Lauren.

Mary left the three of them in the barroom to reach the top of the stairs to the lower floor. The sound of dishes and cutlery clashing together was soft but noticeable. She edged her way down the stairs, slowly and quietly. She had to lead this thing back out into the open but there was no telling what it would do. It had already tried to kill Lauren, or at least scare the life out of her. Mary took each step as lightly as she could, pressing toe to heel, but these stairs were old. Halfway down the step creaked.

Mary winced. The clanking stopped. She froze in place, waiting to hear if it knew she was there. A few of the longest seconds she'd ever known passed. But then out from the kitchen floated three stacks of plates, dishes, and pots. They hovered out in the corridor and Mary stared. Her mind screamed at her to move but she was frozen in place. Any second now the barrage would start, she needed to move. Move dammit!

A dish settled, causing the stack to clatter, and this kicked Mary into gear. She pressed hard with her foot and leapt up the stairs to the sound of plates and dishes crashing onto the floor and wall behind her. The columns of crockery were at her heels as she entered the barroom again, the constant fire sending shards of broken kitchenware dancing around her feet. The three women who were left in the barroom immediately ducked under the bar counter. Mary felt the number of crashes dissipate and looked around to make sure the ghost was still following. The columns clattered as they separated out. Every last piece of crockery was held up, poised in the air, and aimed entirely around Mary. She stepped backwards, unsure of what she should do next. She was trapped.

Then Wat appeared from behind the crockery holding a body over his shoulder. He dropped it to the floor with a clunk and fiddled with its back. There was a click and immediately the dishes and plates dropped to the ground. They all shattered, Mary flinched as the shards scattered out around her. She was mostly fine when she finally looked up to see what Wat had done.

MARY AND THE WAND

It looked like a ventriloquist's dummy, an old wooden one with a square bottom jaw and painted-on face, with a purple top hat sitting slightly askew on its head. Its eyes had angry eyebrows drawn above them in a couple brush strokes, and on closer inspection, there was a faint glow from behind the white-painted wood. Wat picked it up and sat it on the counter with its legs hanging off. Mary finally approached Wat as the dummy was beginning to move. The head rocked slightly from side to side. The eyes rolled around randomly before settling together in one direction. The jaw made its up and down motions and then a gurgled sound began to emit from the dummy. It wasn't good quality, it was the quality you got from an old car radio or from the speakers found in most cheap toys or holiday jumpers. But when the dummy spoke they could just about get the gist of human speech. The eyes and head moved around to look up at Wat and look at each person individually. The jaw also moved in time when the dummy first spoke, 'Oh for fuck's sake.'

'Can you hear me spirit?' asked Wat.

'I 'ear ye,' said the dummy.

'You've caused me a lot of damage, spirit.'

'Aye, but it was funny. Did you see that lass' face when I dropped 'er?'

'You could've killed her.'

'I weren gonna kill nobody! I'ma nonrable man.'

'Is this the ghost?' asked Mary, pointing at the dummy, which then turned to look at her with glazed eyes.

'Yes,' said Wat, 'I've just trapped him in this conduit.'

'Why the hell have you got that Wat?' asked Lauren.

'Because of situations like this where people free poltergeists,' snapped Wat.

'You already freed me once from my cursed accordion! I'd been trapped for hundreds of years. So kind of that lad to let me out, but why didn't ye let me out earlier!? I bet you knew I was in there sir.'

'What accordion?' asked Wat.

Mary sighed as Lauren vocalised what she'd realised, 'Oh Rob had found an accordion upstairs! He'd tried to play the damn thing.'

'What's your name?' asked Mary.

'I be John Milton Heather, but they called me Feathers on the sea,' said the dummy.

'So, you were a sailor,' said Mary.

'More like a pirate,' said Wat.

'I was a man who did 'onest work and got paid for it! Was none o' me business if someone got hurt when they didn't do what we told em!'

'So why did you do all that stuff with me and Lauren and the wand?'

Feathers, the dummy, chuckled, 'I thought it be funny. O and it be!'

Mary scowled, 'Fine, what do we do with him.'

'Common courtesy would be to banish him and disperse his spirit back to the beyond. Someone obviously cursed him to haunt the accordion for a reason though so I'm tempted to put him back,' said Wat.

'Er, now ye be forgettin you could 'elp me out? Give me a vessel, let me walk again, and I'll be a loyal servant to ye,' said Feathers.

'You think I have a vessel just sitting around here?' asked Wat.

MARY AND THE WAND

'Please don't put me back in the accordion, 'aving your spirit attached to an inanimate object like that is cruel! You can understan that, right Stone?'

Wat eyed him, 'Like I say you were punished for a reason.'

Feathers' head lolled and the dummy's eyes rolled to the ground, 'aye, I understand. No man would take pity on a ghost such as meself, especially not one with such 'istory as me,' the dummy milked his voice for all it was worth, 'then have pity and release me. I'd rather joins the rest of the spirits and attach meself to something or someone aff-livin at least.'

Wat considered this and bit his lip, 'You've caused me some serious damage.'

'Abeen stuck innan accordion, give me a break!'

'How long was your sentence?'

'Forever.'

'I'd be letting you off light then wouldn't I.'

'I've an idea,' said Mary, stepping up, 'leave him in the dummy.'

Wat laughed, 'this is only meant for communication. It's almost as bad as the accordion but with the bonus that he can talk,' his smile then dropped, 'actually that's more a minus.'

'I'd rather be released than be stuck in the dummy.'

'It'll give you time to think Wat. We'll decide what we'll do with you,' and she pointed at the dummy, 'later. But we'll give you some time to make your case.'

'From this thing?' said Feathers.

'Would you rather the accordion?'

Feathers growled as best she could tell from the speaker and his head turned to face away. Wat gave a soft smile and said, 'That's a good idea, Mary. Let's let our friend sit out a couple weeks here in the bar,' and he moved Feathers so he was sat in the corner on top of the bar counter.

'You think it's safe to leave him in view?' asked Neo.

'We'll tell our customers he's a gimmick, just some new novelty technology. Like those old fortune tellers,' said Wat.

Feathers' eyebrows dipped, 'you best not be usin me to make money. I'd rather be locked in the accordion than be used as some freak show!'

'Okay decision made; I'll get the accordion.'

'No, I'll be good! I'll stay,' said Feathers and Mary heard the distinct sound of defeat.

She gave Wat a victorious smile that he shared until he wiggled his finger and pulled Mary to the dining room. The place was still an absolute mess and Wat had to pinch the bridge of his nose.

'Wat I'm sorry about all this,' said Mary.

'It seems you're becoming increasingly involved in magical matters,' he stated, 'I think that needs to change.'

Mary gulped but stood straight and looked him in the eye. She half expected him to call her out on everything. She hadn't acted professionally recently at all. She wanted to apologise and explain it all away, she'd return to focusing on what she was being paid for.

'I'll have a talk with No. I think he's best to introduce you,' he said.

'...introduce me to what?'

'Magical matters,' Wat said, 'the basics. What me and this whole pub is involved in.'

'You mean you actually "want" me to be involved?'

'Absolutely, it seems I can't stop you,' said Wat.

MARY AND THE WAND

Mary let go of her hands that she'd been clasping so desperately, 'well I appreciate the offer, Wat, I won't let you down! I'm sure I will provide essential help to you and your business.'

'I hope so too,' said Wat and touched the back of his head, 'this can get dangerous if you don't know how to deal with it,' and he gestured around.

Mary nodded but she couldn't stop smiling giddily. Then Wat gestured to the room again, 'Now if you could help the others clean all this up and I'll ring some local charities to see if they have any furniture going.'

Mary groaned in her head, 'Yes Wat,' and as he left the room she twirled around, 'thank you,' she added.

'Just stop breaking my pub,' he half-joked, 'you're meant to be saving me money, not costing it.'

SNOW AND FIRE

Outside it was overcast. A gentle and cool breeze was causing a draught through the conservatory meaning that everyone had retreated to the dining room for breakfast. The tree in the courtyard was now completely bare, its leaves collected on the floor by the benches in the grass, which were slick with dew and wet soil. It had been raining in the early hours but had now drawn to a close. No commented on it when Mary met him;

'Usual November weather, just a murky mess,' he stated.

She sighed, 'So is this my brief?'

'This is your introduction to magical affairs, yes,' state No, 'Are we getting breakfast?'

'I already ordered something, Kam will bring it out soon.'

'Great,' he tapped his mug, 'well so let's start with the fact that magic exists. It's existed for a very long time.

'I'm aware,' said Mary.

'It exists as a form of energy that can be tapped into and converted into other energies.'

'So far so good,' said Mary, 'where does it come from?'

'Spirits. Souls,' said No, 'the dead.'

Mary frowned at that, 'now you've lost me.'

'You know the generic idea of a soul? When you pass away, your soul will detach from your physical form and join the billions of others that float amongst the void. It's not just humans, any living creature has a soul.'

'Even parasites? Bacteria?'

'No. Not from what we can tell.

'So, where's the line in "living creature"?'

No sighed, 'We don't really investigate magic; many people used to think of it as a sacred art, not something to be questioned.'

'A little dismissive,' said Mary.

No sipped from his tea again and rolled his eyes, 'look let me give you the run-down of what we know then you're free to do with it what you like,' he said, 'including interrogate us.'

'Fine.'

No continued to explain and Mary listened intently. No explained that souls acted as the energy source for magic, that detached souls congregate to something they identify strongly with. When Mary asked what he meant, he said that often a parent's soul will resonate strongly with their child's. A dog's soul may strongly identify with the person that raised it. That person may then tap into that power, or "pool", with the appropriate training.

SNOW AND FIRE

If that person passes away, then their pool dissipates and finds a new 'vessel'. The person also releases their own soul.

The power of a soul is correlated to the age of the person who had it – the older you are, the more power your soul has.

'Think of a clam with a pearl inside. It grows bigger the longer it gets until at some point it releases that pearl. People are clams, and souls are pearls. Those who can cast magic are the clams with a pearl necklace.'

Then he explained that using magic literally uses up the energy - consumes the souls tied to a person. So, all magic has a limit.

'What about your own soul? Could you use your soul to cast magic, wouldn't it get used up too?'

No shook his head, 'Right now your soul isn't "ready" yet. It can't be used for magic.'

'That's a relief.'

'Breakfast?'

Kam had appeared with a plate and was proffering it toward Mary, who had been entranced in No's explanation.

'Yes sorry.'

She began to start eating to let No continue when he gestured to Kam and said, 'Hey Kam, can you show Mary some magic?'

Kam looked up and around the room, 'few too many people. I can show you in the kitchen.'

Mary stopped eating, wiped her face and launched to her feet. 'Lead the way.'

Kam did so; in the kitchen, she stepped to the centre of the room and lifted her forefinger and thumb. She snapped her fingers and a flame the size of a candle's light sat atop her thumb. It didn't seem to be hurting her but she let it go out shortly afterward and wafted her hand.

'Sorry, it starts to burn after a bit,' she said.

Mary laughed, 'That's amazing how do you do that?'

Kam looked to No who then proceeded to pin down the basic premise of conjuration, or in Kam's case, heat manipulation.

'She channels the heat from one place to another.'

'Like this,' she said and reached out to touch Mary on the arm. She relit her thumb and Mary felt her arm suddenly grow very cold and she pulled it away. Frost had formed on her clothes in a handprint.

'Ouch that's sudden,' she said.

'It's a lot of heat energy,' said Kam, 'usually you just take it from the air around you or inside you.'

'But it uses souls. Kam comes from a long line of fire magicians; they're no strangers to this type of magic. And so, she has a large pool of resources to drain,' explained No.

'Not as much as No here,' said Kam.

'Why, what pool do you have?' asked Mary.

No looked around, visibly uncomfortable with the question, 'My family are just very powerful.' He then smiled politely.

'Alright I need to feed the kids now so out of my kitchen,' said Kam, shooing the two of them out.

Mary and No returned to their seats and Mary began eating again as No attempted to explain how magic had existed for so long. She half listened, but her mind was away thinking of the potential.

'Can I cast magic?' she asked.

No sadly shook his head. Unfortunately, it was very likely that Mary, along with most people on earth, had not many souls tied to her so her pool was too small for

SNOW AND FIRE

her to make any effect. She asked how many No had. He said a lot. She asked how many is a lot. He said a lot. He tried to dodge the question some more, making a few quips, when Mary's hand ended up on his arm and she tried to plead with him to tell her.

That was until their attention was drawn away to what sounded like a heated argument. Kam was shouting loudly, Rob was leant back watching her, and Snow, who had her arms crossed, wasn't meeting Kam's eyes.

'If you don't want to eat, that's fine by me. But don't you dare try that bullshit with me,' she stated, 'I'll be letting your father know.'

'Fine! I don't care. Tell my father everything! Tell him I hate him, I hate this place, I hate all of you!' and the girl stood up and left.

Rob closed his eyes, to which Kam put her hands on her hips, 'and just where were you?'

'Don't get me involved, I ate the bleeding thing. I thought it was good,' said Rob.

Mary instinctively got up; once upon a time she would never have gotten involved in any such outburst. But being so tied into events, she felt a compulsion.

'Everything alright Kam?' she asked.

Kam shook her head, 'I've known that girl most of her life. I never thought she'd end up being such a brat. She was trying her underhand insulting crap, and I'd had enough of it. She needs teaching a lesson,' said Kam.

Mary nodded in understanding; she knew just what Kam meant. Snow would often comment on Mary and what she was doing; are you really going to eat "that"? My dad did hire you, didn't he? As in, you're meant to be working for us, doing work? I thought accountants were very smart and boring, but I guess that's only half true.

'I swear, I was this close to smacking her,' she said.

'You can't smack a child Kam, she doesn't know better,' said Mary.

'She's not a child anymore, or she sure doesn't act like it! She best understand that the world doesn't revolve around her as much as she thinks it does,' and with that, Kam collected the plates on the table, including the almost full plate that Mary assumed must've been Snow's.

'I think it's O'Nerry,' said Rob, 'he was a bad influence.'

'And still might be,' said Mary, which caused Rob to jerk his head in a grimace.

Kam left the room and went into the kitchen again.

'She seems really annoyed,' said Mary towards Rob, egging him to try and calm her.

'Of course she is,' said Rob,' Snow is becoming more and more of a rebel.'

'And look at you, the pristine good boy,' said Mary with a smirk.

'I've got better things to do,' and he stood up slowly, which again took Mary by surprise at how tall he was. Then he left, likely to go tend bar.

When Kam returned from the kitchen, she still looked flustered. Mary caught her and pulled her aside.

'Are you going to be alright?' she asked.

'Oh yes, just got a little annoyed,' she said, 'I've looked after Snow for a long time now. You know how I showed you-' and she made like to snap her fingers which Mary nodded to indicate she understood, 'Snow is adept at magic as well.

SNOW AND FIRE

'Wat wanted me teaching her. It's been difficult though. Just like you said, O'Nerry's put some troubling ideas in her head.'

'I wouldn't be surprised,' said Mary.

'O'Nerry is a bad egg. He's got power but he uses it selfishly. One of the important things as a magician is that magic is a tool to be used sparingly and never blindly. O'Nerry thinks he's some new-age magician.'

Mary considered the idea, '…is there a ministry then? Of magic?'

Kam gave her an unimpressed look, 'Mary, do you really think there's some secret society dedicated to witches and wizards of the country?'

'I didn't believe in magicians at all until today,' said Mary.

Kam shook her head, 'alright fine there is a society. The National Society for the Management of Magical Activities. Some people call them the Top Hat Society.'

'Classy.'

'They're exclusive but joining them you get some perks,' and then Kam pulled out her purse and showed Mary a card with the Six of Diamonds on one side, and the other side all her details in white on black:

Kamala Jha, Third Grade Magician, West Midlands District, Tel – Email – Book

'Book?'

'Book message. Old secret,' she tapped her nose, 'I've not partaken in any of their events for a while. I guess that's just how societies go nowadays.'

'So, you all get together and what, learn about magic?'

'Can do.'

'What about the law? How does someone stop a magician?'

'Same as you stop anyone,' and she made her hand into her gun and pretended to fire it at Mary's head. She laughed and relented, 'Come on, what do most people do when they see weird stuff?'

'They hide it?'

'They rationalise it and pretend it didn't happen. It's unspoken that we attempt to "hide" magic, but it's not as if everyone can do it. In the end, it kind of self-manages itself. Like knives.'

'Knives?'

'What's to stop you from taking a knife, Mary, and stabbing someone with it?'

'I don't want to.'

'Exactly,' and Kam lifted her arms and let them fall, 'I think there's meant to be some police departments in central London, but I hear they're understaffed. In the end, turns out that a rare power such as magic is actually really easy to hide in plain view. Take a look at this pub Mary, it's not as if we try to hide it.'

Mary nodded, and Kam went about her business once more. It occurred to Mary that perhaps she'd had more exposure to magic than she'd thought she had. Perhaps she'd experienced it without actually realising it because nobody slapped a label on it and shouted that it was 'magic' and she should take notice. What kind of secrets had she missed? And oddly enough, were they worth finding if they didn't seem to make any impact on the day-to-day life of the normal non-magic society?

'I didn't expect magic was so,' she said softly, 'quiet.'

* * *

For the rest of the day, Mary continued her usual business of making up plans and financial reports. She had had a sit down with Wat about some of the budget cuts he should have started making and where to invest the rest of his money. She was also getting closer and closer to the big problem which was the staff salary. He was going to have to negotiate with everyone possible changes to their contracts as they were all varied, all with their own specific clauses, and then needed standardisation.

But then the night wore on and she was sitting with No drinking in the barroom with Neo, who was serving tables but made an effort to stop by every so often to collect glasses and join the conversation. Eventually, things died down and everyone was getting ready for the night. Neo was cleaning up the bar, Kam had cleaned up in the kitchen and sent the rest of the kitchen staff home, No had retired to his room and it was just the three of them until Wat showed up.

'Has anyone seen Snow?' he asked, 'she's meant to be manning the reception tonight, we're expecting a new guest.'

'I haven't seen her since this morning,' offered Kam.

Feathers perked up in his spot on the counter, 'The lass with the pearl blonde hair? Aye, I saw her leave but she ain't been back.'

'Leave? How long ago?' asked Wat.

'She left around lunch. I remember because that daft man Duncan kept asking if I was some sort of robit,' said Feathers, more disgruntled at his own inconvenience.

'It's past eleven, she should be back by now,' said Wat.

'She's a young adult, I'm sure she can take care of herself, Wat,' said Mary dismissively.

'She knows she's meant to be at reception for me,' said Wat.

'Don't worry Wat, I think I might know where she is,' said Kam, 'I'll go find her. You stay here and look after your counter.'

Mary turned to give Kam a look, then said, 'I'll go too.'

'Mary I think it's best if you stay here,' replied Kam.

'Just try and stop me,' said Mary, as she grabbed her coat off the hooks by the door and opened it up. Kam gave an annoyed sigh before leaving through the door.

The night was chilly, causing Mary to wrap her coat around her tightly. There wasn't a breeze, the air was still, and the sky was clear but the lampposts were still lit casting the road in dim orange. Mary rubbed her hands together as she stepped out onto the road, following Kam. The traffic was non-existent at their crossroads, and only the faint sound of cars came from the high street. Kam was walking the white line on the centre of the road towards the east part of the high street.

'Where do you think she is?' asked Mary.

'I know she's over in the Iron Bull,' said Kam, 'Mary you really don't need to come with me.'

'You're going to talk to her right?' said Mary.

'Yes.'

'Then you'll need support. I'm not saying I'll be able to talk to her myself, but I can help you talk to her. You don't need to do this alone,' said Mary.

'I understand what you're saying, but we're not going to be playing good cop bad cop here. I'm going to find her, tell her straight up she's being stupid, and slap her across the face.'

'I don't think that'll convince her of anything.'

SNOW AND FIRE

'I'm not going to try and convince her that what she's doing has consequences because I AM the consequences.'

The two of them continued until they reached the high street and Kam led Mary down a few side streets until they reached a tucked-away industrial yard and several buildings that ran alongside it, opposite an elevated railway. A train thundered past, its roar echoing around the empty streets, but it didn't drown out the sound of club music, it only joined it. It thumped hard electronic beats that caused the ground to tremor in a rhythm that Mary felt unaccustomed to. She was not a fan of clubs, especially loud ones.

The buildings looked to be closed up and cut off, likely as they were all conjoined on the inside. At the one door that hadn't been bricked up or covered in black wood, a large round man stood with an earpiece and black uniform, hands in front of him clasped together, watching the two women as they approached. There was also the sound of chatter and laughter as there was a roped smoking area where several young people were standing smoking and talking. One was on the ground, their hair pushed back as they stared at the ground, expecting something to appear. Mary grimaced in disgust.

Kam approached the man at the door. She was still half wearing her uniform so it looked a little odd to see her half dressed in chef's whites, her sleeves rolled up, but her black hair was sitting on her shoulders poised like snakes. Mary, on the other hand, still had a business shirt and cravat on with a business skirt and tights. She tried adjusting herself as they approached, knowing she was severely out of place. A couple of the girls in the smoking area saw her and giggled, obviously thinking that Mary must have been out of her mind.

'Ey you're a bit overdressed aren't yah,' shouted one girl, and the rest laughed. Mary rolled her eyes.

The man looked her up and down then thumbed at the door, uninterested. He did the same for Mary. Mary felt a little at ease until they got to the counter behind the door. A glossy eye girl was leaning over the counter and as they approached she outstretched her hand;

'Tenner,' she said.

'I just want to see someone,' said Kam.

'Er no, you gotta pay to get in.'

'I won't be long,' and Kam left it at that.

She walked to the door to the dancefloor, where a larger-built man had his arms crossed. The man held up a hand to Kam.

'Don't let her in, she hasn't paid,' said the girl at the counter.

The doorman then stepped in front of Kam.

'Let me through, I just want to find someone in there.'

'Not until you get a stamp.'

'Listen, I will hurt you if you don't get out of my way.'

'Well, now I'm not letting you in at all. You'd better leave.'

'Let them in!' called the girl at the counter.

The doorman frowned, then gave Kam a harsh look, before stepping out of the way.

'You get it now? I've a reputation.'

'More like I just paid the entry,' said Mary, grabbing Kam's shoulders to ease her through the doors, 'I'd rather we didn't end up in a fight just outside the club.'

SNOW AND FIRE

Inside, the music was deafening. Mary instinctively surveyed the floor. It was full of bodies, likely human, and it smelt of all sorts of alcoholic substances and body odours. It was also crammed so they had to jam their hands between people dancing to make room. Kam made her way across the bar to a set of stairs that lead up with fervour. The atmosphere of the club really felt different when you were stone-cold sober – you could ignore the smell, the sound and the bad manners when you were off your head.

Mary could see that there was a balcony above the floor, where there were even more people dancing and moving to the beats. She followed Kam, avoiding the group of boys at the bottom of the stairs with each other's hands in their trousers. She then dodged the girl carrying another really drunk-looking girl whose eyes were stained and red, her makeup running from her eyes. At the top of the stairs, Mary found there were booths set up along the edges of the walls for "private" encounters. Kam walked on past some that contained couples whose faces were mashed together. One contained a girl on the brink of tears with her girlfriends attempting to comfort her but just looking bored. Finally, Kam stopped at the end and Mary gasped in disgust.

Richard O'Nerry, the despicable silver-haired sore had his tongue embedded in Snow's throat, and a hand down the back of her shorts.

'You!' shouted Kam. O'Nerry somehow managed to hear her over the music and prised himself off Snow to turn around slowly.

He frowned in recognition of Kam, 'You. What do you want?'

But Kam wasn't looking at him, and her hand raised to point at Snow, 'Come here, you're going home.'

'No thanks,' said Snow, narrowing her eyes.

'This isn't up for discussion, you're coming home with me right now,' said Kam.

'Sounds like she's pretty happy here with me,' said O'Nerry.

Mary almost vomited at the idea of the man and the girl and had to turn away for a second. She grasped the balcony bannister, careful not to look down as Kam continued.

'If you don't come with me right now, don't bother coming home at all.'

'Fine.'

Kam's blood boiled over, 'That's it,' and she stomped forward and grabbed Snow's arm harshly, yanking her and tearing her from her seat.

O'Nerry stood up and grabbed Kam before pushing her back, to which she loosened her grip, 'Hey! She said she didn't want to leave alright?' he spat.

'Oh, you think you know what she wants?' said Kam and pushed O'Nerry with two hands.

The man laughed almost manically before pushing Kam back, harder and almost sending her toppling over. Mary caught her and helped steady the woman as she stood up again.

'I think you better leave,' said O'Nerry.

'Not without Snow,' said Kam.

'I'm not coming with you!' shouted Snow.

At this point, the doorman from downstairs appeared as if from nowhere.

'Not you two again. Are they causing you trouble?' he asked O'Nerry.

SNOW AND FIRE

'Yes, they just started pushing us for no reason; that brown one is trying to start a fight.'

The doorman grabbed Kam's shoulder from behind to edge her to the staircase, 'you need to leave,' he stated bluntly.

'I'm not leaving without Snow! Come on O'Nerry, come on! Take me on, I could take you,' said Kam, trying to wrestle from the doorman's grip, but he just held her tightly by the shoulders.

Mary put a hand to her head in embarrassment and helplessness.

'You're not my mom, you can't tell me what to do!' shouted Snow.

'I sure am not your mom! Your mom would've kicked your arse much earlier on!' shouted Kam from behind the doorman. But Snow began to follow her.

'You don't know my mom!'

'I know that she would've regretted a brat like you!'

'Shut up! You think you know me, you don't know anything!'

'I don't know anything!? I'm your teacher, I know everything!'

Snow was still following her up until Kam was taken outside and let out on the street. Tears were streaming down the girl's face and her lips were red raw. Mary followed slightly behind, as did O'Nerry, who was just letting Snow lead him.

'You keep trying to act like you're my mom but you aren't! You're just some stupid cook my dad hired! My dad hires loads of people and he hires them all the time, you're replaceable!'

Kam stood up straight facing Snow, who was standing opposite her on the road now, screaming her eyes out. O'Nerry sidled up behind her, a small but smug smile on his face. Mary took up a similar position behind Kam but she was concerned. This was not what she expected when Kam said she was going to talk to her. It was no longer about Snow it felt, it was about Kam getting to give Snow a good smack to make herself feel better.

'You are nothing but a spoiled brat, who thinks she deserves everything. You're not coming home after this, you hear me? Not after you've been hanging around that monster.'

'I love him! And he loves me,' shouted Snow, 'why don't you all just leave me alone!'

Snow stamped her foot in time with her yelling and wiped her arm across her face.

'How do you not see!? He doesn't love you! He'll hurt you, he'll use you to get what he wants!'

'Shut up, you don't know anything!' shouted Snow, and stamped again.

'Fine! Fine, go ahead and stay with him. When he leaves you, you'll be homeless and you'll have nothing. And all I'll say is good riddance to you!'

'Shut up!' shouted Snow once more and her hand lunged for Kam, grabbing the older woman by the arms.

Suddenly Kam shouted and Mary could see a white crust of ice spreading out on Kam's arms; the same frost that Kam had left on Mary's own arms when she was showing her magic. Mary was about to try and step in but Kam pushed out and away from Snow's arms and then caught Snow's forearms in her own grip. She lifted them up so Snow's hands were above her head and she stared deep into her eyes.

SNOW AND FIRE

'Don't you dare use that shit on me,' said Kam, and Snow began to squeal, 'I taught you that. I could've taught you so much more.'

Mary could then see small wisps of smoke running from Kam's fingertips and she realised what Kam was doing.

'Kam, stop,' she said, putting a hand on Kam's shoulder.

Kam didn't listen at first but after a couple of seconds, with Snow's pitiful crying face screaming hard, she let go.

And immediately threw her right hand against Snow's cheek.

Snow flew to the ground and crumpled up, sobbing. O'Nerry bent down over her and cradled her in his right arm. He used his left hand to turn her and brush the hair from her face. On her cheek was a bright red handprint that stood out on her pale skin. She then screamed hard in anger and the ground around her crystalised. It spread out in a fast circle, freezing the ground into a sheet of ice. The man at the door to the club almost slipped off his feet, the girl who had been sitting on the ground waiting to throw up found she was stuck, and the girls who had been laughing earlier slipped and fell as their heels were frozen fast to the ground. Snow continued and a streak of ice spread up through a lamppost, up into the bulb, and shattered the glass sending it falling to the ground, orange light still glowing from the filament.

'Don't you listen to her,' said O'Nerry, 'you're powerful. Much more powerful than her.' He then stood up and put his hands on his hips with the same smile still on his face as if he had been enjoying the show. 'I think you ladies best leave.'

Mary felt a terrible fear creep up through her. It wasn't the same dread she had felt before, this time it was the fear he'd built up inside her. The trauma she'd felt from their last altercation caused her skin hair to stand on end. She stepped back.

'Kam, let's go. I don't think there's anything else to be-'

And then she was on the ground. Her head collided with the ice and her head went dizzy. She'd felt her feet being snatched from underneath her and she was being dragged away from O'Nerry and Snow. 'Kam!' she cried out.

Kam eyed O'Nerry then ran after Mary. She grabbed hold of Mary's arms and struggled to pull her but the ice was too smooth. Mary just held tightly onto Kam's one hand until Kam freed her other hand and pressed it down to the ground. In seconds the ice was now just water and her hand glowed a soft orange. Then she lifted her hand up and created a burst of fire; a ball of fire to Mary's eyes. Mary looked down at her legs and could see what had got her: it was a shadow. A great shadow had somehow latched itself to her own shadow and was pulling her away.

'What do we do!?' she screamed.

'We get rid of the light!' said Kam.

'What!? I thought shadows hate light, we want more light!'

'Shadows only exist because of light!'

And Kam, still holding tight onto Mary's hand, turned around to the streetlights standing around the road. She pointed a finger at each one and expertly fired what must have been a small bead of fire directly at each filament. One by one, they puffed and went out, causing the girls in the smoking area to scream.

SNOW AND FIRE

When it was pitch black Mary felt her legs drop and whatever shadow had got her was lost in the overall darkness.

'Quick, let's get out of here,' said Kam, pulling Mary to her feet and rushing her down the road. Mary glanced back but O'Nerrry and Snow were gone. All that was left were scared clubgoers and the doorman who had slumped down on the step; likely knocked unconscious from his fall.

* * *

Wat was at the reception, nodding off. He perked up when Mary and Kam appeared but when he saw the state they were in his face dropped.

'She's not coming back?' he asked in a tone that meant he knew the answer.

Kam didn't answer him. She grabbed her coat and then instantly left, slamming the door behind her.

'What happened?' he asked Mary.

'They had an argument. I think Kam just wanted to have a fight, I don't think she went there with any intention to convince her she had to come back,' said Mary, 'I'm sorry Wat, she's in too deep.'

'It's my fault,' said Wat solemnly, 'I know it is. I've never been a good parent, Mary, you can ask Rob that. Snow has every right to hate me.'

'She doesn't hate you,' said Mary, rubbing his back, 'she's young! She's just going through a phase right now.

'I heard what O'Nerry was saying to her – she's in love with him Wat. She's young, in love, she's going to be reckless, doing things like this.'

Wat laughed, 'sounds like her mother.'

Mary paused before she asked the burning question, 'Who was her mother Wat?'

Wat sighed, but with a long desirable sigh, 'She was a goddess. And I don't mean that metaphorically, she was a real true-to-life goddess. The coming of winter, the fairy queen, the north wind. I called her Snow.'

THE NORTH WIND

Back when Nancy and I had finalised the divorce and Rob and I had settled down, I took some time for myself. I set myself back up in this pub with my dad and he looked after Rob with me. He needed a little stability, you see, Nancy and I had been a whirlwind pair. Caught a lot of things in our wake. Caused a lot of destruction, some of it actually physical.

So, one day I packed a bag, left Rob with my dad in the pub and flew out of the country. I landed in Tokyo but I didn't stop. I caught a train, then a bus, then a cart and found my way into a remote part of Japan's rice fields, a small village with an old hut they occasionally let.

Why are you looking at me like that? Why Japan? Well, I wanted to get away and Japan is about as far as you can get. I know, I know, a bit extreme, but like I say Nancy and I were destructive.

Whilst I stayed in the village, I took to hiking the highlands surrounding. The mountainous areas weren't very populated so you could really be alone with your thoughts. About a week in – yes a week Mary – I found my way on a trail that led around a very narrow cliff face. It wasn't well mapped but I wanted the adventure. Lo and behold, the trail hit a steep precipice and I thought to turn back.

But I saw on the other side of this ridge was a cavern and I wondered what had made people trek toward this cavern in the first place.

Now I was rather encumbered I have to say, I had a large backpack on at this point. I wasn't going for an afternoon stroll. I was equipped to hike. I set my bag down, pulled some rope out, and began to make my way to this cavern.

The ledge was tight, it only just fit my toes. I pressed myself as much as possible against the edge, which had patches of moss and felt smooth to the touch. I struggled to find handholds with each step I took. I didn't look down, as the way down fell into a meshed canopy of trees and woodland, so I couldn't even see the ground.

I made it about halfway across when a harsh wind blew across the mountain face. I held on tight. Now, being the professional I was, I had been securing my rope along the way to the face of the mountain so if I did fall, the rope would catch me and I'd be able to pull myself back up against it. However, I did not count that the wind would somehow, and you can take a guess at exactly how it did it, jostle those damn cams and leave a few of them loose.

I got a little further when another gust almost took me but I remained flat against the mountain. It was at the very end that the wind found a few holes in my clothing and actually yanked my hand from the wall. The surprise caused me to lose my footing.

THE NORTH WIND

As expected, my last placed cam basically meant I swung out with my foot as a pivot. Until the cam snapped; the pivot didn't work and my feet lost their place and I swung into the mountain face about three metres below where I was. I didn't hit my head here though, no, no, because another cam was wrenched from its place leaving me to fall another metre and then another, and so I swung against the wall again and this is where I hit my head.

It probably knocked me out for five minutes and I woke up with a grand view of the illustrious wooden canopy below me. I scrambled a little in mid-air until I had adjusted to the fact I wasn't falling. I was gently swinging on my rope that was (hopefully) still secure to the first cam I put it in.

I desperately hoped.

I observed my surroundings for a way I could get back up. I knew I could climb up the rope, but knowing how badly my cams messed up I couldn't trust any others wouldn't fail me. So, I noted that below where I was, there was a smaller cavern that I could just about reach. If I swung myself.

Not sure how much swinging would provoke a failure, I decided to take a chance. I gently rocked myself on this rope to and fro, aiming for the smaller cavern. I wasn't far off. A couple swings and I'd make it.

I heard the jangle of carabiners on the rope as I swung in a larger arc. I could almost reach the edge with my foot when I stretched it out. I tucked back and aimed for a larger swing. As I went back, I felt the gentle lurch of something give way, and as I swung toward the cavern the rope started going slack.

Started. It slipped as I swung, so I reached out with both my arms as the rope fell away from me and I managed to use my momentum to grab the edge. The other end of my rope fell away down into the canopy and I heard it thud. I ignored it at this point.

That was until I found that when I tried to pull myself up, the rope went taut again. The bloody thing had gotten caught on a branch below me.

How long was the rope? Ten metres? Twenty? I wasn't a mile up in the air Mary, I'm not insane, this was just a generic cliff-face!

I realised I had to cut the rope but it meant I wouldn't be able to use it to get back up to my bag. I hoped that the cavern would lead to a tunnel and a way out. By removing the carabiner, I secured my fate in whatever was in that cavern. I heard the sound of my folly clattering down into the trees.

In the cavern it was not that dark, the natural light fell on the inside pretty well. I could see it was a dead-end, and that it hadn't been explored by any human for a long time. I knew this because at the far end of the cavern, sitting on a stone stool, was a tetsujin.

I'm sure you've never heard of a tetsujin before. They are incredibly ancient spirits that are fuelled by intrinsic spiritual belief. This one had laid dormant for hundreds of years and the iron of its casing was rusting away. You can think of them as robots if you like – robots inhabited by magic. The spirits that inhabit them are often natural spirits. In the West, these spirits often inhabit smaller, weaker and almost childish forms, but the tetsujin build bodies from iron. This was a wood spirit, like our gnomes. The thing had grown inside its iron body; wooden limbs sprouted out from it and fed into cylinders that acted as its hands and feet.

THE NORTH WIND

I tapped on the glass dome in the middle of its body. The thing didn't move so I knew it was asleep. Unfortunately, you cannot wake the creatures up easily. They were much more powerful hundreds of years ago when natural spirits pervaded much more of our culture. In the modern age, they have grown weaker and usually succumb to being monoliths or statues.

What? The North Wind? I'm getting to it, Mary! I know I go on a bit, it's important! This is how I met the woman alright? And first I need to tell you about the tetsujin because it helped introduce me. How?

Well, I sat down and started making a plan for how to get out of my situation. I needed to either go up or go down. I decided that going down was probably going to be safest, and going up was riskiest. I analysed the rock face from the cavern. The trees were, like I say, only fifteen metres down. It was steep. If I still had the rope I could've tried abseiling down carefully rather than attempting it freehand. Without it, I needed to judge my eye well. Luckily, like I said, the face was patchy with moss. The points where there was moss I marked were likely best to grip.

So, I sat down for a moment to catch my breath. I took another look around the tetsujin to see if it could help me. After all, being an ancient spirit, I expected it to take pity on such a small and young thing like me. Like a gnome would. Gnomes are generally helpful.

I tried to press it in a few places. The thing was weak. I tried rapping the wood in between its limbs. I even started to prise off the bark. I expected to find it was rotten inside; no lo and behold it was green and alive.

So, of course, the thing woke up.

Its glass dome fogged up and its limbs creaked and cracked the bark. The tetsujin stood up from its stool and actually observed the damage I'd done. I was petrified. I waited for the thing to turn around and eye me.

The dome was fogged with the image very similar to a human face with eyes and a mouth. But these ancient spirits were ancient, they didn't understand our modern tongues or expressions. It looked half similar but it swirled and disappeared making it look blank in expression.

It was frightening. The thing was two metres tall, it towered over me. It extended an arm and three thick blocky fingers and a blocky thumb bent and extended themselves. It was stretching, getting used to being awake again. I watched it as it did this, frightened the thing would lift a hand and smash me into the ground. Or wrap its hands around me and squeeze me to death. Or just grab hold of me and throw me around like a ragdoll.

It looked me over, then turned around. It marched to the cavern's entrance and instantly dropped like a rock off the edge. I heard it bang and crash down into the trees. I didn't run after it, in fact, I just sat on its stool. It didn't stop, the crashing continued as if it were walking in a straight line through branches, and trees, knocking them over perhaps? When I finally got up to see what it was doing it was creating a path through the woodland.

I wondered what I had done. What had I unleashed on the world?

So did she because then Snow decided to appear and she asked me, 'What had I done.'

THE NORTH WIND

Yes, she appeared. She was beautiful, just as beautiful as my daughter. I turned around and she was standing behind me, hands on her hips. She was short, shorter than me, with long white-gold hair that ran down her back, big cold blue eyes, and a young face with a sharp chin. She was dressed in a white gown that was loose and didn't cover the whole of her torso. The floor around her froze and dancing snowflakes instantly formed in the air around her.

'What have you done?' she asked me again, 'you let it loose!'

I didn't know how to respond. Eventually, I did, 'I was just walking…'

'You could've left it alone! Why did you touch it!?' she asked, 'the thing has been quiet for so long! You would've thought you'd have gone and died like I wanted when I first tried to blow you away! But no, you went and did the one thing I DIDN'T want you to do.'

'I'm sorry,' was all I could stutter out.

So you see, when we first met it wasn't love at first sight.

'Do you understand the magnitude of what you've done? Do you know what that is?'

'A tetsujin,' I said, to which she gave me a frustrated look.

'Do you know what it's going to do?'

That I couldn't answer.

'It's going to march over to the closest village, destroy it a little, move on to the next one, and repeat.'

I was shocked, 'but why?'

'Oh just never mind, how about you throw yourself off the edge now and I'll deal with this thing,' she said and marched to the cavern's entrance.

'Wait!' I called out, 'maybe I could help?'

'What on earth makes you think you could help?' she said.

And then she leapt off into the wind. She unravelled, her clothes fell away and she seemed to fold herself into the air. All that was left was a great gust of wind which almost blew me off my feet. Well, I wasn't going to stop here, I had to get after her.

I began my descent, using the moss-covered patches of the cliff face. I know what you're thinking, moss isn't great for grip, but it was growing in the most level points on the face. I held on tightly with every handful. It was a grinding process to ensure I had a secure foothold and handhold as I eased myself down. By the end, I was exhausted but I couldn't stop. I was at the forest level and I could see where the tetsujin had made its pathway of destruction. I took off in hot pursuit.

Compared to the descent, it didn't take me as long to catch up with the spirit. It was sluggish as if it hadn't used its joints in thousands of years. Yet although its pace was slow, it was uninterrupted; trees would topple as soon as it nudged them, and logs would crumble to bark when its legs trod on them. The thing was strong and lord knew what it would do to the village when it arrived.

When I caught up, I wasn't sure what to do.

'Hey!' I called out, trying to get its attention, 'Hey you!'

You have to recognise at this point everything I had been saying to Snow, everything I'd been saying to the tetsujin, was in Japanese. Of course, these were native spirits, they'd have no idea what I was saying if I was speaking British English! I know I didn't make that clear but I'm making a point of it now because the tetsujin didn't respond.

THE NORTH WIND

'It won't understand you,' came Snow's whisper.

She had a thing for doing this; have you ever heard of a whisper on the wind? Her voice would carry on her breeze and so she didn't appear this time, just sent a gust of wind right through my bones.

Now that I knew vocally I couldn't get this thing's attention, I grabbed the nearest stick and threw it upside the spirit's head. It clanged and it stopped on its next step. Its torso creaked and the bark inside broke as it turned to try and face me.

'I've an idea,' whispered the sound of Snow.

Then the wind strengthened, almost tossing me off my feet before it dissipated. I was alone with the iron giant as it were. The dome swirled and it almost looked angry, peering at what I was doing and interrupting its tirade. I smiled weakly and tried to talk to it again.

'Hi,' I said, 'can you understand me?'

It turned its full attention toward me and I thought I had made a breakthrough. Unfortunately not, as it raised one of its arms menacingly and I realised I'd better jump. I jumped. And its fist collided with the ground, shaking the earth so that I couldn't get to my feet again easily. It raised its other fist and attempted to squash me again. It did not succeed as I threw myself into the forest and behind a tree. It then grabbed the tree and uprooted it as if it were a twig. I jumped to my feet and ran. It was slow, but it leaned back and threw the tree overarm at me. It hit the ground into a quick roll, shattering its branches on the ground and I managed to dive for cover as it came to a rough halt.

I really want to calm this thing down but I realised that I was way over my head in unfamiliar territory. I had to wrack my brain whilst also making sure I didn't get killed. Part of me wished Snow were there, even if she had wished that one of the tetsujin's hits had landed.

I ducked into the growth again behind another tree as it attempted to throw another plant at my head.

It was at this point that the wind returned, yet not quite in full force. Snow's whisper echoed;

'Here,' and my bag landed in front of me.

'You're human, you're got torches?'

'I've a box of matches.'

'Good, we need to light this thing on fire.'

I looked for the testujin that was scoping the area around for me. It was just turning around, not eager to come and find me. It knew it was slow.

'That's horrific, I can't do that,' I said.

'You're going to have to, this giant is going to destroy a whole lot of lives.'

'Can't you talk to it?' I said, 'If it can't understand me, can it understand you?'

'There's no point, it's quicker to just kill it.'

To which I had no words. You see, it had not occurred to me that when she had said she'd been trying to kill me, she actually meant it. This was Snow.

When I'd soon find she was a sylph and perpetrator of the North Wind, I'd understand that her disillusionment of life was due to having lived so long that a human's life was as short as we consider the mayfly's. She was accustomed to us dropping dead without any impact on the world. It was the way of the world.

But right then? She sounded like a monster who just wanted to see everything die.

'You need to talk it down, I'm not killing it,' I said firmly.

'You'll just let it destroy the town then?'

THE NORTH WIND

'Why does it want to destroy the town?'
'That's all it did last time.'
'Talk to it.'
'It's a waste of time.'

'Fine,' and I picked up the bag and calmly walked out from behind the tree.

I stepped right into the testujin's line of sight. Seeing me it began its slow approach. It was about five steps away.

'What are you doing,' whispered the wing, 'this is crazy.'

'Tell him to stop and talk,' I said.

'I'll just let him smash you,' she said.

'With my matches?'

Three steps.

'You said you wouldn't burn him anyway,' she said.

'Not unless there's no other resort,' I said.

Two steps. Its arm was rising, ready to squash me.

'It's in your hands,' I said.

The tetsujin was in range and a great roar of wind carried an old tongue I'd never heard. The tetsujin did not land a hit, it stopped and waited. Her voice continued in some ancient form of what might have been Japanese' predecessor, but I could not understand it.

Whatever it was, the giant understood it and lowered its arm.

'What did you say?' I asked out loud.

'I asked him to stop,' she said.

I had to process that for a moment because it sounded absolutely ridiculous.

'You're kidding.'

'I didn't think it would listen. Or understand,' she said.

We waited. The giant stood still. Its dome filled with uncertain grey whisps.

'Now what?'

'Tell it to go back to sleep?'

She spoke up in her ancient dialect. It seemed she said something like 'nerre' with a long drawn-out 'r' and as she did the dome showed less of a mist. It cleared and the giant creaked. I held my breath and waited. It didn't move. When I tried to wave and grab its attention it didn't respond. I relaxed and gave a sigh of relief. Somehow, it had stopped.

Somehow.

Snow appeared again. She observed me.

'You were a bit too willing to let yourself die,' she said.

'You were a bit too willing to let me die too,' I replied.

She asked me who I was. I told her. I asked her who she was. She seemed to gain some stature and threw back her shoulders to stand proudly as she stated:

'I am the North Wind. Fujin, they sometimes call me! Or Ritto! Or sometimes I go by Yuki.'

* * *

'We ended up leaving the iron giant where it stood. Nobody questioned it as it was a remote part of Japan. I'd guess someone would eventually find it and wonder where it came from but at least Snow knew how to send it to sleep if it ever woke up again.

'We spent a long time together. She and I enjoyed my time in Japan. However, eventually, all things must end and I realised I had to return. She showed me a great deal and I loved her for it, but Rob needed me.

'When I got back to England I had reset and was ready to take everything I'd learnt with Snow and apply it here. Democracy, talking, and learning the cultures; those were the qualities Snow imparted.

'About a year after I'd arrived, you can guess what happened. We received a package on our doorstep. I don't blame her, she was a sylph. She couldn't raise her. So, she left me a child. And I named her Snow.'

Mary was entranced. When she realised the story was over she lifted herself up. She wiped a tear from the corner of her eye.

'That was it?' she asked, 'you never saw her again?'

'No, she couldn't come back with me. From what I understand, north winds are fairly territorial.'

'Did she try and convince you to stay?'

'Of course she did, but again I think she knew I wouldn't last. I was a mayfly in her eyes.'

'So Snow-'

'Is the daughter of a sylph, yes.'

'How is that even possible?' said Mary incredulously, but Wat gave her a look, 'I know "how" Stone, but surely the-' she meshed her fingers together, 'magic and human doesn't work.'

Wat shrugged, 'There are many examples out there. It does mean she will have a great number of wind souls attached to her I expect. She may end up becoming our own coming of winter. Who knows,' and Wat lifted his arms in general acceptance.

Mary shook her head, 'and now she's with O'Nerry.'

'Yes. That's not good. I bet he's using her for that very reason,' said Wat.

'So what do we do?' she said.

'What can I do Mary? She may be part god, but she's also a teenager. I can't make her do anything,' said Wat.

'I think you need to do just what you did when you met her mother,' said Mary, her eyes concerned but direct, grasping Wat's hands with her own, 'you just need to get her to talk.'

WHEN NIAMH MET MONA

Jo was one of the kitchen staff. Jo had golden skin and dark brown eyes. She wiggled when she walked, she jumped when she was excited, and she made use of every womanly aspect she had. Mary didn't find her a colleague of interest at first and often left her, along with most of the kitchen staff, alone. If Jo was waitressing, she made sure to swing by the elderly men just to see them twist in their seats. Mary found it distasteful, but as No never seemed to give Jo a second look she was complacent.

Then it came to be a Thursday, and Mary was snacking in the barroom as Neo cleared tables. Jo entered the room and bounced over to Mary's table, leaning forward so her chest squeezed into view and Mary couldn't help but give an annoyed grunt.

'Mary right? I've heard that you've been looking into the staff's salaries?'

Mary paused with a peanut in her fingers. At which point Wat wafted round a corner, the spring in his step a little weak.

'Wat, you haven't been talking to anyone in the establishment about our business evaluations, have you?' Mary asked.

Wat looked like a deer in headlights, 'well…'

'So yeah I wanted to make sure you weren't going to shrink anyone's paycheck is all,' said Jo, swishing her body behind her like a dog.

Mary gave her an annoyed look, 'Ms Mistri is it? I am not willing to talk about this here, especially as the decision is not up to me, is it Wat?' and Mary's tone switched to indicate she hoped that Wat would step in to take charge.

Wat coughed, 'Ahem, yes, that would be up to me in the end. And we should arrange a time and a place to talk about such matters,' said Wat, rubbing his hands together, sounding professional, and he looked as if he was about to continue his sentence until he swiftly exited the barroom into the gallery.

'Look, Jo,' Mary continued, realising that Wat wasn't going to help her, 'I understand your concerns. However, the entire establishment is in the air, not just the staff. In the end, just be glad if you still had a job,' said Mary.

Jo looked dejected as opposed to offended, 'I understand,' she said with a pout, 'look if we really think the pub needs to close, I'm happy to take a pay cut.'

Mary raised an eyebrow. 'Really?'

'Of course? This place is bigger than any of us. I'm sure most of us would be happy enough to do it if it meant Wat could keep it,' said Jo simply.

Mary bit her lip, 'Interesting, I did not think of that. Well thank you for the sacrifice, I'll take it into account.'

WHEN NIAMH MET MONA

'So Mary,' said Jo in a leading manner that meant she had more to ask than business, 'I've been meaning to ask, ('There we go,' thought Mary) I've noticed you've been getting pretty close to No; what's happening there?'

Mary's cheeks flushed and then she turned away. She and No had been growing closer, but all the flirting in the world had not yet moved them toward anything physical, apart from that waltz they had a few weeks ago. They'd talked a lot and they were spending time together in the pub, but they hadn't gone on a date at all, let alone anything a little more private.

'We're currently just friends,' said Mary.

'Currently?'

Mary froze as she realised what she had said, 'That's not what I meant.'

'What did you mean?' asked Jo, propping her head up with two hands, 'he comes here every year, did you know? And he's never gotten on with anyone as well as he has with you. Not even Wat!'

Mary felt herself feel a boost in her ego, 'really?'

'Yeah, he's always been very quiet. Hangs around the pub like a ghost. He never goes out - you should take him somewhere!'

'Like where?'

'Like for dinner, or to see a movie, or to do like some arts and crafts. I hear they opened a hipster wine and pottery place on the other side of town,' suggested Jo,' a guy took me there and it was so sensual.'

Jo disappeared into her thoughts, a soft smile on her face.

'I don't think he'd be interested in that,' Mary dismissed, 'but dinner might be a good idea.'

TALES FROM THE KING GEORGE

'Oh, then I know the perfect place for him! This place around the corner from the high street on Crooks Road. It's brilliant. Trust me. Ask him,' Jo said with intensity.

Mary gave her a sceptical look. Almost on time, No arrived in the barroom. Jo turned around, shot up to her feet and bounced on her heels.

'Hey No,' she said, in a slightly higher pitch, 'how are you?'

Mary noticed Jo was trying to put her wiles to use, but No gave her a glance and then looked toward Mary, 'Hi Jo, I'm fine thanks. Mary, are you taking a break?'

Jo turned to Mary with a knowing look, then jerked her head in his direction.

Mary stuttered a little, then spoke, 'Actually, I need to get back to work, but No,' she paused, 'would you like to get dinner later?'

'Sure, I think they're doing a deal on food and a drink tonight-'

'I meant somewhere else. Do you know Crooks Road? Jo was saying there's a good place there,' she asked.

Jo backed her up by nodding and giving a thumbs up, 'Very nice place.'

No hesitated, then he smiled softly, coughed and said, 'I don't know it, but if you want to get dinner there. Together. That'd be nice.'

'Good!' said Mary.

'Yes,' said No.

There was an awkward pause.

'I should get back to work then. Does seven sound reasonable to leave?'

'Sure, that sounds fine,' said No, his hand on the back of his neck.

WHEN NIAMH MET MONA

Mary nodded and then got up. 'I'll see you at seven then,' she said and left the room.

She was halfway down the staircase to the lower level when Jo called after her;

'There you go! Trust me, you'll have a great time.'

At which point they both ran into Niamh who was emerging from the bedroom at the end with the 'Mum & Dad' sign, her hair done up and still adjusting her dress. When she saw that Mary and Jo were in the corridor there was another moment's pause where they acknowledged one another.

'Good morning Niamh,' said Mary.

'Good morning Mary, lovely to see you bright and early,' she said, putting a smile on her face, 'I don't believe I've met you,' she said motioning to Jo, 'everything alright? You're bright red.'

'She just asked No to a date,' said Jo out loud, receiving a nudge from Mary.

'It's nothing.'

'You're going on a date!? How exciting! Say, me and Wat are going out tonight as well, we should make it a double date!' Niamh rolled on her heels in anticipation. Mary felt her stomach turn inside. 'Where are you going?'

'To this place on Crooks Road,' said Mary.

'Oh I see, Wat and I were going to go to that fancy Italian, I forget the name, then go to the theatre. Some town performance of Midsummer Night's Dream,' said Niamh a little dismissively, 'if you can cancel your reservation then-'

'No, I'm afraid not,' said Mary suddenly, getting an odd look from Jo.

'Never mind! There'll be other times. Do let us know when you decide to go out. I'm so happy for you,' and Niamh gave her a half hug.

She then proceeded to leave up the stairs and out of sight. Jo gave her a questioning look, 'Why didn't you take the double date, she seems great,' and Jo turned back to see if she could still see Niamh. Mary realised Jo had actually watched Niamh leave but shook her head.

'That woman is not who seems,' said Mary, 'she's all superficial.'

'Mm,' said Jo, who sounded as if she wasn't really listening, 'alright well you got the date!'

'I did,' said Mary and she opened the office door, 'I'm not sure what to make of it.'

'What are you going to wear? Are you going all out, or subtle? Or sexy?' asked Jo.

'Actually Jo, I need to get to work,' and Jo's face fell a little into a pout, 'but we can discuss this later.'

'I'll find you,' said Jo.

And she left back up the stairs as Mary entered the office and pressed her back up against the door. At which point yet another person decided to involve themselves in Mary's life as Mona traipsed down on a string of webbing.

'A date huh?' she said with a hint of smugness.

Mary gave the spider a tired look and then took a seat at her desk.

* * *

Mary had been donated an old computer from Neo, who had said she'd bought something newer, and the machine was too old for her to sell. For Mary, it was perfect – she had booted it, installed some of the software she used, and then ran through the concepts with Wat. She also ran through it with Neo who had taken an interest after hearing what her old computer would be for.

She uploaded all the information she had had on her laptop onto the machine and was able to complete her work in the safe knowledge she wasn't storing mass amounts of Wat's data on her own personal devices. It would be very useful when she eventually handed her final report over, though she felt bad that all the effort would be thrown away when the pub closed. She pushed through anyway.

As she worked, tapping away, Mona pressed for all the information she could about her coming date with No: what Mary was going to wear, what they would talk about, what she would order to eat. Mona was adamant, 'Don't order garlic. Trust me. Nobody wants to be smelling that stuff on your breath, especially later in the night.'

Eventually, Mary needed a break (from work and from Mona), so she returned to the bar room to find Boz getting her hair stroked by Jo as they talked in hushed whispers. Boz was gazing longingly into the distance. When Mary walked in, she almost jumped. 'Ah Mary,' she said, 'I didn't see you there.' Mary simply nodded in understanding as Boz returned to bussing glasses. Just then, Wat and Niamh returned to the scene arm in arm from the dining room. Niamh left without a sound and Wat greeted Jo and Mary both.

'Ah, you two again,' he said with a touch of anxiety in his voice.

'Don't worry Wat, we'll talk about it later,' said Jo and she sauntered away.

'Well Mary, how are things?' he asked, 'how's our diagnosis?'

Mary didn't realise he meant the pub at first – after she clocked on she bit her lip, 'fine. So far fine. I think we should have a chat soon.'

Wat gave her a trusting smile and that caused Mary's heart to sink. Did she actually feel bad? But the evidence she had been compiling was compounding. The income wouldn't take Wat as far as he had thought and she would need to break the news to him.

Eventually. Not right now of course, maybe a little later. She just had to tidy a few more notes and make a few more graphs.

She had done her due diligence. And the agency was happy with her work. The fact that she was coming to the appropriate conclusion was just what they all wanted. What Mary wanted, what the agency wanted, what Niamh wanted even with her impatient little meddling. Mary knew she would be pleased when she revealed the news. Mary despised how Niamh would probably be jumping for joy at the prospect of selling Wat's home.

Wat told Mary about the evening's plans;

'Yes, she wanted to go to that Italian for a while now, it's just rather expensive. Plus, the theatre! We're not West End, so I'm not expecting big things,' he said plainly.

'It should be an experience,' said Mary, 'Midsummer Night's Dream, I bet you've had the real-life experience.'

'Twice.'

'I was joking Wat,' said Mary, '...really?'

'Faeries are tricky creatures,' he stated wistfully.

Mary then bid goodbye and returned down the stairs just as she heard the master bedroom click closed. She found the door to the office slightly ajar which was not how Mary had left it. She rolled her eyes; Niamh. She had probably been snooping around again. When she entered, she found the filing cabinet open and a splash of tea in the corner of the room. She tutted and then checked that her files were not left in disarray.

The files were left organised so Mary glanced through, making sure nothing had been taken. For sure, Niamh had been looking for her report. It was lucky she did everything digitally – all Niamh had access to were physical copies of accounts and letters, but that hadn't stopped her from searching for any tiny bit of evidence she could use against Wat.

Mary shut the cabinet and then checked her computer. Her account was locked for twenty minutes; another clue that Niamh was trying to poke her nose where it didn't belong.

She leaned back in her chair and then she realised the mug she'd been drinking from was gone as well. She considered that Niamh had probably knocked it off by accident and broken the thing. It was a shame; she liked that mug. It had a few painted spiders in webs over it.

'Mona? Did you see what Niamh was doing?' she called out softly before unlocking her computer account.

There was no answer so after a few moments Mary called again, 'Mona?'

Still nothing.

'Mona? Are you there?' she asked a little more insistently.

Panic began to creep in as she remembered the last time when Niamh was snooping around her documents and the black smudge on her paper pile. She couldn't see any signs of a struggle but then what kind of struggle would you have with a small spider like Mona anyway?

She began to quickly check that Mona's remains weren't just cast somewhere and pressed into the floor. Just the thought made her feel sick and guilty. But when she couldn't find anything, she thought about what she had found.

Her mug was gone.

Could it be that Niamh didn't just find Mona, she had taken her? Could she have thrown her out the window? No, the last spider Niamh had seen, she had destroyed on the spot; if she had seen Mona, she would've tried to kill her.

So, if she had used a mug, she wanted to keep her alive for her own means. She must've heard Mona talk. Whatever plans Niamh might have had, they were not going to be beneficial to Mona, Mary, Wat or anyone else for that matter.

She stepped out of the office and whispered, 'Mona?'

She crept into the kitchen first. The place was not as worse for wear as it usually was, but there was a lot less crockery. And mugs. There was no sign of her mug, but she could see that the tin foil had been ripped out unceremoniously and left on the counter. Mary put two and two together - she didn't expect Niamh had been making sandwiches.

Then she crept toward the master bedroom, 'Mum & Dad'. Through the door she heard the faint sounds of a shower; Niamh was probably getting ready for dinner. Mary pressed her ear closely to try and tell how good her chances were - Niamh was definitely in there, Wat was not. She risked it and reached for the door handle, slowly turning it and waiting for the faint click.

WHEN NIAMH MET MONA

It did faintly click, and when she opened the door Niamh's showering didn't stop and she didn't call out. In fact, it sounded like Niamh was attempting to sing "Uptown Girl". It didn't sound too bad but you could tell Niamh wasn't aiming for a career in show business. Mary closed the door softly behind her but didn't close it all the way in case Wat found his way in. She scanned the room.

It was a mess, there were women's clothes everywhere. The dresser at the side was covered in makeup and packages of all sorts, and the floor was caked in tight-fitting dresses, large cupped bras and a few other sultry matters. Mary almost tripped on a pair of Niamh's knickers and she felt a little disturbed at the idea of her and Wat together in bed. She saw on the bed Niamh's bag along with some more of her matters. Mary's mug, however, was not in sight. It wasn't on the dresser, on the bedside table - she didn't expect Niamh to have taken it with her into the bathroom. She rounded over to the wardrobe and opened up to peer inside. Upon seeing she knew this was Wat's domain. It contained neatly hung-up shirts, trousers and a set of ties, all in their place. Tidy wardrobe, messy kitchen? Wat was a strange man indeed.

'Mona?' she whispered.

Nothing.

'Mona!' she whispered a little more loudly, and she winced, hoping that Niamh would still not hear her sneaking around.

A faint voice came up from out of the bag, 'Mary?'

Mary felt joy spring from her to know Mona wasn't dead. Unfortunately, then she realised the shower had stopped running. She froze in panic. She couldn't grab the bag and run for it, Niamh would certainly catch her and then what? Try to pretend she didn't know about a talking spider? Things could go badly, and their unsteady alliance would fall into chaos.

She looked around and then felt the door of the wardrobe. It was tidy. There was none of Niamh's clothes in here. She sprang backwards, grabbed the wardrobe doors and closed them. The doors left the smallest crack, but she couldn't peer too closely; she had to stay out of sight. She crouched and pushed herself away from the doors, listening as she heard Niamh moving around the room.

When Mary glanced out, she saw Niamh, heard her humming away, and saw her proceeding to get ready for the night. She took her towel off, revealing herself, to which Mary huffed in annoyance. She put her makeup on, chose the nicest of dresses from the ones on the floor, tried some shoes on, tried some dresses on, tried some shoes on, found the outfit that suited her, and by the time she was finished Mary's knees were aching, her body was cramping and she was ready to claw Niamh's eyes out. Finally, Niamh gave herself a wink in the full-length mirror on the back of the door, grabbed her bag with Mona inside, and walked out of the bedroom.

Mary waited for a minute before she bowled out of the wardrobe and rubbed her legs roughly. When the feeling came back, she ran out the door. Then when the idea came to her, she raced into the barroom. Niamh was there talking to Wat and No was in the corner.

'Niamh!' she said, catching her attention.

'Mary? What's wrong?'

'Niamh turns out my reservations fell through. Perhaps we could go on that double date after all?'

WHEN NIAMH MET MONA

Niamh's face lit up and she clapped her hands excitedly. 'Yes, yes! Absolutely, are you ready now? In fact, of course you're not, let me give you a hand.'

'Sure,' said Mary shrugging, her mind still reeling from whether this was a good idea or not, but before Niamh dragged her away she found No at the bar talking to Jarrett. She swept in behind him and said, 'Change of plans. We're doing a double date with Wat and Niamh.'

'A double what?'

'Trust me, we need to do this. I'll explain later.'

'...Okay.'

And then she was dragged away by Niamh.

* * *

That night in the restaurant, Niamh was almost wholly superficial. As she spoke, Mary felt herself just wanting to crawl further and further inside herself. No was also not a fan, shrinking back whenever the conversation was being roughly taken in her hands. All the while, Mary had an eye on Niamh's bag. She still had to find a way to get the mug without Niamh knowing she'd taken it. There had to be some kind of distraction she could make.

Unfortunately, grabbing the jar would be one thing - getting it back without Niamh noticing was another.

'And that's when we all laughed!' said Niamh as she ended her latest anecdote, laughing on cue and getting a forced laugh from everyone else. Mary hadn't paid attention at all.

'Now, when did you two get so close?' Wat asked Mary and gestured to No.

The two of them looked at one another.

'Well, she liked reading-'

'-he was so quiet-'

'-I just said hello one day-'
'-we danced the waltz-'
'-he saved me from O'Nerry-'
'-we just talked-'
'It just sort of happened,' finished Mary and looked up at No.

She wasn't sure what they were and whatever label Niamh was trying to put on them didn't fit. Or maybe it was he didn't think it fit. They hadn't discussed it at all and if Wat hadn't just asked about them directly, Mary was sure they would've touched on the topic at all.

'Well, I think it's lovely. You're from out of town aren't you No?' asked Niamh.

'Yes, my family comes from Italy actually,' he said.

'What brings you here then?' she asked.

'The weather mostly,' said No, to a surprised reaction from Niamh; Wat seemed unphased, 'Yes the weather just seems to suit the time, don't you think?'

'Clouds?' said Mary in disbelief.

'Yes, November; a time for clouds. I like the bonfires that begin, though I could do without the fireworks,' explained No, 'as the month goes on, I often find myself very reminiscent.'

'I see,' said Niamh, 'what about your family back home?'

'They travel a lot. I think my sisters have actually spent some time travelling East recently,' continued No, 'my sister Avril was in Iran for example.'

'That sounds a bit dangerous,' said Niamh.

No gave her a blank look, 'why?'

'Do you think you might do some travelling?' asked Wat to Mary, trying to move off the subject.

WHEN NIAMH MET MONA

'I do have work planned for December so I will be returning back to London. I will likely end up in Canada early next year-'

'You're leaving?' asked No, a little out of the blue.

Mary stuttered, 'Yes, I'll be finishing my work with Wat by the end of the month.'

'Oh,' said No, his voice downfallen, 'I didn't realise, I thought you'd be here a lot longer as a permanent employee.'

'Permanent? Really?' said Niamh.

'No that's not the case at all,' and she gave Wat a look to help defend her.

'That is right,' said Wat, 'she won't be staying on.'

No looked crestfallen. Mary felt a little embarrassed at the sudden topic. Niamh judged the room and realised what had happened.

'Say, I need to visit the little girl's room. Mary, you want to come with me?' she asked, picking up her bag and opening her hand.

Mary saw, not only a window to escape but a window of opportunity. 'Yes.'

Before she knew it, she'd followed Niamh into a large yellow-tiled room, a mirror spanning a set of sinks opposite five stalls. The room was empty when they entered, the stalls all open. Niamh put her bag next to the sink and checked herself in the mirror.

'That got a little out of hand there,' she said.

Mary nodded and mumbled in agreement.

'I guess I must've forgotten to tell No I was leaving,' said Mary.

'Forgot? How long have you two been-'

'We're not together. We haven't even had a first date yet,' said Mary.

Niamh then realised what exactly she'd gotten herself into, 'I'm sorry I wrongly assumed. This is embarrassing.'

'It's okay, we hadn't really talked about what we were,' said Mary.

'Better talk to him soon about it then if you're leaving,' said Niamh, 'look after my bag would you?'

And Niamh sauntered into one of the open stalls. Mary had the chance. She waited until the click of the door lock.

'Do you think he wants a relationship?' she called, as Mary quietly popped open Niamh's bag.

'I think we get on well enough for that to be an option,' responded Mary, rummaging and finding the mug hidden under an open book and a makeup case.

'But do you think he wants one where you're in the city and he's god knows where? It sounds long distance.'

Mary put the mug into her own bag. It was tight, but she got it to fit, 'I'm not sure, I've never really thought about it.'

'Long distance doesn't work trust me,' said Niamh, 'the distance is hard to deal with. Physical contact is important in any relationship, ignore what the articles tell you online. I know! I know this first-hand.'

The toilet flushed and Niamh stepped out and then proceeded to wash her hand. She checked her face; Mary prayed she didn't need to touch anything up. She didn't and picked up her bag without a second thought.

'Let's get back to the boys then,' she said.

Mary smiled and the two walked back to their table, where Wat was talking to No about the second world war. No looked as he always did but this didn't comfort

WHEN NIAMH MET MONA

Mary; whenever she talked to him, he had this spark in his eye. The spark was missing now.

The night passed and they ate and drank, talking about all sorts, until Niamh checked her watch.

'We'd better go if we want to catch that play,' she said.

'I think I'll pass,' said No, standing up from the table.

'Really?' asked Niamh, sounding disappointed.

Mary, who was much more surprised at the change in No's tone, stood up as well, 'What do you mean? I think we could enjoy it.'

No gave her a soft look, 'I don't really feel up for it anymore.'

He began to leave. Niamh and Wat both had concerned looks before Niamh tried her best with her eyes to say 'Mary, you should talk to him'. Mary eventually picked it up and, after checking the mug was still in her bag, went after him. He had stepped outside and was gearing himself up in the cold when she reached him and put a hand on his shoulder.

'No, what's wrong.'

'I thought you were going to stay a lot longer.'

'Is that a problem?'

No gave a shake of his head.

'You have to tell me what's wrong,' said Mary.

'I'll be leaving at the end of the month,' said No.

'...and yet you're upset that I'm leaving?'

No huffed, 'If you were here I wouldn't.'

'Well that's sweet to say, but I have a life and career in London No. I've liked spending time here, but-'

'Not enough to stay.'

Mary felt affronted by the sudden coldness in No's behaviour, 'what, were you expecting I'd stay here for you?'

No gave her a sad look, 'That's not what I meant. I just…'

'I like you but my life won't go on hold for you,' and Mary folded her arms.

No looked like he didn't have anything to say. After a prolonged silence, he said, 'Ah.'

'Ah,' repeated Mary, 'so I guess this is it?'

'It's probably for the best,' said No, and he turned around.

Tears swelled in Mary's eyes as she too realised what they'd decided. She watched him walk away, hoping he'd stop and turn around. But as he reached the corner and turned into it, she realised that was it. She shook her head to compose herself and wiped her eyes.

She was about to call a cab when the door to the restaurant burst open and a flurry of curls bounced into view. Niamh was pissed. She almost ran into Mary, but seeing it was her, Niamh halted dead in her tracks.

'You!', and she looked over Mary's person. Spying her handbag she tried to snatch it from Mary.

'What are you doing?' said Mary, wrenching it back.

'You took that spider, didn't you! Of course you did, you're just like the rest of them right!? Oh, Niamh doesn't get to know because she's a ditzy blonde and wouldn't understand, is that it?' accused Niamh.

Wat found his way outside to the altercation and grabbed Niamh by the arms, but she pulled them from his grip.

'Niamh, stop this!' said Wat.

WHEN NIAMH MET MONA

'You and your bloody secrets Wat, you can keep them for all I care!' and she shoved Wat away, marching away from him.

Mary was agape. Wat called after her, 'Niamh wait!'

Niamh threw him the finger, 'screw you!' she yelled with tears in her voice.

Wat looked helplessly at Niamh and Mary. He ran a hand through his hair and dropped the tension in his shoulder. He saw the tears in Mary's eyes, 'are you okay Mary? What happened, did y-'

'Me and No just had a falling out is all,' said Mary, wiping her face, 'what about you and-'

Wat shook his head as if he didn't want to talk about it. 'I'm sorry,' he said, and he took Mary into his arms and hugged her.

Mary reciprocated and dried her eyes on his shoulder. He rocked her gently and she liked that. When he let her go, she sniffed but felt a little better about it.

'Sorry for getting emotional,' said Mary.

'It's fine, let's get back to the pub,' said Wat leading Mary into a walk, 'I hadn't expected things to go like this at all. Is Mona okay at the least?'

Mary wanted to say something but she couldn't think of anything.

'All fine here Mr Stone,' said Mona as seductively as she could from within her mug.

'You know about Mona?' asked Mary.

Wat fetched the mug from Mary's bag and pulled the tinfoil off, allowing Mona to crawl out onto the back of his hand.

'I do now. You know Niamh intended to sell your story to the papers?'

'She told me as much, yes.'

TALES FROM THE KING GEORGE

Wat shook his head but didn't say anything. Neither did Mona. And nor could Mary. There was a solemn silence upon them as they walked the way back to the pub. Until Wat laughed unexpectedly and suddenly, causing Mary to jump a little.

'What's funny?'

'Just before Niamh and I got up, I was looking through the bill. I was doing the maths when she realised the mug was gone. She asked about it, accused you, I asked what was so important, she told me, we argued, and then she stormed off. And as soon as I heard your voice, I raced to stop her in case she hurt you,' he laughed again,' and we just walked off! Looks like I can't go back there again, we just left the bill.'

Mo the Sceptic

Of all eighteen staff employed at the Mad King, the most elusive to Mary was Mohammed (Wat referred to him as Mo) who worked the night shift. He worked half the days in the week from twelve at night to six in the morning. Wat was grateful to have him as it meant he and his family didn't have to suffer from twenty-four-hour shifts every day of the week.

Because Mary's own schedule was so rigid, she'd never bumped into Mo until she awoke one night feeling a deep unsettling emptiness. She realised that she had gone the day without eating much and she was now famished. She could eat a horse. She wanted to eat a horse. Unfortunately, that would probably be unreasonable to request at such a late hour.

When she finally broached the topic with her legs, she made her way downstairs with a great deal of effort – it was almost three in the morning and she was exhausted but her starvation pushed her forward.

When she reached the reception, she heard the rustling and clinking of cutlery. Curious, she poked her head into the barroom. There was a flash as the ghostly pale blue eyes of Feathers swivelled into view.

'Jesus Feathers, you gave me a fright,' she said.

'Sorry lass, didnae mean to scare yer,' he said quietly.

'How are you doing?' she asked, sparking some small talk.

'Bin doin as good as I can. To be onest it's mardy bein stuck as yer talkin doll; erbody's just askin me to talk fo'em,' shuddered Feathers, 'when are yer letting me go?'

'When you can atone for your actions,' said Mary, 'maybe we'll let you go at the end of the month.'

'Thar'll be soon enough fo'me,' said Feathers in a sad tone. Mary couldn't help but feel a little bad for the ghost.

Her attention was reignited towards the kitchen when she heard further clattering of cutlery.

'Who's that in the kitchen?' she asked.

'The boy o'works at night,' replied Feathers, 'ere aff t'week.'

Mary realised he meant Mo and immediately ignored her hunger for food in favour of her hunger for knowledge. She walked through the barroom and opened the kitchen door.

Mo was a gangly boy with a sharp short haircut. He also had the beginnings of a moustache that hadn't yet grown out. His eyes were big and dark brown, yet tinged with an utter disinterest that Mary felt was thrown over her when she entered. While he did display a minute frown, it disappeared almost immediately and he greeted her with a stark and unyielding;

'Yeah?'

'Mr Tahir, I don't think we've met,' and Mary raised her hand for a shake.

MO THE SCEPTIC

Mo observed her before he put down the cutlery he was holding and walked over to shake her hand, then went back to polishing the cutlery.

'I'm just polishing cutlery,' he explained.

'So I see,' said Mary. Watching him polishing reminded her why she'd woken up in the first place, 'god I'm starving. Is there any food around?'

Mo put down the fork he was holding and reached into one of the cupboards that was actually an on-hand fridge. He pulled out a couple plates – one looked to be a roast dinner and the other was filled with chips and some salad. He set them down on a counter;

'Knock yourself out.'

Mary inspected the food before picking up a chip, 'thanks.'

'Wat makes sure they leave me something for my shift,' Mo explained, 'I tell him I eat beforehand but he doesn't listen.'

'Sounds like Wat,' said Mary who dug into the leftovers.

The pub was eerily quiet apart from Mo. Watching him work he was very focused on what he was doing. It was very relaxing and given the hour Mary had to be careful not to find herself drifting off to sleep whilst standing.

'So you work the night shift,' she said, 'see anything out of the ordinary?'

Mo shook his head.

Mary immediately found that hard to believe, 'Come on.'

'I used to get up at ungodly hours in my parents' house,' said Mo, 'never saw a thing. Same with this place.'

'Never seen a ghost?' asked Mary.

'Nope,' he claimed, 'I don't believe in them.'

Mary had to stifle herself, 'Come on, really? You know there's a ghost in the barroom right now?'

Mo raised his eyebrow at her. Mary nodded enthusiastically and then pointed the way. She led Mo out into the barroom where Feathers was still sitting on the counter.

'Feathers here is a bonafide pirate ghost, stuck in a dummy,' she stated and pointed at the puppet. Mo turned on the lights so he no longer had his ghostly glow.

'You mean the doll? It's just a robot,' he said.

'I'm a pirate, arr,' said Feathers without much enthusiasm.

'See!' said Mary.

'See? That's just one of the many programmed phrases in his arsenal,' said Mo.

'No, it's a ghost! Watch, Feathers say something else.'

'Er, shiver me timbers?'

'Another generic pirate phrase?' said Mo, folding his arms unimpressed.

'Feathers,' ordered Mary, 'say Mohammed Tahir.'

'Mohammed Tahir,' said Feathers.

Mo tutted and then walked back into the kitchen leaving Mary unsure what to do. She gave Feathers a look of bewilderment and then dashed to follow Mo.

'What was that, do you still not believe me?' said Mary.

'The others are always trying to get me to believe some crazy story. I'm not that gullible okay?' said Mo who'd returned to polishing.

'But this is the truth! Feathers is a ghost trapped in a ventriloquist's dummy!' and then Mary closed her eyes and realised what she was saying was completely insane, 'no but seriously, I know how it sounds.'

Mo paid no further attention to what she was saying and focused on his work.

Mary was getting frustrated. She wasn't crazy, this stuff was real, it was really real! How could Mo not see it?

'I've got it,' she said, throwing a finger in the air, 'the dragon in the oven, Cocharil!'

Mo shook his head, 'I've heard that one before. It's just embers and fire in there.'

'No it's a salamander! Look,' said Mary and she crouched down to the grate of the oven.

When she looked in, she felt silly because Cocharil did look like a pile of embers. She called to him softly, 'Cocharil! Cocharil!' but the embers shifted slightly as if the salamander were only stirring and nothing more. She was amazed at how easily the creature camouflaged but even more frustrated that she just sounded crazy again.

'Honestly, it's a salamander. He choked on broccoli and almost drowned in the common!' said Mary, attempting to reason with him.

Mo shook his head. Mary snapped her fingers.

'The common! Now you won't know this but in the common is a unicorn-'

'Ms Woods, I'm trying to work here,' said Mo in a half-pleading voice, 'look I get it might be funny but everyone tries to make a fool out of me like this. It's not happening. Can we drop it?'

'Mo I'm not trying to poke fun at you,' defended Mary.

Mo scoffed at that and picked up the pile of cutlery he'd polished, 'I'd just like to do my job please.'

Then he exited out to the dining room, likely to set up for the morning. Mary decided to drop it and went back through the barroom. She passed Feathers and realised they'd left the lights on so she went towards the light switch situated by the reception.

'Didnae believe yer lass?' Feathers asked.

'No, not at all,' said Mary, and then she paused, 'You are a ghost right? I didn't imagine that?'

'I am, dead as a doornail.'

'Good. Stay that way please.'

* * *

The next morning Mary broached Wat with the topic.

'Wat, one of your employees is a sceptic. What are we going to do?'

Wat was mid-sip in a cup of tea and reading the newspaper in the other hand. The sudden appearance of Mary caused a wave of concern to rush over his face even before she began talking. It took him some time to realise what and who exactly she was referring to and, even then, he looked incredibly cautious as if he was about to tell her some bad news.

'Are you talking about Mo?'

'Yes, I met him last night and he doesn't believe in magic. At all.'

'He's always been that way ever since I first hired him,' said Wat, a little reminiscent.

There was a pause as Mary expected him to continue but when he didn't, she tried to nudge him, 'so what are we going to do? One of your staff who must deal with the magical every day doesn't believe it exists!'

'I don't think we really need to do anything. If he doesn't want to believe I won't make him. If anything, it makes my job a little easier,' and he chuckled. Not

MO THE SCEPTIC

seeing Mary chuckle with him caused him to stop, 'no but seriously, it's not a mandatory initiation.'

'But how can he just explain away all the weird happenings!?' said Mary.

'With ease, he does it with everything.'

Neo appeared to clean the table and so Mary pulled her into the conversation.

'Oh yeah he's always thought everything we told him was some joke,' said Neo, 'shame really.'

'Mary, what Mo does is no different to the rest of the world with magic. They just ignore it, explain it away,' said Wat.

'To be honest, I think it's like he always says,' spoke up Neo, 'he's just here to work. He doesn't care for magic.'

Mary let these ideas sit with her but she couldn't shake the feeling that it didn't seem right. She thought that Mo should believe and that he should be aware of everything that went on around him. Was it perhaps the feeling that he thought everyone was just having a joke? Or perhaps it was because she felt Mo was like her, or how she used to be at least, and she wanted him to discover the weird world she now knew existed? She could be his initiator, his guide.

And she knew the only way to convince him was Wesley.

When they'd done with breakfast, she went out of the conservatory into the common. There she didn't have to search hard to find Jordan peering up into some pines with his binoculars. When she called out to him, he turned to face her pointing the binoculars in her direction.

'Ms Woods! To what do I owe the pleasure?' he said, genuinely pleased to see her.

Mary took a deep breath.

'I wanted to check your shed's inventory if that's alright with you? I'm making a record of our current assets,' she said.

'Of course! Of course, let me show you,' and he led her to the shed by the pond.

Around the back was a set of double doors held shut by a padlock. Jordan swung out his set of keys to unlock it and revealed the display of tools and machinery at his disposal.

A ride-on mower sat in the centre, ready to be taken out at a moment's notice if needed. On the walls were various power tools including a strimmer, a chainsaw, a hedge trimmer, a leaf-blower and some pruning tools. There were also a few manual tools stacked in a box, a shovel, rake, and hoe, all pretty old and a little rusted.

'Thanks Jordan,' said Mary, 'do you live in the other compartment then?'

She continued to eye the walls for a key rack or something similar as Jordan answered.

'Yeah, I can show you around it if you like? Make a spot of tea?' he laughed.

'Is it better than the tea indoors?' asked Mary.

'Just a little,' said Jordan.

He shut the double doors behind them and locked up using his set of keys. Then he took her round the front where there was a stable door with a small window cut out the top half.

Inside, a welcome mat was sodden with earth, and the rest of the floor was hardwood. The walls were thick – wood on insulation on wood. A small iron range sat in the corner with its chimney snaking up into the ceiling. There was also a wire-frame bed in the corner with a thick duvet and blanket set on it, and a dresser sat at the end of the bed. The room wasn't much larger than the rooms in the house.

'Are you okay out here Jordan?' asked Mary.

'Oh yes, plenty comfy for me,' said Jordan, and he did just what Mary wanted: he took off his jacket in habit and put it and his set of keys on the coat rack by the door. Then he set to making a boiling kettle on his stove. He had some live embers so he blew on them to get them going, then threw a log into it to make it hotter. 'I spend most of my time out in the common or in the pub.'

'I suppose it's comely,' said Mary, making note that the keys were right by the door.

She couldn't take them now and she had no good reason to ask for the keys off Jordan either. But if they were this easily accessible, it shouldn't be hard to borrow them later in the night.

'One sugar or two?' asked Jordan, lifting up a rounded blue mug.

Mary smiled sweetly, 'One please,' and she felt sorry for Jordan.

She'd have this cup of tea with him to ease her guilt.

He rubbed his hands and picked up the small glass bottle of milk off a shelf. Once the water was done boiling, he strained the tea through some loose leaves. As he did so he chatted with Mary about some of the things he'd seen. He chatted about how the fieldfare had been arriving recently due to the hawthorn they'd been growing near the centre of the common. He'd been watching one hop around in the hedge a little earlier.

When the tea was done, Mary gripped her tea in both hands and accompanied Jordan out to the bench set by the pond near the shed.

'It's a good bit of work this common,' he said, 'I've been doing this almost thirty-odd years you know?'

'That's an awfully long time,' said Mary.'

'I used to do work up in the Wyre Forest, but they're dedicated to conservation up there. Here we've not got any rules on what's meant to be where. Birds of any kind are free to flock here as long as I make it attractive for them, you see what I mean?'

Mary nodded.

'In a way, it's just like how Wat does it. It's not like he has any rules governing him on who he can and can't let come in. Truth is, it just attracts people.'

Mary looked at Jordan and realised that perhaps he knew more than he'd ever let on.

'Why this pub though?' she asked, 'surely they'd just spread around?'

'People are like birds,' said Jordan, 'you fly with the flock.'

* * *

Was it a bad idea? Maybe. The premise was simple; one, take Mo to meet Wesley. Two, Mo's mind is blown at the existence of magic. Three, Mo and herself return with a new level of trust and Mo is inducted into the world of magic.

What could go wrong?

Mary's alarm woke her up at three in the morning and she pulled herself to a sitting position. She felt awful but that wasn't going to stop her.

Downstairs she found Mo setting tables in the dining room and bundling the used tablecloths into a bag.

'Where are we going?' he asked.

'Into the common,' said Mary, dragging the boy by the hand.

MO THE SCEPTIC

She pulled him out onto the patio where the security light clicked on. He shivered a little in the cold. When she tried to take him up the trail into the common he pulled her to a stop.

'You're not actually serious, are you? There's no way you're taking me out there,' he said.

'Why not? Trust me,' said Mary.

'I barely know you,' he replied.

Mary huffed, 'I've got a clean slate Mr Tahir, there's not a bad record on me. I promise you I'm not going to hurt you,' then she thought, 'or trick you. This isn't a prank.'

'Fine,' he relented and began to shuffle along with her, 'where are we going then?'

'You know that closed-off area of the common? I'm going to take you inside there and show you what Wat's been working on,' said Mary excitedly.

Mary pulled out the torch she'd brought with her and led Mo up into the common towards Jordan's shed. This was the tricky bit.

'What are you doing?' asked Mo.

'Going to borrow a set of keys,' said Mary.

The lights were off. Mary tried the handle to the door and, surprise, it was open. Of course it was, Jordan was trusting. She edged it open only a little and then reached around the corner. Her hand found the keys. She cautiously lifted them off the hook.

Jordan stirred a little in his sleep, the cold draught reaching him in his bed. Mary pulled the keys out with her and gently closed the door again until it clicked shut.

She turned back to Mo, jerked her head in the direction of the fencing, and led him away from the shed. She jangled the keys a little, happy that she had gotten them. She'd return them when she was done, it was harmless. No one was going to get hurt from this.

When they got to the fence, she looked through the keys to try and work out which ones went where. She gave Mo the torch to point at the fence gates whilst she looked at the keys.

'Er, Ms Woods?' Mo spoke up, gesturing to the gate.

Mary hadn't been paying attention so when she looked up it took her a second to realise what he was referring to. The padlocks were all broken open. The gate was ajar. Someone had beaten her to it.

Her mind raced to O'Nerry.

'Turn the torch off,' she instructed.

'What?'

'Do it.'

Mo turned the torch off and they were drenched in complete darkness. Mary held the keys tightly and listened intently. It was silent save for the wind rustling the trees and the distant sounds of cars but nothing was coming from the field. She put pressure on the gate. It wouldn't move, it was caught on the ground. She pulled up then pushed. The gate eased open.

She couldn't see anything through the gloom. This worried Mary, she should be able to make out Wesley regardless. She scopes the whole field but she couldn't see anything.

'Dammit put the torch back on, we need to find Wesley.'

'Wesley?'

'Put the torch on!' said Mary, a little louder than she meant to but she was scared.

Mo flicked on the torch and swept it around.

'What are we looking for?' asked Mo.

'A horse,' said Mary.

MO THE SCEPTIC

'You brought me here to show me a horse?' said Mo.

Mary ignored him and broke into a jog toward the trough at the centre of the field. From there she scoped out the whole area. She knew there had to be some kind of stable where Wesley slept. She saw it, it was sitting beneath the pine trees, by the fencing on the left side. She changed direction and jogged toward it. Mo followed with his light, keeping the destination lit up across the field.

'Wesley?' she called out.

Reaching the small structure, she found the horse bed made underneath it and Wesley lying down on it. But Wesley was not glowing as he usually did. Mo's light flickered over the unicorn.

Mary crouched down and tried to brush away the straw that was covering him but found that it wasn't straw at all. It was sticky. It was blood. It was matted into Wesley's fur. His eyes were glossed. A strained whiney rasped through the unicorn – he seemed to just be alive. But his neck was cut open, blood clotted at the wound.

'Get Jordan. Wake him up. Knock on his door, break it down, he needs to get here,' said Mary, as she brushed the untainted hair of Wesley's body.

Mo didn't ask any further questions, he ran with the torch out of the field.

Mary sat there in silence, listening to Wesley's laboured breaths. She could feel him trying to touch her, touch her emotions, but he couldn't quite reach her. He was too weak. He tried lifting a leg.

'No, don't, you're hurt,' she said.

Wesley attempted again, his hoof brushing her leg as if physically reaching out to hold her. She gently stroked his leg with her hand.

Mo came back and Jordan was in tow. The old man couldn't run but had walked as fast as he could manage over the grass. When he reached Mary and Wesley, he too bent on his knees to look at him.

'Poor thing,' he said, 'someone's gone and cut him up good.' He looked at Mary, 'Find Wat. I'll look after him here.'

Mary found that she was crying and hadn't realised it. She wiped away the tears and she did as Jordan said. Mo began to follow her.

'So you wanted to show me a dead horse,' he stated coldly.

Mary had to stop herself from throwing a fit so she stopped mid-step and coughed as she held it in.

'That was Wesley,' she said, 'he's a unicorn. I was going to show you a unicorn.'

'A dead unicorn.'

'Mo, this is not the time,' she said, but half of the sentence got lost into sobs and she broke into a run.

Mo didn't run after her. She didn't care.

* * *

Wesley did not make it. Jordan determined the cut was too deep and it was a miracle he lasted as long as he did. In the end, the time of death was approximately three forty-five. Wat closed Wesley's eyes. He then ordered Mary back inside and Jordan to close off the gate and make sure no one else went in. They needed to preserve the area as best they could as it was effectively now a crime scene. They couldn't do anything more until morning when it was light.

MO THE SCEPTIC

The topic of the keys came up. Jordan noted that the keys were stolen when Mo had woken him. He hadn't noticed the locks were cut open as he assumed someone had just stolen the keys to get in. When Mary revealed she had the keys there was an unsteady silence.

Mary hadn't any excuse. She stared into two sets of eyes; one set was deeply confused, the other set deeply saddened. That's when Wat told her to go inside.

She had never felt so awful. She couldn't stop crying. Not just about Wesley but now she had to answer for something dreadful; she'd have to answer for stealing the keys and attempting to show Wesley to Mo.

The next morning, she found Wat in the reception on the phone. His tone was grave and incredibly regretful.

'-thank you. I'm sorry again Therin, honestly I- yes I understand. I understand. Yes, I understand we shall talk when you're here in person. Thank you. Goodbye.'

She noticed that the line had gone dead halfway through his goodbye. When she approached him, he wouldn't look up.

'Wat, I'm so sorry,' she said.

'For what?' he asked, but the tone made it sound rhetorical.

'Everything. I didn't kill Wesley. I hope you don't think that.'

'I don't Mary,' said Wat, putting a hand to his forehead, 'the good thing is we could be with him when he passed on.' He looked her in the eyes. 'The fact you stole Jordan's keys is a whole other thing.'

Mary didn't see anger, she saw deep disappointment. He was looking right through her, trying to suss what was inside her and she felt awful. No Wat, you don't understand, I'm not hiding anything! I'm a good person, please believe me!

'I wanted to show Mo Wesley, to get him to believe!'

'We talked about it the day before. I don't understand why you felt the need to do that. I don't understand why you felt it necessary to take the keys without asking. I don't understand how you could betray mine and Jordan's trust just to get one person to believe magic exists.'

Mary didn't have a sufficient answer for him, so Wat continued.

'If what you're saying is true and you found Wesley dying,' and Wat gritted his teeth at that, 'then it's lucky you did. It's not as if you killed him. If you hadn't taken the keys, Wesley would still be dead. And we would've found him probably about now when he was stone-cold dead, rather than on his last breath.

'Then again, perhaps you were lying and Wesley wasn't dying when you found him.'

Mary opened her mouth to argue but, instead, her emotions caught in her throat, 'you already said that you don't think I did it! Why say that!?'

'Because that's how Van Pelt sees it, and how he will see it,' said Wat, 'it's how someone else might see it. Mary, you don't see what you've done.'

Wat shook his head, he looked almost like he was trembling.

'Mo can vouch for me, he was there,' said Mary.

'Yes, he did,' said Wat, 'and then he quit.'

'He quit?'

'Yes Mary, he decided he didn't want to be a part of whatever is going on,' and Wat lifted his head up, both hands on either side of his head.

MO THE SCEPTIC

Mary had nothing now. She was speechless. She watched Wat, looking for some clue as to what he was thinking. He was blank. Then he roughly stood up and walked away from the counter down from reception.

Mary didn't know how to feel. No one else was there, she glanced around; she wanted someone to come and tell her it was alright.

But that person used to be Wat.

And he had made it abundantly clear that nothing, absolutely nothing, was alright.

CHEER UP WAT

Mary put up her coat on the hooks behind the doors and carried her bags with her into the barroom. The pub was as busy as usual on a weekday, but there was a shroud of discontent. Duncan and Seamus were at the counter being served by Jarrett. Neo rounded a corner and almost ran into Mary.

'Mary!' she exclaimed, 'have you seen Wat? We've not seen him for days, I'm having a hard time picking up after him.'

'Aye, where is the laddie,' spoke up Duncan, 'we're getting worried! We've not had our evening yarn with him since last week!'

Mary bit her lip, and ended up looking down, 'he's been busy. I'm sorry.'

She made her way through reception and down a level to set her bags in the kitchen. She'd restocked a few necessities which she noticed the family were running low on, and that she had been unceremoniously helping herself to. Plus, with Wat out of commission, he'd not been taking as much care of things as he usually did.

Rob had ended up following her into the kitchen noticing her putting away groceries. When she was finished, she almost walked into him.

'Why are you buying us groceries?' he asked.

'I've been taking them so I'm just replenishing what I've taken,' she said plainly.

'Did something happen between you and my dad?' he asked.

'Why would you think that?' asked Mary.

'Just he's gone into some semi-comatose state and you're acting all "proper" and "professional" again,' to which Rob accentuated his tone to mock the word.

'It's for the best, I think I got a little too involved in the business. I'm meant to have an outside point of view,' said Mary, preparing to go into the office.

Rob put a hand on the door as she walked in, propping it open.

'Could you at least try talking to him? You're the only one so far who hasn't,' he said.

'I don't think he'd want to,' said Mary.

'Why not?'

'I did something bad. I think he's upset by that,' said Mary.

'Yeah, definitely not the fact that my sister's staying with a wanted criminal. Or that his girlfriend has dumped him,' said Rob.

Mary gave him a look but she realised he was right. She'd been so focused on her own misgivings she'd forgotten everything that had happened.

'He seemed so happy until now,' she said.

'I guess it all got the better of him,' said Rob, seeing his work was done he began to leave, 'my dad's really good at pretending to be happy.'

CHEER UP WAT

Mary had to sit with the thought. Then she got up and approached the parlour. Behind the curtain she could see Wat sat in his armchair, whiskey in hand, staring idly at the television. It was playing the evening roster but he wasn't paying it much attention. His eyes were glossed as if he were a million miles away.

She left him to it for the moment. She went back into the kitchen and made two cups of tea. She had to make use of a large bright red mug that was chipped on the far side, and an old brown mug in the shape of a goofy face – Wat's personal favourite. She brought them into the parlour and set his mug next to him. He gave it a glance and then lifted his whiskey.

'I know,' she started softly, 'but I think you should ease off that.'

Wat nodded and then set down the whiskey, but he still didn't pick up the tea. Mary sat down in another of the armchairs near him and put her hands together. She considered what she could say.

'People are already asking where you are and it's only been a couple of days,' she started.

Wat nodded in recognition and his eyes lowered to the ground.

'I don't know how you do it, but you've always had this air about you. You've always been able to light up a room without doing much at all,' she said, 'is it magic?'

He smiled weakly, a brief snort rushing through his nose.

She smiled too and continued, 'I don't know how you did it after Snow ran away. I don't know how you did it after your fight with Niamh. It's incredibly strong of you to keep a happy face for all of them, I can see why losing Wesley has sapped all that strength.' She let herself breathe, 'at least it proves you're human and not just another magic being.'

Wat put a hand to his forehead and geared himself up to speak, 'My problems are my problems, I don't want to burden anyone else with them.'

'Wat, as a friend, I can say that's exactly what I'm here for.'

Wat sighed, 'I understand what you're saying, but unfortunately you're not entirely in my good books Mary.'

Mary's heart sank, but she pressed on, 'Well then what about everyone else? Neo? Kam? Everyone is here to help you. You can trust them; you could always trust them.'

He managed to rip his eyes away from the television and it looked like she'd gotten through to him.

'Neo is saying she needs help,' said Mary, 'at the very least, you have to tell her what's up.'

He studied her for a second then nodded in recognition, and he eased himself up from his seat. Mary felt a little proud and she accompanied him up the stairs.

In the barroom, Duncan and Seamus erupted into claps and a cheer.

'Laddie, where have you bin? We got loads to catch up on,' said Seamus, raising his current pint.

Neo wheeled into view, a smile of relief on her face, 'Wat! I need to ask you about rotas, and some other things.'

Wat smiled simply, and gave a gesture to Seamus, 'I'll speak to you later Seamus. What's the issue Neo?'

'First off, what's wrong?' she said and put her hands on her hips as if ordering him to drop and give her twenty.

CHEER UP WAT

He geared himself up to speak but before he could utter a word the front door opened. A slow silence pervaded the room. Everyone paid attention to the meticulous thumps of boots as the well-dressed figure of Van Pelt entered the room. He gave everyone a terse look before taking off his coat and then nodded to the room.

'What's with all the long faces? I thought I was the one who'd lost a fortune. Again.'

He strode to the bar beside Duncan and Seamus where Jarrett poured him a drink, a look on his face that said he was reluctant but knew he had to. Mary walked over quickly to Van Pelt, ignoring Wat's attempt to stop her.

'Van Pelt,' she said as she got there.

'Ah Ms Stone, you're still here. Can you tell me how we managed to let one of nature's most beautiful and powerful creatures die in such a horrific fashion?' he said.

'I'm sorry for your loss,' said Mary.

'Saying that doesn't bring me the money I would've made. I had scholars from all over making bids. All you had to do was keep it alive,' said Van Pelt.

Mary's lips pressed together before she continued, 'Wat feels awful about it as well.'

'So he should.'

'He's really not taking it well.'

'Again, that's what I'd hope.'

'If you please, Mr Van Pelt, I understand-'

'Do you understand?' Van Pelt stated firmly, still not looking at Mary, 'The money I would've made from that creature was beyond anything you would ever dream of. I spent thousands finding it, and I was promised millions, and now you've gone and got the bloody thing killed.'

Mary slammed her hand on the bar bringing his attention to her, 'Mr Van Pelt, do not quote numbers to me! I deal with them every day!

'But whilst you are angry at the loss of a number, Wat is devastated from the loss of a life.

'Do not treat this as some idle mistake, I met that creature and it was the most beautiful thing I'd ever seen. Losing Wesley has hit me like losing someone I knew, and I met it once. So think how much more it's hurt Wat.'

Van Pelt looked her up and down searching for where the anger came from.

'Wesley?'

Mary felt a surge of complete disgust, 'his damn name,' she almost shouted, and she took the cue for an exit.

Out down the gallery, she passed through the billiards room, down the extension to the conservatory, and onto the patio. When she was outside in the cold air, she realised she hadn't a coat. But nonetheless, she needed to cool off.

She should never have gotten involved. She should've stayed in the office with the numbers and documents and told Wat to sell. She should've told him to shut down effective immediately and then none of this would've happened. She felt silly.

This was all her doing – why did she feel she needed to get involved in their lives? This was her fault, her mistake. But starting from now she was going back to her roots. She would tell Wat to shut down. Tell him to close. And that will be the end of it, she could go back

CHEER UP WAT

to the big businesses in London and forget any of this happened.

She looked up into the grey sky, searching for something. She held herself tightly on either side.

'Lass, you sitting okay?' asked Duncan from behind her.

She whirled around to see Seamus as well, with the door open to the conservatory.

'Good talk with Van Pelt, the fucker looked morose as a spanked boy after you left,' said Seamus and laughed with the Guinness in hand.

Duncan had a whiskey but switched it to his left hand as he stepped out. 'I swear, what would Wat do without you?' he asked.

'Probably a lot better,' said Mary dejectedly.

'Nonsense! The boy was half-running a pub, now you're keeping up the other half!' said Duncan.

'He was this close to selling before you got here,' Seamus backed up, holding up his forefinger and thumb a few millimetres apart.

'Really?' Mary was shocked.

'Oh yes,' Duncan chimed in, 'but I remember him saying that with you onboard, there was no way he'd fail. You'd bring him back from the edge!'

Mary hesitated. To hear that Wat had been open to the idea of selling all along…

'Well he'll have to do without me soon, I leave next Friday,' said Mary.

'What!?' said Seamus, spluttering on stout.

'You can't-'

'You're gorgeous-'

'The pub needs you-'

'We need you-'

'We'll be sorry to see you go,' said Wat, stepping out onto the patio.

'Wat, I'm sorry for the outburst,' began Mary but Wat held up a hand.

'Therin apologised to me right after you stormed out. He admitted he's annoyed and he took it out on us,' explained Wat, 'he's still upset about the money though.'

'Wat, I'll do anything to make you feel better. Do you want me to talk to Niamh? Shall I drag Snow back here by her hair?' said Mary, throwing wild suggestions out. She needed him to forgive her.

'You can start by promising you won't take anything without asking first,' said Wat.

Mary nodded.

'Now kiss!' stated Seamus. Duncan laughed, slapping Seamus on his cast and causing the old man to yell out, spilling stout over himself.

'I do need your company, Mary,' said Wat, 'you and I need a chat with Van Pelt.'

* * *

Mary, Wat, Kam, Van Pelt and Jordan were all sitting around a round table in what Wat called one of his 'function rooms'. It was one of the locked rooms in the gallery that he said was reserved for events. This one hadn't been filled with furniture like the ballroom, only the round table, but no chairs. In the end, Wat had found an armchair for Van Pelt, a barstool for Kam, a deckchair for Jordan, an office chair for Mary that she found the back was broken on, and a simple dining chair for himself but that wobbled on two legs.

The room was lit by a lamp hovering above them. Due to the proximity to the barroom, they could hear the patrons talking through the walls, but it was quiet enough and reclusive enough that they knew they could talk in secrecy. Drinks were also spread out on the table.

'As we know,' said Wat, 'Wesley was killed.'

Everyone at the table lowered their heads in acknowledgement of the fact.

'Van Pelt, I'm willing to work out reimbursement with yourself, but the problem we have is that someone killed Wesley. We can't take such a thing to the police, but this person could be dangerous. Not only to us but to any of our patrons,' explained Wat.

'Well I think we all know who our prime suspect should be,' said Kam plainly, 'O'Nerry has been a menace to this family. Especially most recently with Snow.'

'Let's look at the facts,' suggested Mary, 'the locks were broken meaning someone intended to enter the common. Therefore, whoever it was knew that the common existed and knew that something inside was important.'

'Why not just climb over the fence?' asked Kam.

'Jordan and I charmed that fence. Only one way in, the gate,' said Wat.

'They used my bolt cutters, so they also got into my tool shed,' said Jordan, 'I don't know when they disappeared but at least we know someone planned it out.'

'It also looked like they cut Wesley's throat with a kitchen knife, so they made sure to use only the pub's property. That means they must've had extensive knowledge of the inside of the pub,' said Mary, 'A long-standing patron perhaps?'

'I can't think of anyone who would do such a thing,' said Wat, and Mary realised what she'd said – it was someone who knew Wat and probably knew him well.

'Let's think motive,' said Van Pelt, 'why would someone murder a unicorn?' No one answered, so Van Pelt coughed, 'Well I know for a fact the studies that were lined up for the thing were about its use in magic. Unicorn blood is said to hold mystical properties, but it's not proven. Some say it can provide eternal life.'

'Again, I can't think of anyone who: one, believes that, or two, would want that,' said Wat.

'They obviously didn't want wealth,' said Mary, 'otherwise they would've just kidnapped it.'

'So let's say it was O'Nerry,' said Kam, 'why would he kill it? Just to spite Wat?'

'That would make sense,' said Wat, 'Snow would've probably asked him to do it to hurt me.'

'Did she know about the unicorn?' asked Kam.

Wat's brow furrowed, then he leant forward, 'The only people who knew about Wesley before he was murdered were me, Jordan, and Mary. Did you tell anyone about him?'

'Not me, no one asked,' said Jordan.

Mary gulped, 'Only Mo.'

Wat nodded but he kept his eyes on Mary.

'Someone knew Wesley was there without being told?' said Kam, 'could they have overheard a conversation about him perhaps?'

'We kept it close to our chest the whole time,' said Wat.

'Was there anyone who really wanted to know?' suggested Kam.

'Niamh,' said Mary, 'Niamh would've desperately wanted to know.'

CHEER UP WAT

'But why would she kill it?' said Wat, 'she wouldn't do that.'

'If motive doesn't pinpoint anyone,' summarised Van Pelt, 'and nor does method, then all we have to go on is that it was probably a regular to this pub.'

'Which is a lot of people,' said Wat, 'not easy to shortlist.'

'I still think it's O'Nerry,' said Kam.

'I think it could be Niamh,' said Mary.

'And I think it could be Mo,' said Wat, throwing his arm dismissively, 'we've got no basis for these accusations. We've no proof.'

'I can take a look at the crime scene,' suggested Van Pelt as he stood up, 'sounds like that's one of the only things we can do right now.

'There has to be a way we can scope the crowd, lure out the killer?' said Kam.

'If it's someone we know we can scope the crowd by holding an event,' suggested Mary, 'karaoke?'

Wat shook his head, 'We'd need something that everyone would turn up to. Then if they don't, we can use that to shortlist. Something that draws everyone together,' he began to think, 'You've got a birthday this week don't you Mary?'

Mary felt a little shocked at the suggestion, 'Yes but what does that have to do with anything?'

'Ahh,' said Kam, 'everyone knows who you are, it would be very unseemly not to appear. Especially as you're leaving soon, we could say it's everyone's chance to say goodbye.'

Mary had her mouth agape, 'honestly? You think people would turn up for me,' at which point she too stood up, 'I see what you're suggesting here but I would not feel comfortable having my name attributed to the notion. Mr Van Pelt, perhaps I can help with observing the crime scene?'

Therin nodded, to which Jordan also got up, 'I'll let you into the common then.'

He didn't look Mary in the eye when he got up which left Mary in the lurch. Van Pelt followed him and that left her with Kam and Wat.

'Perhaps a pub quiz?' suggested Mary, 'I just don't feel it would be appropriate for me to be the face.'

She left it at that and joined Therin and Jordan. The two men walked up to the enclosure without a word passed between them. Mary didn't feel comfortable breaking the silence and so she just kept up. When they reached the enclosure, Jordan let them through under the rope that he'd hung up with a sign that said 'DO NOT ENTER; INVESTION UNDERWAY' and a small '^GATI' underneath it.

Therin looked around the field, 'So this is what you kept it in. Not bad,' he stated, 'where is it now?'

Jordan pointed toward the stable. Rather than leaving him in the open, Jordan and Wat had wrapped a blanket and tarpaulin over him tightly to keep the flies away.

'I've some men who'll take the body away. It's still pretty valuable,' said Van Pelt looking over the size of the body.

Mary couldn't help but feel repulsed at the notion that Van Pelt was still going to sell the beast.

'You mind if we open it up?' asked Van Pelt.

Jordan shrugged and went about unravelling the rope he'd used. When they opened Wesley up again Mary had to look away. Van Pelt crouched close to the creature to see what he could. He followed the blood trail.

CHEER UP WAT

'Cut the neck whilst it was sleeping,' said Van Pelt, 'that's amazing.'

'Amazing?' spat Mary, 'please don't use that word.'

'It is amazing Ms Woods. You don't realise what it took to capture this beast. It senses living beings within a hundred metres and I don't believe the murderer could make a hundred-metre sprint and kill this beast faster than it would've killed the murderer,' said Therin, 'somehow they were able to actually sneak up on this creature without it knowing.'

'Perhaps it wasn't a living being,' suggested Mary, 'you know I'm fairly certain Boz is a zombie.'

'The other thing is that they're vaguely telepathic, it would've known you were going to kill it,' said Therin, 'looks like we've got a handprint from whoever did it.'

'That was me,' said Mary, 'I thought it was straw in the dark and accidentally put my hand in the blood,' she lifted her hand and considered it as if it was still blood-stained.

'You did that twice?' asked Therin.

Mary looked round, 'no, just the once. On his ribs.'

'Someone put their hand to his neck as well,' said Therin, 'right-hand. If that doesn't seem occult…'

'So they were a magic user then,' said Jordan.

'Can't say,' so Van Pelt stood away, 'maybe Wat knows more.'

The three returned back to the pub. Mary finally decided she'd have to broach the sore subject with Jordan so she tapped him lightly as they were walking in and said,

'Jordan I'm sorry, I didn't mean to hurt you,' she said.

Jordan gave a huff, 'if anything it was bad timing,' he said, 'You would've gotten away with it if it weren't for

Wesley dying and all.' Mary smiled at that. 'I know that you didn't hurt the thing.'

'That means a lot,' and the two of them entered the dining room where Kam and Wat were talking across a table.

Van Pelt sat next to Wat and leaned in, Mary and Jordan standing just behind him.

'We got footprints, but I don't know how we'd match those subtly,' Van Pelt explained, 'and we also have a hand-print on his neck. Again, unless we're going to organise finger-painting lessons…'

'Missing bolt cutters, handprints,' Wat listed as if he were naming items on a shopping list, 'it feels like everything's coming apart.'

'At the moment, everyone's a suspect,' said Van Pelt, 'essentially everyone had access. And no one has a good reason to do it.'

'Looks like the party's back on the table,' said Kam.

'We've not got a lot of time,' Wat acknowledged, 'but it could work in helping us narrow down our suspects.'

Mary groaned, 'I understand it's for the greater good but,' she gave Wat a sympathetic look, 'are you going to be okay organising it?'

Wat didn't turn to look at her but stood up. He put his hands on his waist and stretched his back. His dirty blonde hair fell back away from his face. He then reached up and adjusted his waistcoat.

'Yes,' he said. Then he lowered his voice. 'I believe we've already made it apparent that we know that the unicorn is dead. Van Pelt shall have his men take Wesley away and that'll buy us some time. With Van Pelt gone, we'll continue business as normal.

CHEER UP WAT

'Then when Friday comes, we meld with the crowd and see if we can goad the details from every one of their particular whereabouts. It has to be someone who's been staying here, who knows about the common,' and Wat bit his lip.

'Understood, I'll get the staff on it,' said Kam standing up as well.

'I'll get my boys in,' said Van Pelt.

'I'll let you in to retrieve Wesley,' said Jordan.

'And I'll,' began Mary, 'act natural?'

'Marvellous,' stated Wat and dismissed the group.

Mary stuck around, 'Are you sure you're okay Wat?'

His mouth crinkled into a smile but Mary knew it was no more than a mask. She wondered how often, if ever, he dropped it in front of anyone.

'I'm always okay, I have to be,' he said under his breath, 'listen, about what we were talking about earlier this month, I think you're right. The pub should close.'

Mary's soul shifted gear, 'You can't!'

Wat gave a weak shrug, 'with this, things are dangerous. I can't continue to operate if everyone's at risk.'

'You could've closed months ago! Why now of all times?' pleaded Mary against her own will. She couldn't believe what she was saying, 'You can't throw in the towel!'

'Because before I was the only person at risk! I could handle that. Not this, not my daughter, not my patrons,' he gave a defeated sigh, 'this was always my uncle's pub and it always will be. But I'm not him. My dad taught me everything I know. He was an explorer and loved to find the new and undiscovered.

'Me, I just wish I had a better handle on what I've already got.'

Mary's Birthday

Mary eyed the banner with distaste. Rob had a nail gun in hand as he raised the message 'Happy Birthday Mary' in bright lettering. Two thoughts rolled through her head; one, she absolutely hated celebrating her birthday, and two, this was a little underhand to use her birthday as a way to notice anyone missing or acting suspicious. She had her arms crossed subconsciously so when Kam tapped her, she suddenly dropped them and a smile spread on her face.

'Yes sorry,' Mary said.

'Just enjoy yourself,' said Kam, 'this day is for you.'

'Indeed!' came Wat's call, 'Mary I don't want you to worry, I've planned every little thing.'

'Oh I can see, the decorations are going well,' she said.

The lunchtime crowd was watching Rob as he went about putting up the other decorations that Wat had given him. She gave him a smile to let him know she appreciated it and he just shrugged before sending a few more nails into the woodwork. The image of

TALES FROM THE KING GEORGE

Feathers' head turning slightly, popped up in her peripheral vision.

Wat circled around her, exclaiming, 'Not only decorations but food too.' He was moving towards the kitchen so Mary followed. When he opened the door, Mary gasped.

A giant of a man was putting the finishing touches to an enormous cake that was sitting on a trolley at the end of the row of counters. The man was so tall and big, his chef's hat was crushed into the small gap between the ceiling and his head. His face had stubble and his eyes were beady and unforgiving. When the giant looked down on Mary, there was no discernible emotion on his face; she couldn't tell if he was pleased or annoyed to see her.

'Wojciech,' she said, her hand pressed to her chest, as she realised who this was.

The giant grunted at the sound of his name, and spoke with a harsh Polish accent, 'You want I should make it bigger?'

'No no it's perfect Wojciech, thank you,' said Wat in response, 'he's been working on it all day.'

Mary was astounded and rounded the cake but, as she tried to admire it, she couldn't help but stare at Wojciech and the size of him. Wojciech noticed her staring and grunted again, 'Yes I am big, but cake is big too yes?'

Mary nodded. His voice was as untinged with emotion as his face was.

'Oh did I never get around to introducing you to Wojciech?' asked Wat.

'Everyone kept saying it was a bad time.'

'All time is bad time,' said Wojciech, 'I cook without distraction.'

MARY'S BIRTHDAY

'And he cooks brilliantly. Kam is always jealous when he's on shift but today we've got them both! Of course, Kam is just here for the festivities, Wojciech will be our main chef,' explained Wat and patted Wojciech on the back of his thigh.

'Kam cooks hot. I cook meat,' said Wojciech and he moved to the other side of the kitchen as if to prepare something else.

Mary watched with a slight nervousness as he did so. Wat put an arm around her and lead her into the dining room;

'Like I say, everything's covered.'

'Thank you, Wat,' she said, 'have you noticed anyone missing so far?'

'I haven't seen much of Tilly, but that's no different from usual. I haven't seen No around recently but I'd expect that may be because of…' to which Wat trailed off.

Mary ignored the feeling of sadness that attempted to creep into her head, 'okay so the plan is just to interact with as many people as possible and suss out the bad egg,' she said.

'Yes it all seems a little,' and Wat searched for the word, his grin disappearing, 'distrusting.'

'Are you going to tell everyone about the closure too?'

'That can wait. Today's a celebration,' and he left Mary to go back into the kitchen.

Mary remained in the dining room, thinking. They'd discussed putting the pub on the market and severances for the staff. Wat was going to tell the staff of the pub's closure before he proceeded with any of the paperwork and solicitors. This also meant talking to Niamh again, which Mary was not looking forward to.

Neo passed by bringing some dishes to the kitchen from empty tables, 'hey Mary, you excited about tonight?' she asked.

'Oh yes, colour me stoked,' Mary replied, throwing a thumbs up at her.

* * *

Later that night, the pub felt more alive than it had been in a while. In fact, it felt just as packed as it had been for Halloween which was an achievement for Mary. The drinks were pouring, the food was everywhere, and Mary had found herself talking to Boz and Jarrett, the designated bartenders for the barroom. Van Pelt was at the counter with an eye around the room. There were some people she didn't recognise, but it was mostly staff from the pub and the regulars who'd seen her, and the regulars who just came to the pub every night regardless of whatever event they said was happening.

Eventually, Mary found that someone had caught her eye - it was No. He was sitting in the other room, talking to Lauren as far as she could see until he noticed that Mary was looking at him. Mary immediately threw her gaze elsewhere and met Jarrett's eyes that seemed to question her.

'You alright Mary?' he asked.

'It's No, he's over there,' she said.

'Ooh, let's get him over here then!' said Boz and threw her hand up to call him over, 'who's that with him?'

'Lauren?' suggested Mary.

'It looks like Jo's at that table as well,' said Boz, 'he's not coming over, he's shaking his head.'

'Jo!?' said Mary and whirled around to see that Jo was indeed laughing and had her arm on No's.

MARY'S BIRTHDAY

She couldn't help but fixate upon this before she turned back to the counter and Jarrett took the hint. In five seconds Mary had a shot of sambuca in front of her. It was gone before Boz could protest.

'I thought he didn't pay her a second glance,' muttered Mary.

'Well looks like he has no choice now,' said Jarrett.

'I don't get it, he liked me, didn't he? We all saw it,' said Mary.

'I saw it,' said Boz, 'what happened, didn't you two go on a date or something?'

'Yeah they did,' said Jarrett and motioned to cut the conversation off to Boz.

But Boz ended up continuing, confused, 'Did it not go well?'

'I said I'd be leaving in December and he got weird about it. He said he was leaving too, but would stay if I stayed. I said I'm not staying for him,' Mary groaned, 'I don't know, I was hoping he'd say he'd come to London to visit, but he didn't say that. He just said "Ah".'

'Ah?'

'Ah,' repeated Mary, 'I like him, but I guess I messed it up.' Jarrett passed another shot to her.

'He's coming over now,' said Boz.

'What?'

'Jo's bringing him over.'

Mary turned around to see Jo with No in her arm. With a smirk on her face, she stopped in front of Mary and said, 'he wants to talk to you.'

No nodded. He was dressed up now: his long coat was gone and his scarf was still around his neck but it acted more as a cravat. His face was fully visible and he took off his glasses to reveal stoic grey eyes. Then he looked into hers and began to talk.

'I'm sorry. I shouldn't have assumed that you would wait for me like I wanted to wait for you.'

'You know London isn't that far, right?' said Mary, 'it's not as if I'd be gone forever.'

'No I know,' said No, and he realised that everyone was watching the two of them. He motioned with his head to talk to her alone.

She obliged and stood up from the bar. The two of them walked into the gallery and No led them into the courtyard. It was empty and not even the lamp was on.

'I like you,' said No. Mary opened her mouth as if to say something but No continued, 'I get busy during the year travelling. It's pretty lonely. And when I'm with you, I don't feel so alone.

'I've decided I've never felt this way about anyone before. Not that I can remember and I remember a lot,' said No, 'you've made my time here feel beyond anything I've ever felt.'

Mary suddenly felt a pit in her stomach, 'That's very sweet No.'

He took her hands in his and continued, 'I know this might sound rash but you've made me feel something special. Do you feel the same?'

'I definitely feel something No,' she said and squeezed his hands, 'I'm just concerned I don't want you to fall too hard for me. I'm away a lot, I'm not that interesting, I'm a little too strict and ordered and-'

'And that's what I love.'

The lamp lit up and suddenly the doors to the courtyard opened up. In rolled Wat with the cake and a crowd of guests. A cheer rose from the crowd and then

MARY'S BIRTHDAY

a song of Happy Birthday began to waft on everyone's voices.

Mary suddenly felt a strange feeling wash over her and tears welled. She realised that she'd never had such a fuss made about her birthday and the fact that this many people cared about her enough to do it - well it brought her to tears. Her hands went to her face and No wrapped an arm across her shoulders, squeezing her. Kam stepped forward with a knife held up, ready to cut the cake. As the song reached its climax, Wat began the applause before passing her a flute of champagne from off the trolley. He then lifted one of his own and shouted 'Speech!'

Soon the crowd was following the call and 'speech' was being repeated all around the courtyard. Mary lifted her own glass and then took a moment to think about what to say. Perhaps it would be best to sum up how she felt about the Mad King in all?

'Thank you, everyone, thank you so much for everything, the party, the company, the drinks…

'I guess I should also thank you for showing me that there's more to this world than what meets our eye. I can't say just how much my life has changed since I've started working here and every single one of you people have been a positive influence on my life,'

She reached up for a tear and wiped it away.

'I'm going to miss you all when I leave, I-' and Mary couldn't stop herself from sobbing.

Lauren, who had been in the front row grabbed her by the hands and assured her it would be alright, whilst the crowd awed and applauded.

No squeezed Mary, reminding her that he was still there. She turned her face to him and leant in. He took the hint and kissed her. Wat grabbed the knife from

Kam, who was too distracted, and began cutting the cake which was met with a round of laughter. The music suddenly increased again and when No released her, Mary was on cloud nine and flying higher.

'Who wants a piece?' shouted Wat.

* * *

The cake ended up in the centre of the barroom, open for anyone to take a slice. Mary ended up talking to almost every person she'd ever met - Duncan, Seamus, Jarrett, Neo, Boz, Kam, (not Wojciech for obvious reasons), Jo, Lauren, Blue who'd also joined the party, Jordan, Van Pelt, Wat, Rob and even Sebastian the rat, which Wat had let out to rummage for some pickings. But then someone else piqued her interest at the corner of the room. Dressed in a blue formal dress and wearing her blonde hair in curls, Niamh was laughing with Wat once more. Mary leant to Jarrett to point it out.

'I thought Niamh was gone,' she said.

'No, she's still around,' said Jarrett, 'I think they had a falling out but she's forgiven him.'

Mary felt a strange feeling of confidence well in her. Maybe it had been the cake cutting or maybe the liquor had finally hit her but before she knew it, she was marching her way across the barroom to their table. Wat happily greeted her;

'Mary! Enjoying your night?' he asked.

'Wat, what is she doing here?' she asked.

Niamh gasped, 'I'm sorry, am I intruding?' Her words came out slimy and tainted.

'I thought things were over between you two,' Mary continued.

Wat coughed, 'It was only a little fight.'

'You can't still be falling for her trick, can you?'

MARY'S BIRTHDAY

'What trick?' said Niamh, sounding offended.

'She's using you to get the pub! She just wants you to sell it so she can get the commission!'

'Well obviously,' chuckled Niamh, 'not the "using" part, but you realise how much I can get as a commission from this place? Anyway, I thought we wanted the same thing here?'

'Maybe at first,' said Mary, causing Wat to give her a confused look, 'Wat, Niamh hired me to make a predetermined conclusion; I was told I would be paid if I told you to close.'

Wat stood up quietly, 'I don't understand.'

'Niamh paid the agency I work for to ensure that, regardless of my evaluation, I would tell you to sell. And I was going to, but I changed my mind. You need to stay open! Regardless of what anyone else wants or thinks, you have to remain open. You can do it! Honestly, it wouldn't be too much of a stretch it just-'

'Wait, Niamh hired you?' Wat asked, backtracking.

'No I did not, I never did anything of the sort!' shouted Niamh standing up, 'what kind of money do you think I have!?'

'The game is up Niamh, I know it was you.'

'And I can tell you you're wrong! I certainly had no part in bringing you here,' said Niamh, 'I thought you would make it easier but you've been against me at every turn.'

The pub was quiet again.

'What do you mean you had no part? Someone hired me to shut the Mad King down,' stated Mary.

'It wasn't me,' said Niamh, holding her hands up in denial.

'You wanted me to shut down?' Wat asked Mary softly, and Mary saw the look of hurt on Wat's face.

The patrons in the bar were now picking up the conversation going on and they began to murmur. Calls for confirmation came; 'is the pub closing?' 'Are you really closing up, Wat?'

Mary turned to them all, 'no it won't! We can make it work, there may be some sacrifices made and some modifications, but the establishment doesn't need to close. I put my reputation on it; I'll stake my entire career on it,' she turned back to Wat, 'Don't sell Wat, please don't.'

Wat didn't answer. His face was contorted into confusion and distrust.

Niamh stepped up, 'I should never have trusted you,' she stated coldly.

'And he should trust you? After what you did to Mona?' said Mary.

Niamh scowled at her, 'Mona?'

'The spider.'

Niamh's eyes lit up and pointed her finger at Mary, 'I knew it! I knew you took that spider from me. She was going to make me famous!'

'At what cost?'

'It was a talking spider!'

'SHE is my friend.'

Niamh began to advance toward Mary menacingly.

'I can't believe you, waltzing in here and acting as if you're the big boss. And all this time you were working the same angle as I was! What about me? Why don't I get to be involved? Why do you exclude me? Is it because I'm pretty? Am I too "dumb" to understand? Do you think I can't keep secrets?'

The pub had become entirely silent as Niamh demanded an answer from everyone.

'It's not like that,' Wat started to try and say.

MARY'S BIRTHDAY

'Is that why you couldn't tell me about the unicorn either!?' Niamh spat.

Mary locked on, 'how do you know about Wesley?' she gasped upon realisation, 'it was you who broke into the common!?'

'It was the only way to find out!'

'Why did you kill him?' moaned Mary.

'Kill him? I didn't kill the thing, I just saw it and took a bunch of pictures,' said Niamh, 'so I had proof this time!'

'You broke into the common?' said Wat, his voice wavering.

It was the same betrayal all over again.

'You don't tell me anything! The spider, the unicorn; what else are you hiding? And why are you hiding it from me?' shouted Niamh.

No one said anything. That was until Feathers turned his head and said out loud; 'probably because you're a nutjob?'

Niamh screamed. Her legs gave out but Wat caught her as she scrambled backward. Mary sighed out loud. 'Really? Now of all times, you talk?'

'What is that?' screamed Niamh in terror.

'Calm down,' said Wat.

'No,' stuttered Niamh and she stood up, 'I don't trust you anymore! What the hell is going on?'

'You've got poor taste in women Wat,' said Sebastian, who was now on the floor around Wat's table.

Niamh screamed again, banging into the cake trolley, causing the cake knife to fall to the ground right beside her. When she saw the knife, she grabbed it roughly and pointed it directly at Sebastian. Seeing the threat, he scampered away.

Niamh scrambled to her feet, brandishing the knife around the room defensively. A few of the patrons backed up to the other side of the room while the staff emerged from the ranks to help get a handle on the situation.

Wat kept his focus on Niamh. His voice was low as if all his emotions had been sapped. 'Niamh, give me the knife,' he spoke.

She regarded him. 'Tell me the truth! What is going on!?' she demanded.

Wat sighed, 'We try to reveal it slower than this, but this pub is special.'

'What the fuck does that mean!?'

'It means I sometimes hire special people, and my patrons are special people too, looking for an escape. Looking for sanctuary – a safe place. Please put the knife down,' he said, reaching for it.

'No, get away!' she said, 'this is crazy, that puppet talked! That spider talked! That rat talked, everything talks! Do the chairs talk, is this Beauty and the fucking Beast!?'

Everyone stepped back, apart from Mary.

'Please Niamh, we're not trying to trick you. We won't hurt you.'

'That's right,' said Neo, stepping forward too, 'we're sorry we left you out, but it wasn't on purpose.'

'It was for your own safety,' said Jarrett.

Neo, Boz and Jarret stepped forward creating a circle around her, barricading her from leaving.

'Let's just talk about it alright? We'll tell you everything,' said Mary, 'and you can know exactly what's been going on.'

'Everything, I want to know everything,' stuttered Niamh, 'I don't want any more secrets.' she sniffed.

MARY'S BIRTHDAY

'We promise,' said Mary, who threw her hand at the staff to keep them from getting closer. Instead, she alone approached Niamh reaching out slowly.

Niamh just watched her but she didn't stop her from getting closer. Niamh's makeup was a mess, her mascara was running from her eyes; open wide in terror. Mary looked past it and saw a scared woman; she had a hand on the knife's handle now. Niamh sobbed. Mary gave her a weak smile and looked at Wat. He didn't look at her at all. When she looked back at the staff, their faces were at ease but they still looked concerned.

Boz stepped slowly forward, 'Now let's give up the kni-' but she lost her footing and tripped.

She fell forward into Niamh who in response lifted her hands. Mary lost grip of the knife, letting Niamh's hand and the knife dig into Boz's chest.

Mary screamed in surprise as Boz and Niamh went down to the floor. Niamh let go of the knife, she rolled Boz over and her hands were everywhere as if she was trying to grab Boz's soul before it left. Boz was paralysed by shock, eyes wide open, uttering a gasp. Niamh finally ran into Wat's arms, shrieking 'I'm sorry I'm sorry I didn't mean to hurt anyone I'm sorry.'

Instantly Kam and Mary were at Boz's side. Mary initially grabbed the knife but Kam pushed her away, 'no we might cause more damage if we try and remove it!'

But there was no blood.

Kam looked over Boz but in the end ripped open her uniform, displaying her chest and the knife and handle sticking out of it. No blood.

Boz came to from her paralysis and saw what they could see; that the knife was stuck in her. And here she was. Still alive. No blood. No pain. She muttered 'dammit.'

Everyone's mouths were agape. No one said a thing for the longest period that anything had gone unsaid. Until Mary stood up and pointed at her.

'I knew it!'

* * *

It had all calmed down by closing. Boz had been sewn up and explained that, yes, she was undead. Yes, she couldn't feel most types of pain but she'd learnt to mimic it. No, she didn't eat brains. And yes, she would apologise to Niamh for giving her such a scare.

But Niamh had left after calming down. Wat had taken her home. Everyone agreed it was for the best.

Everyone went home, the celebrations couldn't continue as they were. Mary helped to tidy up but none of the staff would look at her properly. They kept their responses brief and she didn't try to get much more out of them. She'd broken everyone's trust.

Wat eventually returned, and when he did Mary attempted to talk to him but he held up a hand. He didn't want to hear it. He left the staff to finish cleaning up.

Rob was the first of them to try talking to Mary.

'What did they offer you?' he asked, the anger sitting delicately behind the words.

Mary felt withdrawn, 'A lot of money. But I won't do it.'

'You were gonna.'

'Yes but before I knew everything about this place.'

'My dad thought you were really great you know? He thought that he'd convinced the best accountant in the country to come and help him out of sheer goodwill. He wouldn't stop raving about it, he thought you were

MARY'S BIRTHDAY

the best thing that was going to happen to this pub. He thought with you onboard he'd never close down,' to which Rob shook his head, 'turns out, none of that was true.'

Mary didn't have anything to say to that. She watched him leave hoping she'd think of something that would make it okay.

But there was nothing.

Shadows

Mary was sitting in the office. She had papers open and she was trying to track down a transaction from maybe two years ago. But the night had worn on without her realising. It was only when Mona piped up and said, 'Mary, are you going to sleep at all today? It's past one,' that Mary realised just how engrossed she'd become.

She checked what time it was exactly on the computer and it hit her that she'd spent the whole evening down in the office. She hadn't dared return upstairs. No one would talk to her. Everyone had turned a cold shoulder to her now.

'I'll just finish up here,' she said.

She finished it up after a half-hour. She left the office and entered the kitchen where she made herself a quick sandwich and headed up the stairs to the reception.

It was deathly quiet. She could hear every step she made. She poked her head into the barroom just to see it. Feathers glowed a pale blue in the darkness.

'Feathers,' she greeted softly.

The puppet blinked, 'Ello lass.'

'Up late?' she said.

'I dinnae sleep,' he replied, 'I cannae.'

Mary nodded, 'what's it like? Being dead?'

The puppet rolled his eyes and static seemed to rumble through his speaker, though it was probably an attempt at a sigh without having lungs, 'ye realise that the time ye had alive was enough, and everyfin beyond that is borin. It's like constantly waitin fe ye to hit port.

'Except I winna. I affte sail these seas eternally. It's maddenin to know that yarna getting any closer to yer destination and yet ye man the deck as if you may just run into it at the last second.'

Mary approached him and sat at the counter, 'what were you like when you were alive?'

The puppet gave her a look that made Mary think he had never been asked the question before, 'I wissa pirate.'

'What was that like?'

'Compared to now, a lot mo active. I scrubbed decks, manned sails, and sometimes we'd plunder. Sometimes we'd get a little stock and then we'd sail into port, sell it all for some coin and then spend it all in one night.

'Do you miss it?'

'It's quieter now,' mused Feathers, 'I dinna have to worry about being hungry, tired or bleedin. The company's worse though.'

Mary laughed at this, 'You prefer the company of pirates?'

'Ye all talk of these phones and internet, I've never eard of it. Ye all talk of other sides of the world as if it's all known. There's no mo' exploration. No mo' "what do you think" just "what is".'

SHADOWS

Mary nodded, 'I understand,' she thought back to what Wat had said, 'would you prefer being "dissipated" then?'

'It's where I belon,' he said, 'At least let me back out to wander the earth?'

'You mean, turn you off?'

'And set me free, yeah.'

Mary chewed her lip, 'I'll talk to Wat tomorrow. I can't do anything without him knowing.'

Feathers closed his wooden eyelids, 'I appreciate that lass.'

Mary got up off the stool and was about to head to bed when the front door began to rattle. She stopped where she was and waited to see who was trying to get it. Trying was not the right word, there was a click in the lock. Then the door opened, gently.

It was Snow. She peered inside and when she saw Mary she jumped.

'Snow?' said Mary, 'you're back.'

Snow ducked behind the door for a second, looking back, before she eased herself inside and closed the door behind her. Mary wasn't sure what to say. The girl didn't look upset, but she didn't look happy either. Her eyes were wide open and her breathing was fast. Mary could almost hear the young girl's heartbeat. She seemed scared.

'Are you okay?' asked Mary, 'did you run here?'

'Yes,' answered Snow, a little uncertain.

'Do you want me to get your dad?' asked Mary.

Snow shook her head quickly, 'no, no, I-' she caught herself, 'Ms Woods, I'm sorry about the club with Kam. I didn't mean to hurt you.'

Mary smiled sweetly, 'Listen I want to talk to you. Your father told me about who your mum was,' hearing this Snow frowned slightly, 'I understand that you're upset not knowing her on a personal level.' Snow's frown continued. 'Your father loves you a lot, he's willing to do whatever he can to make you happy. He's been worried sick since you left. He's trying so hard to fill the gap she's left on you and he wants you to forgive him.'

'What do you know of my mum,' whispered Snow, almost too quiet for Mary to hear her, 'you can't know more than me and I don't know anything.'

'I know she was a powerful wind goddess. And I know you have that same potential inside you,' explained Mary.

'Did you know that one day I'll be the North Wind here in England?' said Snow, 'did he tell you that? Did Kam tell you that? One day I'm going to have to take my place as some goddess rushing around in winter,' the floor began to creak and a cold draught blew from the doorway where she stood.

Mary was a little taken aback, 'no they didn't say that.'

'One day I'll be like No, I'll be a shell for the North Wind. That sounds fun doesn't it?' said Snow sarcastically, and the floor cracked as frost appeared on the wood.

Mary would've asked her what she meant by this but she knew it wasn't the time or place. Instead, she stepped back and raised a hand, 'Snow, is this what this is about? Is that what O'Nerry's telling you?'

'He's showing me I'm not limited to whatever Kam tells me. I have great power,' and she lifted her hands, 'I can do things beyond imagination. I don't have to listen to what people tell me to do. Especially you!'

SHADOWS

Mary stood a little straighter, 'that's true you don't. You choose,' Mary raised an eyebrow, 'so have you chosen O'Nerry?'

Snow crinkled up her nose and marched toward the reception. Rather than go in, she slammed her hand up against the wall, onto the light switch. The lights came on. Mary looked around, a little blinded by the sudden glare and confused about what Snow was doing. She lowered an arm as she saw Snow pull the door open. She was glaring directly at Mary as she did it.

As the door opened, the shadow of O'Nerry draped its way over the floor reaching her feet. It wrapped itself around her own shadow and Mary felt herself bound together, unable to move.

'Mary! We meet again!' announced O'Nerry.

He was standing in the doorway. He waited until he was sure she couldn't escape and then strutted into the pub. Snow flocked to his side, arm around his, still staring Mary down angrily.

'What do you want O'Nerry, what more could you possibly want?' Mary spat.

O'Nerry walked right up to her and stroked her cheek.

'I'm here for the thread. That's all I want, it's all I ever wanted,' he said.

Mary narrowed her eyes, 'what?'

'The thread that Wat's been hiding here! You're his accountant, Mary, surely you've found it amongst his assets, right? That's what he's paying you for?' he lifted his arms theatrically, then stopped to whisper into Snow's ear. She then skipped from his arm into reception.

'I've not heard of any thread,' said Mary.

O'Nerry put a hand to his head, 'Alright I'll bite. So, turns out some busy-body wasn't too happy about people who could detach their shadows,' Mary felt her bonds tighten, 'so they made a thread that could be used to permanently reattach them. Turns out that Wat has the bloody thing here somewhere. The key word is somewhere,' he then edged in closer, 'strangely enough, I'd feel a lot better if I had it. Keep it close to home you know?'

'Is that it?' said Mary, 'and you think Wat would hand it over for Snow?'

'Snow?' said O'Nerry, 'oh you think this is some kind of handover? No no, Snow is with me because she wants to be! I keep her around because she's useful, and a bit of fun if you know what I meant,' and he grinned – Mary felt like vomiting.

'You think he'll just give it to you then?' asked Mary.

'The plan was to just take it! Can't find the thing though, Snow has been trying for months,' said O'Nerry, 'I thought when you got here, I could convince you to help find it but you were not in a negotiating mood…'

'That was a negotiation?' laughed Mary, 'you're pathetic. I can't believe it. I bet that's why you murdered Wesley too, trying to scare us into giving us the thread?'

'Wesley?'

'The unicorn!' said Mary, annoyed she had to clarify.

O'Nerry's grin widened and he tilted his head. He shook his head. Mary reared her head up in disbelief. No, he had to.

'You had a unicorn?'

Mary's heart dropped, 'you didn't know?'

'That's a shame, if I had known beforehand I could've used its power. Unicorn souls are incredibly powerful, you know.'

'You can't just use someone's soul.'

'No that's right, but what no one tells you is that you can force a soul to bind to you. It's not a pleasant experience by far, you want to know how it's done? I've got some time,' and O'Nerry sat down, 'I'm sure you know a soul binds to an idea it identifies with a lot when it passes on. The easy part is releasing a soul,' and O'Nerry traced a line on his neck, 'but how do you make it identify so intensely with yourself?'

Mary didn't answer, she just stared him down. He laughed.

'I'll tell you. You need a powerful emotional connection. Family members attach to family often because of that. But you know what else is a powerful emotion? Anger. Vengeance.'

O'Nerry leaned in, 'You make that person hate you, you force them to despise you, and then you kill them. They pass on with an unbridled vengeance directed to you and it only goes towards making you stronger! Pretty horrific right?'

'That's awful,' said Mary.

'Oh it can be, torture goes a long way. I myself don't do that,' said O'Nerry standing up, just as Snow entered the room again, 'I prefer keeping people alive. People are much more useful when they're alive.'

'I've frozen all the doors shut,' said Snow.

'Good, then I'll go into the attic and have a look around,' said O'Nerry, 'we'll leave shadow here to hold Mary.'

'Oh will you now?' said the ghostly voice of Feathers, 'and what if I have something to say about it.'

Intrigued, O'Nerry approached the doll, 'And what are you?'

'I'm your worst nightmare sonny,' said Feathers.

O'Nerry picked up Feathers with two hands and jostled him, 'What are you, some expensive toy?'

He looked at Snow who shrugged, 'I remember he appeared before I left.'

'Do you have an off switch? So I can shut you up?' said O'Nerry.

Feathers' eyes rocked side-to-side quickly, 'no.'

O'Nerry laughed to himself. Mary struggled to look round to see what he was doing, 'you leave Feathers alone!'

O'Nerry rotated Feathers and looked at his back. Sure enough, there was a big old switch. 'Oh, what have we here!'

'Don't touch that!' said Feathers, 'or I'll knock your block off!'

'I'll hold you to that,' said O'Nerry and flicked the switch.

Feathers' eyes closed. O'Nerry set the puppet on the counter.

'Well, that was eas-' but before he could finish his sentence a bottle hit him round the face and sent him to the ground.

Snow screamed in shock, 'No!'

Mary realised what had happened and attempted to struggle at her bonds. She felt the shadow kick her out and onto the floor. She coughed a little but she could see the shadow bending and darting around on the floor. It shifted and moved, narrowing, running up onto the wall and onto the ceiling as if chased by something. As if chased by Feathers.

SHADOWS

She had her moment now, she needed to wake someone. Anyone. Mary got to her feet and raced into the reception. Snow tried to stop her, throwing her foot against the ground and causing the wood to freeze.

Mary felt the steps down to the basement freeze over and she lost her footing. She slipped and fell backwards, thumping down on her rear. When she reached the ground, she scrambled to get back up. She could see Wat's door at the end, there was ice around the frame. She needed to get him up. She pelted as fast as she could towards the door and swung her shoulder in front of her. When she collided with the door, she hit it with all the force she could muster. Ice shattered and she fell back to the ground.

'Wat!' she shouted 'Wat, I need you out here!'

Snow was gone, she wasn't following her anymore. Mary realised that she and O'Nerry were still in here and were going to get that thread. She had to stop them, right? She had to stop O'Nerry for sure. She had to stop Snow. She had to help Feathers. They couldn't just barge in here and take what they wanted!

What she needed was the thread. It was the only way to stop O'Nerry.

She rushed toward the office. She had to have some record of it. She flicked on the light and struggled to the desk – the bruise on her legs was starting to feel worse for wear.

Mona spun down from the ceiling, awoken by the ruckus.

'Mary? You're back-'

'Mona, did you ever see anything about a thread? Any documents about a black thread?'

'No, I don't think so, why?'

TALES FROM THE KING GEORGE

'O'Nerry's here and he wants it. He's going to rip this pub to shreds to find it,' said Mary, 'but if I can find it before him I can use it to stop him.'

'How?'

'Don't know yet. First I need to find it.'

Mona spun down to the filing cabinet, 'you got any clues?'

'No,' said Mary, until she thought about it, 'O'Nerry said he was going to the attic. Saul's junk was up in the attic. Maybe Saul was the one who had it and that's why I've not read any documents about it!' She slammed the filing cabinet shut.

When she got out of the office, Wat's door was rhythmically shaking until it burst open in a shower of icicles. Wat stood dishevelled in a dressing gown.

'Mary? What's going on?' he ordered.

'Wat! Where did your uncle hide his things? Are all of them in the attic?' she asked quickly.

'Yes, I think, why?' said Wat.

'No time, O'Nerry's up there searching for the black thread!' said Mary, running back to the stairs up into reception.

'O'Nerry? Thread? What are you talking about?'

'O'Nerry's here! With Snow!' Mary ducked into the barroom. There was no sign of O'Nerry, Snow or the shadow. 'Feathers?' she called casually.

When she got no answer she ran back the other way, through reception and up the stairs. She could hear loud bangs now and crashes. On the next floor, some bangs were coming from people's doors as they realised they were trapped in their own rooms. The rest came from up in the attic. Wat finally caught up with Mary as she got to the ladder to the attic.

'Mary wait!' shouted Wat.

SHADOWS

One of the doors at the end of the corridor burst open into shards of wood. Out stepped No wrapped up in a dressing gown and pyjamas. He looked irritated.

'No!' said Mary, 'we need your help. O'Nerry's-' she looked up and jumped out of the way as a suitcase dropped down the ladder and smashed against the floor. The contents fell over the carpet and rolled around. Wat cursed under his breath. He ascended the ladder as fast as he could.

No reached Mary and helped her up. She checked herself, noting the cut in her leg.

'Mary, are you okay? I'll get a bandage,' said No.

Mary grabbed him by the arm, 'no, I'm fine,' and she pulled herself up, 'Let's get up there and help Wat.'

No lifted her up so she could stand. Determined, Mary got onto the ladder and entered the attic without a pause for breath. No was close behind.

In the attic, lights were on again. But the shadow was holding Wat down on the ground. Snow watched him, terrified. O'Nerry was kneeling down close to him, speaking in his ear. When he saw No and Mary had arrived, he stood up straight. Suddenly the shadow whipped back to O'Nerry's side.

'Ahh, No I see you've joined the fight,' said O'Nerry.

No stood up above the hole. Mary took to his right. She wasn't sure what she was going to do but she wasn't going to stand idly. It'd at least give O'Nerry one more opponent.

'Looks like you may have met your match though,' said O'Nerry proudly, 'Snow? Could you show Mr No the window?'

Snow threw her hands up in front of her. A torrent of wind surged against both Mary and No. Mary felt herself being flung up and backwards into a mannequin and knocking into an antique globe. No felt the same effect but for longer, the wind carrying him further and higher up and into the small window pane in the wall. He cracked against it but it was too small, he slipped down the wall onto a pile of cardboard boxes and they fell apart as he fell onto them.

Mary lifted herself up and felt her head, knowing she'd smacked it hard on the floor. She saw blood on her fingertips – only a little. She got back up to see No also rising up to his feet.

'It's time to sleep, little one,' he said loudly. Snow stared him down defiantly. 'Nerr-' Snow immediately threw her arms up and greater gusts of wind blew but this time encircling No and Mary. She couldn't hear a thing, the roar of the wind too loud, drowning out everything. She couldn't move, the chill winds blew around her.

Then she saw the snowflakes begin to form and she felt her body temperature lowering. She lost her footing and careened onto the floor. When she tried to get up it was too cold and the snow was filling the air, blinding her. It was just white. She crawled in a direction, reaching out for something, anything. Her teeth started chattering and she couldn't feel her hands. It was as if she'd been sent to another world, to the Arctic. She wrapped her arms around herself, willing for it to stop. She attempted to cry out.

'Snow, please!' she shouted, 'Snow!'

And then it stopped because someone was choking from the other side of the room; the side where O'Nerry had been holding Wat. Richard has his fingers tightly pressing into Wat's neck, lifting the man the full breadth of his arm which ended up leaving Wat an inch off the floor. Wat struggled, grasping at Richard's arm, his legs jerking out but too tired to lift up and cause Richard damage.

'Stop, don't hurt him!' shouted Snow, breaking her concentration, 'Dad, just tell us where the thread is!'

Mary was still shivering, she stayed in her foetal position on the ground, listening to them. It wasn't long before No was by her side again and he wrapped his gown around her to warm her. He looked like he'd been hit by the same storm.

Wat gurgled with fingers squeezing his throat, 'What thread?'

'Don't play dumb with me. I'm tired, Stone,' said Richard, breathing out heavily, 'the black thread. The shadow thread.'

'The shadow thread?'

'You know what I'm talking about!'

'You want the shadow thread?' said Wat, and he began to laugh, or at least wheeze, 'I can't believe it, you're here for the thread!?'

'What thread?' reiterated No.

'There is no thread. There was no thread! I made it up,' laughed Wat.

'Don't play games with me,' said Richard, tightening his grip. It almost caused Wat to laugh louder.

'You really believe that I had the thread, a thread that has the power to bind a detached shadow back to its owner? Honestly Dick, how many people do you know in the world whose shadow is a free being?' laughed out Wat, 'I made it up years ago to keep you away. If I had known it would've only drawn you here I would never have done it,' and his coughing turned to a slow wheeze, 'that's ironic,'

Richard eyed him before he dropped him and Wat instantly collapsed into a fit of gasps and coughs.

'Honestly,' he rasped, 'you really broke into my home and kidnapped my daughter to get that thread?'

Richard had a look of disbelief etched over his face, but behind it were the flames of rage licking around his eyes.

'He didn't kidnap me,' Snow spoke up, 'I love him and he loves me.'

Hearing her voice, Richard turned around to her. Mary's heart dropped. She could see the rage being directed towards her.

'You didn't know this?'

Snow was unprepared for his reaction, 'I had no idea, he never told me-'

'He never told you? Is that your excuse?' and O'Nerry advanced on her.

No was back on his feet ready to react. Wat was still on the floor trying to catch his breath.

'I can't believe you, you had me breaking in here? You couldn't have just asked him? You knew that's what I wanted, you couldn't have just asked your pops here, "Hey Dad! Do you have a shadow thread anywhere"!?'

'Richard, I love-'

O'Nerry's hand flew through the air and ended up sending Snow down to the floor. Mary gasped. No was about to run at him, but O'Nerry's shadow found its way around him. With the ounce of strength Mary recovered, she lifted herself and crawled toward Snow.

'Don't you touch her!' shouted Wat as he pushed on his knee to lift himself up, 'you get away from her.

'I can't believe this,' spat Richard, looking around the room before throwing his arms up in defeat, 'you're no use to me now. You were a good little fuck but I've wasted my time here.'

He whirled to face Wat who had his fists up again. He was bruised badly, his face swollen, but he was prepared to try and land some hits. But Richard was sullen and his eyelids lowered and he sighed deeply to show he was disappointed.

'Yeah, it is ironic Wat.'

O'Nerry shook his head. He walked past Snow without a look and passed Mary to the stairs. He let himself down without another word. When he was gone, his shadow released No and dropped him to his knees. Then it disappeared with O'Nerry down the attic ladder.

Snow was paralysed, the girl gulped and stared at where Richard's feet had been. She was breathing fast. Mary reached her and tried her best to soothe her, rubbing her back. Wat fell to a knee and crawled to her. Snow didn't dare raise her eyes but Wat pushed his arms around her and pulled her up to him under the armpits as if she was just a little girl again. The tear ducts in her eyes gave way and water ran down his back, solidifying as they went until he had icicles forming at the end of his shirt. She stuffed her face in his shoulder and muffled the sounds of her broken heart.

* * *

Wat considered Feathers' doll. He'd propped it back where it was but the familiar pale blue glow was gone.

'Where do you think he's gone?' asked Mary.

No had his arm around her, rubbing her back.

'I expect he's just somewhere else,' said Wat, 'the door was open.'

'He helped me Wat, I think he deserves it,' reasoned Mary.

Wat nodded in agreement and a smile appeared on his face, 'he can have it. I've got my little girl back. A little broken maybe but she's home.'

Mary reached out and gave Wat a hug.

'He didn't kill Wesley though,' she whispered.

'He didn't?'

'He said he didn't.'

'And you believed him…'

'He's got no reason to. He didn't even know you had a unicorn,' explained Mary.

'If it wasn't Niamh, and it wasn't O'Nerry, then who could it have been?' wondered Wat out loud.

Mary shrugged. She didn't have a clue; their most likely suspects were struck out.

'Perhaps best to think about it tomorrow,' suggested No and rubbed Mary's shoulder.

She reached around and held him close. Somehow, she still felt cold. No also felt extremely cold but she knew she'd feel warmer with him.

'Good idea, let's get back to bed,' said Wat and rubbed his neck, 'I think I'll take tomorrow off.'

The First of December

Mary found herself looking at the screen in half a daze. She felt somewhere between desperate fear and incredible relief and hence her body has resigned her to stay seated. On the screen was the email she'd received from Ralph; his reply to her last correspondence. The gist was disappointment, and Ralph said he would have to terminate her employment and Mary felt that was for the best. Or perhaps she didn't know how she felt.

She sat up from the chair. She leant back in the chair. She felt restless. She finally stood up and opened one of the cabinet's drawers.

'Are you okay?' asked Mona, spinning down to drop on Mary's shoulder.

'Yes,' said Mary, and after she thought about it she said, 'no.'

'What's wrong,' said Mona, attempting to massage her shoulder with her small front legs.

Mary shuddered at the feel of her tiny legs stroking her, 'The deed is done. I am no longer employed by my agency. My contract with Wat is at an end. I'm going to be leaving tomorrow.'

'How does that make you feel?'

Mary couldn't answer it because she wasn't really sure. There clearly was something tugging at her heart when she thought about leaving. She thought it was No at first but it wasn't him; it was as if something had pierced her heart, but this feeling was like a bruise. Something inside her had changed. She couldn't just go back to accountancy that was for sure.

'Mo left without a word,' said Mary aloud.

'I don't think anyone knew him that well,' Mona said, gripping tightly as Mary wound around the other side of the desk, 'you've made a much bigger impact.'

'You're telling me,' said Mary, 'take a look at Niamh, O'Nerry…' and she trailed off, 'maybe Wat would be glad to be rid of me,' feeling sorry for herself.

'You know that's not true,' said Mona.

As if the gods were listening, Wat made a soft rap at the door before letting himself into the office.

'Hi Mary,' he said, a little solemnly but the hint of a smile was stashed in the corner of his mouth.

Mary stared at him, her hands clasped together tightly, 'Wat. Hello,' she patted herself down and crossed her arms awkwardly, 'I have finished up my evaluation.'

'Good,' said Wat.

'I've contacted our solicitors and reverted all our work. I've filled out a strategic twelve-month plan that should keep you afloat with some adjustments to your incomings and outgoings. As long as you stay within budget, the King George won't need to close for some time.'

Wat nodded. Mary waited for him to speak. 'Some of the staff said they'd be willing to sacrifice pay as well.'

THE FIRST OF DECEMBER

'That's very noble of them,' said Mary.

'Yes my staff are incredibly loyal to a tee,' he stated.

'Wat, I-'

Wat held a hand up to stop Mary, 'thank you,' he began, 'I know what you're about to say…'

'I got fired.'

Wat paused, 'Okay I wasn't expecting that.'

'I can't begin to tell you how sorry I am for everything that I caused. I know that this isn't enough to forgive me, but please know this – I want you to stay open. And I must plead you do,' said Mary.

Wat opened his arms. He stepped into a hug, grasping Mary tightly which Mary reciprocated. She let out a sigh and softened in his hold. Then she felt a tear run down her cheek and held Wat tighter.

'How's Snow?' she asked, still tightly grasped.

'She's holed up in her room watching videos in bed,' he replied in her ear, 'she'll be fine eventually. Thank you for helping to bring her home.'

'It wasn't really me,' said Mary and Wat gripped her arms and held her in front of his face.

'It was absolutely you,' he said and Mary felt a little better hearing him say it, 'come on let's have a break upstairs.'

Mary let him take her, not feeling Mona jump off her shoulder at the last second before she shut the door. He led her up the stairs into the barroom where he went behind the bar to fetch something to drink. Jarrett was cleaning glasses when she arrived. Mary felt uncomfortable knowing the cold shoulder she'd soon receive.

'So we're seeing you off tomorrow are we?' he asked, not looking up. Mary was not preparing for that and found herself speechless. 'We should be holding something to see you off,' said Jarrett meaningfully, putting down a glass.

'But,' Mary struggled to say something, 'but there have been so many events lately-'

'-and events bring business,' said Neo, rounding the corner is a tray full of plates.

'More money,' said Jarrett.

Mary felt bad, 'but I betrayed you all.'

Jarrett shrugged, 'I think of it as we won you over. Also just try and stop him.'

'Stop him?' her smile dropped, 'oh don't tell me. Has he done it already?'

Jarrett straightened up and coughed loudly, 'I don't know what you mean,' whilst nodding his head. Neo laughed as she rolled out another flyer that she'd been sticking on the outside of the Mad King.

'Yes, what do you mean Mary?' asked Wat, coming out with a teapot.

Mary shook her head, 'who did you invite?'

'Everyone,' he said, 'again.'

'It's going to be just as amazing as the last one,' said Jarrett, 'except Seamus is in the hospital again.'

'And Wojciech isn't in,' said Mary.

'And Boz has taken time off for "trauma" even though she didn't feel a thing when she got stabbed,' said Neo.

'Just as amazing,' repeated Jarrett sarcastically.

Wat gave a disappointed shake of his head, 'Not with that attitude.'

The three of them exchanged looks and Mary helped herself to a cup of tea. On the cup was a barrage of autumn leaves that enshrouded the surface, and were covered over by both her hands. Being regarded as a friend again felt good.

THE FIRST OF DECEMBER

It wasn't long before Mary had finished up her work and was back in the barroom to be greeted by a room filled with people. Another banner was on the wall saying 'Good Luck' and 'Best Wishes' and everyone cheered as she entered. Wat called out, 'a round for everyone!' to which Mary responded, 'Have I taught you nothing.'

Everyone laughed and the night continued as it had in the past; beers were drunk, food was passed around, Wat told stories of past calamities in the pub, Kam told stories of a young Wat, Jarrett shared his own barrel of jokes and so on. Halfway through the night of hearing multiple well-wishes, No appeared in the room and Mary gave him a tight hug.

'No, where've you been?' she asked.

'Grabbing something,' he said, 'you're leaving tomorrow?'

'Yes my train is in the morning,' she said.

He kissed her, 'Then we've only tonight,' and he sounded far-off as if his mind was elsewhere.

'Do you want to stay down here or…' she asked, suggestively.

He smiled, 'Let's go upstairs.'

She waved to the rest of the staff and they went upstairs. When they'd calmed down Mary found herself in his arms lying in bed.

'You should stay,' said No.

'I can't, I've got no job,' she said.

'Work here,' he said, 'Wat would take you.'

She sighed. She needed to let him down easy here. 'I know he would but I don't belong here – don't take that the wrong way. I do love it here, but I am a city girl. It was nice for the time away, but I have ambition.'

'Ambition?'

'I wanted to reach real heights with my accountancy firm. Now I need to think about everything, my whole life has changed.'

'For the better?'

'Entirely the better,' she stroked his chest, 'but my future isn't here. It's somewhere else. Tomorrow I'll head home and I'll figure it out from there.'

'What if tomorrow never came?' asked No.

'Oh sure No, if you could stop time then I'll stay,' she said sarcastically – obviously that was the only thing keeping her here.

No became unnaturally quiet and Mary felt as if she'd said something wrong. But then he raised his arms around her and she settled into a deep sleep knowing her alarm would wake her bright and early the next morning.

* * *

It was not the first of December. To Mary, it didn't feel like it. And when she woke up and looked over at her clock, which read it was the thirty-first, she didn't pay any mind to it. When the radio said that today marked the thirty-first of November, she felt that was exactly what day it should be.

No was gone. She rolled over and looked around the room for him. There was no sign that he was in the bathroom. In fact, it looked as if he had left with no intent to return. She considered that it was for the best and sat in her bed for a while thinking that to herself.

When she finally went downstairs and saw Wat in a panic with the rest of the staff, she realised she no longer found it concerning but her heart began beating at the promise of something curious.

'Everything alright?' she asked.

THE FIRST OF DECEMBER

'No, no, everything's wrong. Have you seen No?' Wat asked her immediately and intensely.

'Not since last night,' said Mary, avoiding providing further details.

'We have to find him,' he stated flatly, 'This is bad. This is extremely bad.'

Kam lifted her head out of her hands, 'where would he have gone?' she asked, looking at things pragmatically.

'Mary, did he say anything to you about where he would've gone?' Wat asked Mary.

Mary shook her head, 'Not that I remember. We just talked about how I would be leaving tomorrow.'

'You mean today,' said Wat.

'I leave on the first Wat, don't you remember?' said Mary.

'Today IS the first,' he said, leaving Mary confused, but he turned back to the group before she could ask him to elaborate, 'we need to search the whole area then. Mary will stay here in case he comes back. Neo, Jarrett, you take the east side of town. Kam you take west, I'll take north.'

'What if he went south?' suggested Neo.

'He'd never go south. Too warm. Let's go.'

The four of them clustered to the coat rack and rushed out the doors, leaving Mary on her own in an empty pub. Feathers' old puppet form lay lifeless on the counter, she half considered sitting him upright and having half a conversation. Instead, she decided she'd get a bite to eat and so made her way downstairs. She entered the kitchen at the same time as Snow was leaving; her hair was dishevelled and her face ghostly pale. Red eyes looked up at Mary and then looked away, embarrassment, defeat and heartbreak running across her face. Mary took pity on the girl and wished she could say something. Snow shut her door gently and Mary continued on her quest.

She had a cup of tea to start things off and was considering making toast when she heard the front door open. She took the tea with her as she entered the barroom. She found just the person everyone was looking for; No was looking this way and that, and when he heard Mary enter his head whipped her way.

'Perfect!' said No, 'grab your coat, we're leaving.'

He looked slightly different, but Mary couldn't put her finger on it. He was dressed the same in his long grey coat, his grey eyes, his scarf, sharp hair, and fogged glasses from being out in the cold too long.

'Everyone's looking for you, where are we going?'

'We need to get away from here,' said No.

Mary wasn't having that.

'Why is that?'

'I'll explain on the way, but you have to trust me,' said No, 'please.'

Mary eyed him. He definitely seemed different: it was an air of confidence. Some new-found strength from within him. She had to think practically; even though she didn't trust him, if she stayed with him, she could alert the others.

'Alright,' she said finally and went to grab her coat.

No kept a lookout until she was ready, then he grabbed the door and the two stepped out. It was chilly and overcast as per usual, causing Mary to pull her coat around herself as close as possible.

'What happened, why are they looking for you?' she asked.

'Because they want to put me away,' he said.

'For what?'

THE FIRST OF DECEMBER

'They think I'm crazy; I am but I'm crazy for you Mary,' said No.

Mary bit her lip, 'That's sweet, I like you too, but I don't want you getting into trouble over me.'

'It's not just you Mary, I've never stood up for myself. But now I am, I'm taking a stand!' said No.

They entered the high street and crossed over, but Mary still wasn't sure where they were headed. It looked like they were heading west which meant Kam was likely closest. She pulled out her phone and sent her a text saying 'With no. headed your way'.

'Where are we going?' asked Mary again, prodding for answers, 'I've got work to do. I'm leaving tomorrow No.'

'No you're not, you're leaving December the first,' said No.

'Which is tomorrow,' said Mary.

'Not this year,' said No. Then he stopped suddenly, 'shit.'

Kam was at the other end of the street.

'Stop right there,' said Kam, 'we need a word.'

No was like a frightened bird, darting his head in all directions. When he saw the street to their right was empty, he grabbed Mary's hand tightly and pulled her into a run.

'No, get back here!' shouted Kam, 'Mary!'

Mary could barely catch her breath, but she managed to pant, 'I think we should talk to them, maybe we can come to a compromise?'

No didn't reply and instead tore down the street, turned left to keep them going west, and then took another turn.

'I've an idea,' he said and rapped on the door of a house.

Mary gave him a bewildered look. A woman answered the door with a look of enquiry, but as soon as she saw No her face lit up. Then she stepped backwards, letting him walk in. No complied, not paying the woman a lick of attention and pulled Mary onward. They passed through a lounge to the back of the house, out into their garden, out to the end where the fence was.

Mary looked back, 'who are these people?'

'No clue.'

Then No pressed his hand to the fence and it shattered. Mary had barely enough time to register before No pulled her into the next garden. They went up to the back of the house where a man was inside watching TV. Seeing No he immediately got up from his sofa and opened his sliding door, allowing them to pass through. No did so and raced to the front door, opened it, and walked onto another street. He didn't bother to close the door and continued heading west.

They were on a street of terrace houses, now on either side of them, and the ground sloped down slightly. Further down the road west there was a mini-roundabout that split traffic going further out of town and traffic toward the railway.

They continued running and Mary realised that he wasn't going to tell her anything until he thought they were safe. They ran to the roundabout and turned right which brought them underneath the arches of the railway that passed through town. They stopped for a breather under the arch and Mary checked her phone briefly. No new messages.

'Okay No, what's going on?' panted Mary.

'It's complicated,' said No. He hardly seemed out of breath.

THE FIRST OF DECEMBER

'How did you break the fence and who were those people?'

'Just people. People are very susceptible.'

'I need to know what's going on. How can I trust you when you're keeping secrets from me?'

No sighed then looked around. 'Alright, hold on,' and he dragged her to the edge of the archway and down the brickwork out of sight. He straightened himself.

'You know how we talked about magic being souls? How you've got souls attached to you and the more you have, the more magic you are?

'Sometimes a very large amount of souls will collect with the same sort of idea. If a lot of souls attach to a person, they tend to have an effect on that person. If you've enough souls, that idea will begin to overcome that person until they're one and the same.

'Like Snow - Snow will collect more and more souls that identify with the North Wind until she becomes affected by it.'

'Are you saying you're one of those people?' asked Mary.

'I am the physical manifestation of an idea that many souls are bound to, yes.'

'So then the people-'

'I influenced them. Made them do what I wanted.'

'Wat thinks you're dangerous? That's why they're trying to stop you?' asked Mary.

'Something like that,' said No, 'come on, we're not far now.'

'Far from where?'

'The train station,' he said.

Mary let him drag her but her mind figured that he wanted her to come with him. She was not ready for whatever he had in store for her.

The station was a small one, with a ramp up to the small ticket office which has double doors for an entrance and another set leading to the first platform. There was also a bridge to reach the other platform with a ramp and stairwell up. The place was deserted and the ticket office looked closed, but both sets of double doors were wide open. There wasn't a single person waiting for a train, even though there were several cars parked out front. When they reached the station No fished out his pockets two tickets, passing one to her. She read it and instantly tried to hand it back to him.

'I'm not going to an airport - just where are you thinking of going?'

'Serbia,' said No.

'No are you crazy? You're literally going to run to the other side of the earth?'

No looked dejected and was about to make a case for himself. But his face dropped when he saw Wat behind Mary, stepping in to make an appearance. Mary turned around to see him. Somehow he'd found them. Perhaps he knew that No would be trying to get as far away as possible. A smile crept up on her face without it meaning to.

'That's enough No. It's time,' he said.

'Yes it is, we're leaving,' said No.

'We're not leaving No,' said Mary, stepping away, 'this is stupid, let's talk about this. Maybe we can compromise.'

'There's no compromise,' said Wat, 'he has to stop.'

THE FIRST OF DECEMBER

Mary gave him an incredulous look, 'Wat you can't be serious?'

'I told you,' said No, 'there's no compromise.'

'What's the plan No, are you just going to keep running? How long are you going to drag out November?'

'What is he talking about?' asked Mary.

'You know how I said I'm an idea?' said No.

Wat stepped forward, directly opposite to No, Mary standing to the side. 'Today's the thirty-first of November,' he said as if he was reading Mary's thoughts, 'does that make sense to you Mary?'

'I guess?'

'When was the last thirty-first of November?'

Mary couldn't answer and so she kept quiet. No filled the silence; 'I'm tired of it Wat. No one likes November. It's cold, it's wet, it's dark. The only highlights are sales, thanks, fireworks and memories and none of that is strong stuff. Not like Dec who gets Christmas, Janet who gets New Year, even Octavius has Halloween!'

'So what No, are you going to stick around to the fiftieth? To the hundredth? This can't last forever,' said Wat.

'You're November,' said Mary when the gears clicked.

No gave her a resigned look, 'I am the manifestation of November. The souls that make me are filled with the notion of November, and the public's thought of November keeps me alive.

'When December comes I become weaker until the next time it comes around.'

'That's amazing,' said Mary, 'so what's the problem?'

'The problem is he's making November longer,' Wat said, 'You must have a powerful soul attached to you. A soul that already had a wealth of magic available.'

No and Wat didn't break eye contact. Mary standing in the middle felt like she was missing a large piece of the puzzle.

'I'm sorry Wat.'

'He was innocent in all this.'

'He was just a unicorn.'

Mary turned to No, a look of horror. No didn't meet her stare, keeping his eyes on Wat, but he seemed much more at ease.

'You killed Wesley?' she asked, the feeling of betrayal welling inside her.

'They live a long time, their souls are incredibly powerful,' explained No.

'He was endangered.'

'Most creatures end up extinct eventually.'

'He was under my protection.'

No didn't move, he didn't dare meet Mary's eyes. But when she began to move to Wat's side, he had to.

'Look, I'm sorry, but I didn't think you would notice!'

'Notice!? He was an innocent and beautiful creature. What kind of cruel monster are you?'

'You're too old No,' said Wat sadly and Mary recalled that she'd heard this story once before.

Ancient spirits simply saw the world as such a fleeting thing. The North Wind had when she wanted Wat dead.

No shook his head, 'Look what's done is done. If you want to try and stop me because of that, go ahead.'

THE FIRST OF DECEMBER

'How could you do it No?' Mary asked. When No looked at her, her eyes were welling up, 'was it just for power?'

She could see his façade shatter and he stammered, 'It-it wasn't for power! I did it because I wanted to stay here longer with you!' he dropped his hands, 'look no one likes November. It sounds silly but when you're a physical manifestation of everyone's thoughts it matters a lot. I'm filled with constant indifference, discomfort and inconvenience. No one likes me.'

'But I did,' she said.

He paused for a second, then he nodded, 'but not anymore.'

Mary stood in front of him and put her hands to his face, 'I liked you No, I really did, but I didn't love you. You are a wonderful person, I enjoyed our time together so much even if it was only a month. But this has gotten out of hand, you need to stop this.'

'You won't come with me?'

'I wasn't going to even before you said all this! I was hoping we'd end on a happy note.' No regarded her solemnly and Mary saw the light inside of him die, 'No, were you really going to run from the world with me?'

'Run from a couple thousand-year tradition?' added Wat.

No looked down without moving his head, then stepped back from Mary. The man was no longer looking to run away and Mary saw an embarrassed boy looking for a way out. She looked at Wat who also had realised that No was no longer going to run away. But there were other ways out.

'No? No, I think it's sweet,' she said, causing him to snort, 'no honestly, it's endearing to know you would do it for me. I've never had anyone want to run away with me.

'But I don't want to run away. I actually enjoy my life, I enjoy my work. I don't want an escape.

'That doesn't mean I wouldn't mind a change sometimes. Working for Wat and meeting you was one of the best things that happened to me,' and she stepped up behind No and wrapped her arms around him, 'will you be here if I come back?'

He turned his head trying to see her, but she'd pressed her head to his back. The spirit smiled and put his hands on hers, rubbing them.

'Yes,' he said quietly, 'I'll be here,' and he lifted one of her hands and kissed the back of it.

She lifted herself off him and stood back, unsmiling, watching No. The spirit heaved a deep sigh, stopped smiling and said seriously, 'Things will be weird for a bit. The popular opinion is going to suddenly change.'

'Better late than never,' said Wat.

No nodded, expecting a different reaction but shaking his head, 'Yeah I suppose so.'

He began to walk up into the station as a strong wind entered, blowing intensely. It swept up the loose leaves from around the station and ran them around his body. They amounted into a dense whirlwind of leaves obscuring No from Mary and Wat. They braced their arms up at their heads as the leaves masked everything until the wind died down and No had vanished. Mary shuddered as she suddenly felt a strange sensation that today was not today.

'We'll be expecting Declan soon then,' said Wat, 'I bet he was feeling uncharacteristically tired this morning.'

'Where did he go?' asked Mary.

THE FIRST OF DECEMBER

Wat shrugged, 'when the months change they tend to travel around. He's probably gone somewhere serene and quiet.'

Mary sighed but was suddenly encompassed by Wat, his arms surrounding her from behind. She grasped his arms.

'You're a very special woman to make time stop for half a day.'

She smiled at that.

* * *

'The time is nigh,' said Wat, 'it's been an absolute pleasure accommodating you Ms Woods.'

'It's been wonderful staying here,' said Mary.

She was standing by the door, her luggage placed beside it. The turnout wasn't big – Snow was nowhere to be seen. Jarrett had been cleaning taps so he stood next to Wat, along with Neo. As Mary set her things down, Jarrett grabbed her in a bear hug.

'We're going to miss you,' he said, rocking her.

Neo had her arms folded and gave Mary a nod, 'Yeah it's going to be a lot different with you gone.'

Mary looked between the three of them and licked her lips. She'd left businesses a thousand times in the past and she knew how it went. Sometimes you don't get to say goodbye to everyone how you wanted. But with leaving the Mad King, she felt so much more sorry to see it go.

'I'll be back,' she said, 'next year. Just to check in and make sure you're sticking to my plan.'

'You better,' said Neo.

Mary lifted her arms in finality and then said her final goodbye, 'I will see you then.'

Wat grabbed the door and led her outside as she carried her bags to the taxi that was waiting. She noticed Patel standing outside his shop and he gave a nod of acknowledgement before putting his cigarette back in his mouth and yelling inside.

When Mary placed her bags down and turned to Wat, she felt the air rush out from her as Wat's arms clasped tightly around her.

'Mary thank you so much, you've saved the business,' he said from her shoulder.

'Wat, I'm sure you'd have found a way around it,' she said.

'I really thought we were doomed this time,' he prised himself from her and she saw tears in his eyes.

'Wat pull yourself together! You've handled more than just me leaving without tears,' she said but sniffed as she felt the tears arriving of her own.

'Are you sure you wouldn't rather stay?' he asked quietly.

Mary smiled sweetly, 'Wat you've shown me that there's a lot to the world. But this is your world. I need to think things out and figure out my new path.

'This is not the end, this is just the beginning for me,' she said.

'I like you, Mary, I wish you all the best,' said Wat.

It was painful how time seemed to speed up. Her bags were in the boot and she was sitting in the back of the taxi before she knew it. She pushed the window open and waved to Wat who waved back and the taxi pulled away. Mary watched the Mad King shrink down the road and disappear around a corner. When it did, she sat back and breathed out.

She watched the world around her change in the taxi, on the train, and on the bus. Before, she'd be on her laptop or her phone, but now she watched intently as the houses and apartments were flung through her

THE FIRST OF DECEMBER

eye-line. She wasn't sure what she was looking for, what she was seeking out, but she had to be sure she wasn't missing something – anything.

When she got to her flat she opened her laptop and began the same old job of looking through her emails. The latest email drew a smile from her. Ralph had replied again to her with just what she wanted.

'Dear Ms Woods,

I can neither confirm nor deny that our client was a member of the top hat society. You know I cannot share these kinds of details.

All the best.
Ralph'

And that was the story of how Mary Woods became one of the more interesting accountants.

Printed in Great Britain
by Amazon